VENTURA

+

WINNETKA

J.G. BRYAN

SANTA
MONICA
PRESS
TEEN

Published by: Santa Monica Press LLC
P.O. Box 850
Solana Beach, CA 92075
1-800-784-9553
www.santamonicapress.com
books@santamonicapress.com

SANTA
MONICA
PRESS
TEEN

Printed in the United States

Santa Monica Press books are available at special quantity discounts when
purchased in bulk by corporations, organizations, or groups. Please call our
Special Sales department at 1-800-784-9553.

ISBN-13: 978-1-59580-124-1
ISBN: 978-1-59580-767-0 (ebook)

Publisher's Cataloging-in-Publication data

Names: Bryan, J. G., author.
Title: Ventura and Winnetka / J. G. Bryan.
Description: Solana Beach, CA: Santa Monica Press, 2023.
Identifiers: ISBN: 978-1-59580-124-1 (print) | 978-1-59580-767-0 (ebook)
Subjects: LCSH Los Angeles (Calif.)--History--20th century--Fiction.
| Los Angeles (Calif.)--Social life and customs--Fiction. | San Fernando
Valley (Calif.)--Fiction. | Teenagers--California--Fiction. | Friendship-
-Fiction. | Bildungsroman. | BISAC YOUNG ADULT FICTION / Social
Themes / Friendship | YOUNG ADULT FICTION / Boys & Men |
YOUNG ADULT FICTION / Lifestyles / City & Town Life | YOUNG
ADULT FICTION / Social Themes / Drugs, Alcohol, Substance Abuse |
YOUNG ADULT FICTION / Coming of Age | YOUNG ADULT FICTION /
Historical / United States / 20th Century
Classification: LCC PS3602.R935 V46 2023 | DDC 813.6--dc23

Cover and interior design and production by Future Studio

For Mom

"Praising what is lost
Makes the remembrance dear."

—WILLIAM SHAKESPEARE

Chapter One

Weddy had a cousin.

His name was Marco, and he loved fast cars. Marco was older than all of us, so he was the first one to get his license. We used to go out during lunch in Marco's red Celica, five of us—me, Hank, and Andrew in the back seat; Moose in the front; and Marco at the wheel—and search out dirt roads on the backstreets of Woodland Hills and Canoga Park, where Marco could practice drifting and make 360-degree turns on a dime. He was very good, and we were usually terrified, which made it all the more fun.

While Weddy had told us plenty of stories about Marco, we had never actually met him. For all we knew, Marco had never even been over to Weddy's house. Something about his dad and Weddy's mom not getting along.

Marco had gone to a different junior high than us, but once we hit high school we were all together at Woodrow Wilson. In fact, Marco was in Algebra with me and Hank in tenth grade, and when the teacher did roll call on that very first day of school and we heard Marco's name, we both recognized it and immediately approached him after class was over.

"Hey, man," I said. Marco was still sitting at his desk, and Hank and I hovered above him.

"Yeah?" he asked, his dark curly hair and dark eyes immediately suggesting his Italian background.

"Are you Weddy's cousin?" Gotta love Hank: always

gets right to the point.

"Yeah, I am. I mean, I was. I guess. Did you know him?"

"He was our best friend," I answered glumly.

"No shit!" A look of recognition came over Marco's face. "Weddy told me about you guys. Wait, wait . . . Ronnie and Douglas, right?" he said, pointing first at me and then at Hank.

"Actually, I'm Hank and this is Douglas," Hank clarified, pointing at me.

"Oh, right. He told me about you, too, Hank. And I think I remember seeing you guys at the funeral."

"Yeah, we were there," I said, but the truth was I didn't remember much about that day and was so focused on trying not to break down that I avoided looking at anybody as much as possible. Ditto for Hank. "Ronnie moved away, and we haven't heard from him since, well, I guess since the day of the funeral."

"Texas, right?" Marco said. "I remember my dad saying something about it. My aunt and uncle weren't too happy about Weddy's friendship with that guy. I think they sort of blamed him in a lot of ways."

Hank and I didn't really know what to say to that. We both knew Ronnie had felt guilty about everything that had happened. Hell, we *all* felt guilty. But it really wasn't fair to pin Weddy's death on Ronnie; it's not like Ronnie ever forced Weddy to do anything he didn't want to do.

"Anyway, it's nice to meet you guys," Marco said, rising out of his chair and extending his hand, which both Hank and I shook. "I really miss Weddy," he said with obvious sadness in his eyes. "I mean, our parents don't really get along, so I didn't get to see him too much, but still . . . we were *paisano*, you know?"

Hank and I were both huge *Godfather* fans, so we knew immediately what Marco was talking about. "Weddy was Italian?" Hank asked.

"Well, Weddy's mom is Italian. She and my dad are brother and sister."

"I was gonna say . . . Wedderspoon doesn't sound very Italian!" I laughed.

"Romano. That's my last name, and my aunt Sofia's last name—I mean, Weddy's mom's last name—as well."

"Huh. We never knew that. Did you know that, Hank?" I asked, turning to my buddy.

"No. I mean, Weddy never talked about his uncle all that much. He talked about you once in a while," Hank continued, looking at Marco, "but he always said his parents didn't get along with your parents and what a drag it was because he liked spending time with you."

"Yeah, it's a drag, for sure," Marco sighed. "My dad and Weddy's mom hate each other. I think it has to do with something that happened between Weddy's dad and my dad a long time ago. And even though Weddy's dad divorced my aunt and moved to Arizona, the damage between my dad and my aunt was already done. I think she blames my dad for the divorce—which is totally not fair—but that's just the way it is. I pretty much only got to see Weddy at major, major occasions where there was no avoiding inviting both the Wedderspoons and the Romanos. You know, weddings, funerals, that sort of thing. Every now and then Weddy and I would talk on the phone, but because we were kids and didn't drive, there was no way for us to ever get together, and our parents both refused to do anything to help us see each other. I think they all now realize it was a mistake, and that maybe, just maybe, had I been around Weddy more, he'd still be alive."

This pronouncement from Marco hit me like a sucker punch to the gut. Weddy's parents thought Marco could've prevented Weddy's death? How? By keeping him away from Ronnie? From us? Did they actually blame Hank and me as well?

I looked over at Hank, but he was just staring at the floor. I think his eyes had welled up with tears and he was trying to hold it together.

Marco must have seen the changes in our expressions because his tone immediately softened from his direct, rather gruff way of speaking. "But look, I don't want you guys to think that I agree with them. What happened was just a horrible accident. The only guy to blame was that fucking douchebag who's now sitting in juvie. I hope he rots in hell."

"For sure," Hank and I both muttered at the same time. "Fucking asshole," I added for good measure.

"The thing I never understood," Marco began, "is why the hell were those guys chasing you anyway? I mean, why did that jerk kick Weddy and send him flying into the middle of the intersection?"

"No reason!" I said, perhaps a little too excitedly.

"It was Halloween, and they were just looking for trouble," Hank added. "I always felt bad for the woman driving the car who hit Weddy."

"I know," I agreed. "It wasn't her fault."

After a few uncomfortable moments of silence, Marco asked, "You guys want to go to the cafeteria and get some lunch?"

"I'm always ready to eat!" Hank said with a smile. His mood and the dark cloud hanging above all of us suddenly lifted, and from that point on, and for the next three years, Marco was a part of our group.

Marco got his driver's license the summer before eleventh grade. Like I said, he was the first one to drive, and fortunately or unfortunately for us, he wanted to follow in the footsteps of his dad, who was one of the most famous stunt drivers in Hollywood. I remember one time when we came so close to drifting into a telephone pole, I could actually see the staples in the pole from all the flyers people had attached over the years—looking for lost dogs and cats, mostly, though the occasional plea for somebody's parrot who had escaped would also make an appearance. The pole was just inches from my face as I looked out of the back seat side window into what I thought was our certain death, or dismemberment, anyway.

But at the last minute, Marco would somehow pull his trusty Celica out of the drift and away from the pole, and we would cheat tragedy once again. I have to admit, it was a pretty big thrill.

Until it wasn't anymore.

It was a hot August day, a few weeks before our senior year would begin at Woodrow Wilson High. I was lying around the house, enjoying the air conditioning, when the phone rang.

"Douglas? Marco here. Andrew's at my house, and we're gonna go driving. Want to join us?"

"Sure," I said.

"Pick you up in ten." *Click.*

Marco lived across the canyon. You could almost see his house from our backyard.

"Mom?"

"Yes, honey?" she replied from upstairs.

"I'm going to go out for a bit."

"Where are you going?"

"Just driving around with Marco and Andrew."

"What about Hank?"

"I don't know. I think he's got basketball practice."

"Can you do me a favor and pick up some corn from the stand over on Hayvenhurst? Get a half dozen ears."

"Sure, Mom. I'll ask Marco to take us over there."

"Thanks, honey. Have fun!"

When Marco showed up, he wasn't driving his Celica; he had his mom's brand new 1978 Ford Mustang King Cobra, in all of its bright, red-and-black-accented glory.

"Whoa," I exclaimed as I came out the front door and walked down toward the car, where Andrew sat in the front passenger seat with the window rolled down. "I see we're traveling in style today."

Andrew hopped out and pushed the seat forward, gesturing for me to get in the back. "Marco's mom and dad are out of town," he said, "so we thought we'd test the handling of this fine motoring machine."

"Today's your lucky day," Marco chuckled.

"How's it going, buddy?" I said to Marco as I climbed into the back seat behind Andrew. "Hey, Andrew, move the seat up."

"Fuck you. I need the room. Sit behind Marco."

"You're such a fucking asshole," I said, scooting over behind Marco, who, despite being much taller than Andrew, had his seat set in a normal position, which provided me with at least a modicum of legroom.

I immediately reached for my seat belt, but discovered the buckle wouldn't click.

Marco looked at me in the rearview mirror. "Oh, sorry,

that belt is broken. My mom's taking the car in next week to get it fixed."

"Seriously? Come on, Andrew, move up."

"Oh, don't be a pussy. You'll be fine."

"Gee, thanks," I said. "Where are we going?"

"Oh, I have a few things in mind." Marco smiled that devilish smile of his.

"Hey, I promised my mom I'd pick up some corn for her at the stand over on Hayvenhurst. Hope that's okay."

"What the fuck do we look like, a delivery service? Are we your chauffeurs or something?" Andrew always had a nasty comeback for everything.

"It's fine, Douglas," Marco assured me. "Besides, I want to check out the dirt parking lot over on the other side of Balboa Park. It's pretty close to the corn stand."

"Thanks, Marco. And fuck you, Andrew."

"Yeah, whatever," Andrew said with a wave of his hand.

The rest of the day was a blur. We did spin-outs, 360s, drifts . . . you name it. We drove all over Encino and Tarzana, looking for dirt roads and isolated patches of asphalt where Marco could practice truly frightening and exhilarating maneuvers. There were a ton of places off of Mulholland especially.

We also picked up the corn—in spite of Andrew's continued protestations. "I can't believe we're wasting time on this!" he complained. "I have better things to do."

"Like what?" Marco challenged. "I think you probably already beat off enough this morning."

"Ha, ha," Andrew deadpanned. "I'm getting more pussy these days than both of you put together."

With that, Marco and I burst into laughter. Everyone

knew Andrew couldn't score with the girls. Sure, he was *friends* with some of the hottest chicks at Woodrow Wilson, like Patty O'Shea, the beautiful, redheaded cheerleader, and Lisa Miller, who was a shoo-in for homecoming queen that year. Hell, he even heard the darkest secrets of Tammy Goodrich, who had been having sex with guys since the ninth grade. But that was the problem—Andrew was simply the confidant of these hotties. They treated him like one of their girlfriends, not one of their boyfriends.

"Andrew, we all know you've never gotten your dick wet. You're not fooling anyone."

"Oh, fuck you, Marco. I've had plenty of sex."

"Yeah?" Marco taunted. "Who you dating this week? Your right hand or your left?"

Marco and I exploded into fits of laughter.

"You guys are such assholes," was all Andrew could muster in response. He knew we were onto his bullshit.

As we approached my house, we saw water pouring down the street from the houses up on the hill just south of ours.

"What the fuck?" Andrew said.

"Let's go check it out!" Marco yelled, obviously excited by the possibilities a wet street—especially a wet street on a big hill with plenty of curves—held for a fearless and talented driver like him.

We made our way up the hill, past my house and toward the newer homes that had been built just a few months after we'd left our townhouse and my mom and Art had bought this place in Tarzana, in a neighborhood known as Stromness because of the nearby golf course with the same name. Art belonged to the Stromness

Country Club and liked the idea of living nearby so he could pop over and use the range and even just play nine holes if he felt like it. He was always trying to get me to learn the game, and I tried it a couple of times, but I found it incredibly boring. *And* incredibly hot during the Valley summers. I'd much rather be in an air-conditioned gym playing ball, thank you very much.

Besides, the members of Stromness were just a bunch of old men living some Scottish fantasy. The course was fashioned after the famous links courses in Scotland, and all of the buildings were designed to make you feel like you were in some sort of quaint Scottish village, which always seemed totally bizarre to me since here we were living in the very un-Scottish town of Tarzana.

Actually, my friends and I did get a fair amount of use out of the golf course. We'd often sneak onto the course after hours and play tackle football in the fairways, which made for an excellent gridiron. Another fun thing we used to do was get big blocks of ice from the liquor store and take them up to the course at night and ride them down the green hills that lined the course. What a blast! It was like our own personal Alpine slide. It tore the shit out of the golf course, and we'd be strung up by our toes if they ever caught us, so we reserved that activity for special occasions—usually nights when we were so drunk or stoned that our courage ran high.

Anyway, there was a ton of water coming down the hill above my house, and it only got deeper and deeper the further we climbed. By the time we got close to the top of the hill, the water was running all the way to the edges of the curbs on either side of the street.

"What the hell is going on?" Andrew asked, looking

wide-eyed out the window.

As we rounded the final curve near the end of the street, we got our answer: a fire hydrant had exploded, shooting a massive fountain of water fifty feet into the air.

"Cool!" Marco yelled. "The car can use a wash after all of those dirt roads!" he laughed.

And so it began. Round and round we went, driving beneath the tower of water over and over again, laughing hysterically each time we did it. We'd come out from the dousing, water streaming so thickly down the front windshield that we couldn't even see the hood of the car for several seconds. It was even making its way into the interior of the car, and I could see a small puddle forming at my feet. Talk about a blast!

Needing a break, we made our way down the hill toward the next side street where Marco could pull over before going back up for another pass under the temporary waterspout. However, we saw a man walking on the sidewalk along the opposite side of the street.

"Watch this, guys," Marco said with a devilish look in his eye and a pronounced cackle to his laugh. He proceeded to make a U-turn and drive back up the hill, making his way closer and closer to the curb as we approached the man on the sidewalk. Suddenly Marco inched toward the gutter and floored it, showering the guy in a gigantic wave of water that thoroughly doused him.

"Holy shit!" Andrew screamed.

"Jesus!" I shouted, looking back at the man, who was beyond pissed, shaking his fist at us and yelling what I was sure were obscenities. He was soaked, with water dripping off every part of his body.

"That was awesome!" Marco laughed, obviously

pleased with himself.

"We better get out of here," I counseled, "or else that guy is going to kill us."

"Okay, one more time under the fountain and then we'll boogie," Marco promised.

We circled back around the cul-de-sac at the top and drove under the water one more time. As we made our way down the hill we passed the man, who was still making his way up the hill to see what was going on in spite of his wet clothes. He once again yelled and shook his fist at us.

The last thing I remember was coming around the next big curve and seeing the white DWP truck coming up the other side; a neighbor had obviously called them to come shut off the hydrant. I could feel us starting to drift to the left and watched as Marco frantically turned the wheel in the direction of the slide, hoping, I'm sure, to pull out and straighten the trajectory of the car. It didn't happen.

Apparently, we continued to slide toward the Water and Power truck, slamming into it driver's side to driver's side, and then spinning around until we settled against the curb on the other side of the street from where we had started, our car pointing in the opposite direction of the way we had been traveling, facing directly up the hill.

Because Andrew had refused to move his seat up, I was still stuck behind Marco in the seat without a seatbelt, and had been thrown like a rag doll, eventually coming to rest face down across both of the wheel wells, directly behind the front seats. There were several inches of water in the car by this point, and Andrew would later tell me that he heard me "gurgling" as I cried and tried to breathe with my lips sitting in a small puddle of water. Not that Andrew did anything about it, of course. In fact, Andrew immediately popped out of the car, totally unhurt, and blended into the crowd that had formed—neighbors who had either witnessed or heard the crash—as if he were simply a bystander.

Somehow, while completely blacked-out, I managed to crawl out of the wreckage—make no mistake, the car was totaled—and over to the parkway, where I laid on my back on the grass.

Meanwhile, my mom had actually heard the crash from our house. We only lived a block or two down the street, a few hundred yards as the crow flies.

"Gee, I hope that wasn't Douglas," she later told me she had said to herself. Mom always had a crazy sixth sense. When the operator called to tell her about the accident, my mom didn't even give her a chance to explain; she simply hung up the phone and tore out of the house, hustling up the street toward the scene of the crime.

I woke up to my mom screaming hysterically, looking down at me lying unconscious on the ground. I immediately came back to life.

"Mom, mom . . . it's okay . . . I'm okay," I said groggily. As I tried to sit up, the full impact of what had happened came into sharp focus. There was Marco's mom's Mustang, doors open, front windshield completely smashed. I could only imagine what the driver's side of the car looked like. Marco was still sitting in the car, dazed and confused, his hand held up to his forehead; both were bloodied. I later learned he had smacked his head on the rearview mirror, causing a gash that required a half-dozen stitches.

"You kids have been causing trouble on this street for weeks!" Shit. The guy we had soaked was standing above me, screaming at both me and Marco. He turned to the assembled crowd. "These kids have been pulling stunts like this for weeks. I've seen them driving around here like crazy idiots with my own eyes."

"What?" I managed to say. "No, that's not true. We've never even driven up here." It was a weak defense, I'll admit. I glanced around for some sympathy, and for the first time I noticed ears of corn strewn all across the street, wet and dirty and looking seriously unappetizing. So much for having corn with our dinner tonight.

"You leave him alone, sir." My mom got right up in the dude's face. "Can't you see he's hurt? Can't you see he's just a little boy?"

"Little boy, my ass. He's a menace to society is what he is." Nevertheless, the guy backed off and stepped away. Lucky thing, too, because at that moment Art drove up. He had followed my mom in the car in case they needed to take me to the hospital. Art would make mincemeat out of this guy.

"I couldn't find the keys," Art said as he walked up. "How is he? How are you, kid?"

"I'm okay," I assured him, and my mom, once again.

The ambulance showed up and, after checking both Marco and me out, they decided we should go to the hospital to get Marco his stitches and to rule out any concussions for either of us.

I was placed on a gurney and loaded into the back. Marco was helped into the ambulance and sat next to me and the EMT.

"Don't worry, honey," my mom said as they closed the door. "We'll be right behind you in Art's car."

At one point during the drive to the hospital, I started to say something, but Marco just looked at me and shook his head "no." I think he was worried about liability and didn't want me to say anything that might incriminate him.

They took us over to Tarzana, and we were admitted into the ER, though they took Marco into a different room to stitch him up. While I rested comfortably in a bed, the police showed up. The two officers entered my room and began asking me questions.

"So, tell us what happened, Son. You were in the front passenger seat, correct?"

"Well, no, actually," I explained. "I was sitting in the back seat. Behind the driver."

"Why were you sitting there?" one of the officers asked, confused. He had a very pronounced mole just to the right side of his nose. His name tag identified him as Officer Gordon.

"Because Andrew was sitting in front." I looked past the officers through the doorway, where I could see my mom, Art, and Andrew sitting in the lobby of the ER. I wasn't sure how Andrew had gotten there, but assumed he'd caught a ride with my mom and Art. Otherwise, he would've been stuck high up in the hills of Tarzana with no way to get home.

"Wait a second," Officer Gordon said, noticeably irritated. "How many people were in the car?"

"Three," I said innocently, unaware at this point that Andrew, being the snake that he was, had simply slithered away as if he were an innocent party to the whole debacle.

"Three!" Officer Gordon exclaimed, his voice rising. "Who was the third person?"

I looked out toward the lobby, pointed directly at Andrew, and nonchalantly said, "Andrew. That kid sitting over there next to my parents." With that, the officers turned around and looked directly at him. Andrew went white as a sheet.

The officers marched out of the room and headed straight toward Andrew. I couldn't hear what they were saying, but apparently they were more pissed off at Andrew than they were at either Marco or me. They accused him of "leaving the scene of a crime," and even told him they could arrest him right then and there and take him down to juvie. It didn't take long before tears were rolling down Andrew's face, and his shoulders were heaving with sobs. I knew Andrew well enough to immediately realize this was all an act, a big show. He was a master bullshit artist. All gamblers are, right? Andrew had been gambling and playing bookmaker for all of his friends since the eighth grade. His histrionics worked, however, as the cops eventually bought his tale of running door to door to try to get help.

The truth, Andrew told me later as I lay on the couch in my living room, my body aching from being tossed around the back seat of the car, was that he had leapt out of the car to avoid getting in trouble, and simply watched as I crawled from the wreckage over to the parkway grass.

"Gee, thanks, Andrew," I said sarcastically when he finally confessed.

"I'm sorry, but I wasn't about to fuck up the rest of my life just to help you. And it would've worked if you'd just kept your mouth shut when you were talking to those cops."

Andrew had been on track to become an attorney since the day he was born, and as the years went by, he continued to adopt and revel in his growing arrogance and lawyer-like attitude. But he was such a dufus in so many other ways—a mediocre athlete in spite of his love of sports, his inability to land a girlfriend or even get a real date in spite of his friendships with many of the hottest girls at Woodrow Wilson, the spittle that would form at the sides of his mouth—that it counteracted his trial lawyer demeanor and made you pity him and grudgingly accept him as a friend. Besides, who else was going to organize the football pool week after week?

As for Marco, he got off pretty easy. Insurance paid for the totaled Mustang, and his parents bought his story that we had only gone under the hydrant spray twice and had not intentionally splashed the guy on the sidewalk. "It was an accident, pure and simple," Marco insisted. "The street was wet, and we were going downhill and around a curve. Sure, I might've been going a little fast, but not on purpose. I just lost control of the car."

His dad, being a professional stunt driver, was more than a little disappointed that Marco hadn't properly pulled out of the drift, but he was certainly happy his boy was okay. "When you're feeling better, we'll go out and practice that maneuver," he promised Marco, though from what Marco says, they never did.

Needless to say, that little episode put the kibosh on our driving excursions. Not for Marco, of course, who was not only born to drive, but also had a dad who either looked the other way or just plain didn't care. But for me, Andrew, Hank, and Moose, there would be no more crazy stunts with Marco.

Moose was especially adamant: "No fucking way, man. I'm never getting in a car with that guy again. I'm so happy you guys didn't call me that day." Then again, when Moose turned fifteen and a half, he immediately got his permit to ride a motorcycle, and I almost got killed as a result.

We were coming back from The Wherehouse—where I had unsuccessfully tried to buy the new Fleetwood Mac album only to find out the store was sold out of the insanely popular record—and we were headed home, up to Stromness. I was on the back of the bike, a Honda 200. Pretty basic. We were coming down Valley Vista, right where it hits El Caballero golf course. We made the right onto the side street you have to take in order to wind your way over to Reseda, and up ahead were some kids playing in the street. The next thing I knew, I saw an orange Frisbee come flying across the street in front of us. Only it didn't make it; it was a shitty throw. The Frisbee landed right smack dab in the middle of the street and skidded in front of us just as we came by.

Moose had two choices: either swerve to try to miss the Frisbee and potentially dump me and/or the bike, or go straight over the Frisbee and hope he that he wouldn't dump me and/or the bike. He smartly chose the latter, and we sailed right over the orange disk as if it were nothing but a stain on the pavement. Didn't even feel it. However, the fear I felt the moment I realized we were about to hit the Frisbee was enough to swear me off of motorcycles for the rest of my life, and I've never been on one since. I still have visions of exactly how we would've gone down, the front tire skidding on the slick plastic disk, Moose losing control of the bike as we fell to the left, Steve Mc-Queen-style—only Moose ain't no Steve McQueen. We'd go down hard, the flesh on the left sides of our bodies—arms, legs, face, shoulders, feet, you name it—stripped off as we met the pavement and skidded along the asphalt.

No thank you. Never again.

And refusing to ever get on the back of Moose's motorcycle was a sacrifice. Because where we lived, up in Stromness, any sign of civilization was easily three or more miles away, and while it was downhill to get there, it was definitely uphill to get home. I mean, we were closer to Mulholland Drive than Ventura Boulevard, so having *any* means of transportation was a godsend. Prior to Moose getting his motorcycle, the only way for either of us to get around was with our parents or with our thumbs, and since we lived way at the top of Stromness, it was hard to get a ride all the way back. The driver would normally drop us off about a mile down the hill, unless they were super chill and gave us a ride all the way up and then went back down to where they lived. But usually it was some mom who was in a rush, and who was *so sorry* she had to drop us off down below but she just had to get home to pay the babysitter, let the dog out, make a phone call, get the ice cream in the freezer . . . you name it, we'd heard it.

It's funny that Moose and I had gotten stuck up here together. In junior high we were mortal enemies. Hated each other's guts. Were each other's chief adversary when it came to any sport. But then my mom and Art bought the house in Stromness, and we moved from the townhouse in Encino the summer between ninth and tenth grade. Art's automobile parts business had been doing extremely well; in spite of the downturn in the economy, his sales had actually soared recently, as mechanics who worked on older cars continually sought him out for parts for their customers' vintage automobiles.

While Art and my mom couldn't afford to be in the original part of Stromness—the neighborhood adjoining the golf course with large homes on big lots—they were able to afford a nice, newer part of the development in the hills around the course. Granted, the houses were much more modest in size compared to the homes that lined the fairways, and the lots were far smaller as well, and you were miles from civilization, but at least we didn't share walls with neighbors or have some idiotic homeowner's association to deal with anymore.

The happiest member of the family was undoubtedly L, who I no longer had to take on excruciating walks down to a dusty, weed-infested lot day after day. She now had a backyard with all kinds of places to pee and poop, not to mention her very own doggie door in the kitchen.

We moved to Stromness not long after the Fourth of July. At first I was sad to be moving further away from Hank, but we knew we'd see each other every day at school. As for Natalia, after we broke up, we never talked and barely even said hello if we saw each other. She was going to head off to the all-girls high school where her sister went, so I'd probably never see her again anyway. I never even bothered to say goodbye before we left Encino.

The day the moving truck pulled up to our new house was hot. And I mean Valley hot. Triple digits. I felt bad for the movers.

I walked outside the house just to see what was going on, and who the fuck did I see across the street and two houses down? Moose. He was coming out from inside the garage he had just opened, his enormous frame silhouetted as the door rose and seemed to float up in the air in slow motion above him.

"You?" I said in disbelief, pointing my finger directly at him for added emphasis.

"No!" Moose said, even more surprised than I was. "You're the fucking new kid?" Word had gotten around the neighborhood that a new family with a kid who was going to be attending Woodrow Wilson was moving into the house that had recently sold, and Moose was excited to see who his new neighbor was going to be.

I looked up at the cloudless sky, the sun blasting its rays down at us. "How is this even possible?" I yelled.

But at that moment, we realized we had been thrown in this lot together and had no choice but to accept our fates. Here we were, forced to spend our entire high school years living almost directly across the street from each other, in a far-flung neighborhood named after a Scottish village set high up on the Valley side of the Santa Monica Mountains. We could not change our circumstances.

"Look, Douglas," Moose said. "I know we hate each other, but I've lived here for a couple of years. There are no other kids our age up in this part of the neighborhood. I mean, Leslie Lamb lives next door to you," he said, pointing at yet another of the faux Spanish-style stucco boxes that filled the streets around here. "But that's about it."

"Leslie Lamb lives there?" I asked. I didn't really know Leslie all that well, but she always seemed all right.

"Yeah," Moose said. "Anyway, if you want to have anybody to hang out with up here, I'm your only answer. Believe me, you're the last fucker I want to hang with, but I don't think we have any choice."

He was right, and I knew it. "How about a truce?" I offered.

"Sounds good to me," Moose sighed.

"Let's meet in the middle of the street and shake on it," I suggested.

Slowly, each of us walked toward the middle of the street. We both stopped about halfway across.

"I think you need to come over this way a little bit," Moose insisted, pointing to a spot a foot or so closer to his house.

"No, I think this is good," I replied. "This looks halfway to me."

"You're out of your mind. Look how much closer you are to your house!"

"Does it really matter?" I asked.

"You said 'the middle,' and I agreed," Moose replied. "Just seems like we should meet in the middle if that's what we agreed to."

"Fine," I acquiesced. "How about here, halfway between where I say it is and where you say it is?"

"Fine," Moose agreed.

And that's how our friendship started, with a handshake that was either in the center of the street between our two houses or not. There would be plenty of arguments and compromises in the years to come, but we would never be mortal enemies again.

In fact, what cemented our friendship for eternity took place just two weeks later, on a blistering Saturday afternoon in my new driveway. Art had surprised me by hiring someone to come over and install a backboard and basket above the garage. I had gone out with my mom to run some errands, and by the time we returned . . . *voilà*. There it was.

The driveway, like most driveways, was far from perfect for basketball. It sloped down to the street and rather dramatically at the end, so that you were probably shooting at a twelve-foot basket by the time you were beyond twenty feet or so. But from fifteen feet and closer, it was fairly flat and plenty wide. You could go out a good eighteen feet on the wing on either side of the basket, and while the corners were tighter, the right side featured an opening where a walkway came along the side of the house and then turned toward the driveway. This created a space along the baseline where you could fall away into the corner and extend the distance to over twenty feet, especially if you fell into the bushes while doing so.

I became quite expert at the corner fall-away, if only because it allowed me to get my shot over my much taller brother, David. Being so much older and bigger and stronger than I, David was impossible for me to beat, and even scoring off of him was a huge challenge. He could stop me pretty much whenever he wanted to, and the only time I could really hope to make a basket was off of loose balls or long rebounds. But that right corner enabled me to fall away and create distance between me and him, enough distance that I could get my shot off and over his outstretched arms. Sometimes he'd come so hard at me in an attempt to swat my shot that I'd fall way back into the juniper bushes, planted where the walkway turned and went down the side of the house, snapping off a few branches in the process. It hurt at times, but if I got the shot off cleanly, it was well worth the few scratches the junipers left.

One day, a couple of weeks after we'd moved into the house in Stromness, my brother and I were hanging out. He was using the pool, eating lunch and stuff, while I was lying on the couch, enjoying the AC and watching NBC's *Game of the Week*, the Cubs versus St. Louis, I think.

The phone rang, and I picked up. "Hello?"

"*Bonjour*," Moose said. For some reason, while the

rest of us had studied Spanish in school, Moose had chosen French.

"Hey."

"What are you doing?"

"Lying here watching a little baseball. Trying to stay cool."

"It's so fucking hot out. But I feel like doing something."

"Like what?"

"I don't know. Shoot some baskets or something."

"In this heat?"

"It'll be good for you, Douglas. Make you sweat for once in your life."

"Fuck you, Moose."

"Come on. Meet me in your driveway in five." *Click.*

I looked up to see David eating his second salami sandwich of the afternoon.

"Hey, David. Want to shoot around with me and Moose?"

"Why would I want to do that?"

"I don't know. 'Cause it's fun?"

"Tell you what. How about I play you two-on-one for a dollar each?"

"Seriously?"

"You guys suck. I won't even break a sweat. Even in this heat."

"I'll have to check with Moose, but I'm game. We'll kick your ass."

Needless to say, Moose was more than happy to accept the challenge. "But why only a dollar?" he asked David once we were all out in the driveway, wearing shorts and no shirts. David and I had our Adidas Superstars, but Moose went with old school Converse, plus a red headband on his head and a blue wristband above his shooting hand.

"What did you have in mind?" David was definitely interested in upping the ante.

"How about five bucks?"

"Each?" David asked, wide-eyed.

"Whoa, whoa, whoa, big fella," I said to Moose. "This is getting a little steep for me."

"Five bucks total," Moose clarified. "Our five bucks against your five bucks."

"Well, that's hardly fair," David protested.

"Why not?" Moose insisted.

David couldn't come up with an answer. "Okay, whatever. First one to ten, have to win by two. Douglas shoots for first outs."

"Done!" Moose said enthusiastically before passing me the ball. "Shoot for outs, Douglas."

I hit the shot from our makeshift top of the key, inbounded the ball to Moose, and the game was on. Moose and I immediately shifted into the most obvious strategy: spread the court. There were two of us and only one David, and since it was impossible for him to guard us both at the same time, we instinctively knew that if we spaced ourselves correctly, we'd get open look after open look. All we needed to do was hit our shots. Sounds easy, but our driveway wasn't that large, and David was big and athletic, so he could switch back and forth between us fairly quickly.

Still, as the game wore on, the heat began to affect David and, leading 9–6, I drew my brother out toward the right wing, gave him a head fake to get him up in the air, and then passed the ball to a breaking Moose, who took the ball and . . . blew an easy layup.

"Come on, Moose!" I yelled. "You gotta make that shit!" I was worried that David would reel off several straight baskets to snatch the win from us.

"Fuck!" Moose said glumly. "Sorry, man." Moose had a mental block or something when it came to layups; he was always missing wide-open gimmees right under the basket.

Fortunately, a tiring David missed his next shot under the withering pressure of our double team. Moose did a great job boxing him out, and I snatched the rebound, cleared the ball, and calmly sank a seventeen-footer to win the game.

"Yes!" Moose shouted. "We kicked your ass, David!"

"Shit," David frowned. "I can't believe I lost to you weasels."

"Well, you did!" I enthused.

"Yeah, now pay up!" Moose demanded.

David simply turned his back, flipped us the bird, and walked back into the house.

"Hey!" I yelled. "Where you going?"

"You better not welch on that bet, David," Moose threatened.

David whirled around. "Or what?" he laughed. "You gonna go tell your mommy?" he mimicked in a whiny voice.

"David, just pay up, man," I pleaded.

"I'll pay you when I feel like it," David said, turning and going inside the house.

"*Merde!*" Moose spat. "What an asshole."

"Don't worry. He'll pay. I'll go to my mom if I have to."

David eventually did give us the money he owed, but only after he made us admit that the only reason he lost that day was because of the extreme heat.

Heat or no heat, Moose and I knew we'd kicked his ass fair and square, and we would undoubtedly revel in that sweet victory for the rest of our lives. We certainly let everyone at school know about it.

"Hey, Andrew," Moose bragged while we were standing with our group of friends the first day of school after that summer, "Douglas and I played his older brother David two-on-one for five bucks and kicked his ass!" He would repeat the story of the game, play by play, to anyone who would listen.

Most of our friends, however, were more interested in the fact that Moose and I had gone from worst enemies to close friends seemingly overnight. "What the hell happened to you two?" the other kids asked. Of course, Hank, Marco, and Andrew knew because I had seen them a lot that summer, and we'd even played some basketball in my driveway with Moose. But for the kids who hadn't seen us between ninth and tenth grades, it was still quite a shock.

"He finally came to his senses and realized he was much better off being my friend than my enemy," Moose laughed. "He figured out that if he were friends with me, he'd get to be on my team more often and wouldn't have to always be losing to me."

"Fuck you, Moose," I said. "Hank and I always kicked your and The Big Lefty's ass," I insisted, referring to Clark, Moose's best friend back in junior high.

"In your dreams, Douglas. In your dreams," Moose said, waving his hand as he walked away. While we were now friends, there would always be a bit of an adversarial relationship between the two of us that we would never quite shake.

Chapter Two

The Labor Day weekend before our final year of high school seemed to appear from out of nowhere. Where the hell had the summer gone? I slept in late on Saturday; once school started on Tuesday, there'd be no rest for the weary. I was just in the process of waking up, and as I stretched my arms up above my head and let out a big yawn, I heard the phone ring. Then my mom called out, "Douglas! Hank's on the phone. Time to get up."

"Okay, Mom," I answered groggily. "I'm coming." I made my way out of my bedroom and into the hallway, grimacing as I spotted Art's most recent purchase: a *Garfield* phone. For some reason, Art was a huge fan of the comic strip, and they had recently started selling a phone in the shape of Garfield. When you picked up the handle, the cat's eyes would open. Why in the world someone would want a phone in the shape of an orange cat was beyond me, and even though I despised *Garfield*—"*Marmaduke* is so much funnier!" I would argue with Art—Mom said it was important to Art to have bought the phone for the family, and to just smile and laugh and pretend that I was happy about having to use this stupid phone as my main outlet to the world going forward. Sure, there was another phone in the kitchen and in the den as well, but this one was the closest to my bedroom, and I would sometimes bring it into my room, running the extra-long wire I'd convinced my mom and Art to keep permanently attached to the phone under my bedroom door once I had closed it for privacy.

My mom wasn't crazy about the extra ten or so feet of wire that was constantly sitting in a heap on the floor next to the wall in the hallway, but she knew it was important for me to have some space where I could talk to my friends in private. There was no way they were going to give me my own phone in my bedroom, so she just tried her best to ignore the annoying pile of wire lying on the green shag carpet.

"Hello?" I said, picking up the receiver with one hand while holding the fingers of my other hand over Garfield's eyes so they wouldn't open.

"Hey buddy," Hank said. "You just wake up?"

"Yeah. Trying to get in as much sleep as possible before school starts on Tuesday."

"Sorry, man."

"That's okay, I'd just started to wake up before you called."

"Oh okay, cool," Hank said. "Hey, Simon's Stereo is having a huge Labor Day sale. My parents said I could get a new pair of speakers for my birthday. Want to go over there with me to do a little research?"

"Sure," I said. "What time were you thinking?"

"How about I pick you up in an hour?"

"Sounds good. See you then." I hung up the phone, released my fingers from Garfield's eyes, and ran them through my thick hair. Today would be a good day to hang out in the back room of Simon's Stereo; it was supposed to be triple digits outside, so sitting in a cool, dark room listening to a variety of high-end audio equipment sounded like just the ticket. Pacific Stereo over on Topanga

Boulevard was by far the more popular stereo shop in the Valley, but we preferred Simon's, which was located on a side street just off of Topanga, not too far from the high-end mall known as The Promenade. Pacific was a little too "mersh" for our taste. Sure, they carried the most popular brands—Pioneer, Kenwood, Panasonic, and the like—but if you wanted the super high-end stuff—McIntosh receivers, NAD amps, Denon turntables, and Advent speakers—then the small room at the back of the Simon's store was the place to go.

"Good afternoon, gentleman," the salesman greeted us as Hank and I walked through the front entrance of the stereo shop. "What can I do ya for today?" The salesman appeared to be in his early thirties, tall, thin, and very hip in his tight French jeans and shirt unbuttoned down to nearly his navel, revealing a hairless chest with a couple of gold chains hanging from his neck. One of them included a small spoon, a seemingly new symbol of prestige, as anyone doing cocaine was probably not only a rock and roll or movie industry insider, but was also making a decent living to boot. Who could even afford that stuff?

"Yeah, ah, I'm interested in buying a new pair of speakers," said Hank, trying to sound as sophisticated as possible.

"Well, you're in luck," the salesman said with a smile, turning on the charm while stroking his reddish-colored beard, neatly trimmed and cropped short to his face. "We're having a killer sale and have a huge selection of audiophile speakers." He spun around and gestured with his long arms and fingers toward a wall literally filled with a dozen or so different brands and sizes of speakers.

"Great!" Hank replied. "But I'm actually more interested in the speakers you have in the back room."

"Right on!" The salesman smiled again. "You want to see the primo stuff, eh?"

"Yeah, it's his birthday," I interjected, "so he wants something really special."

"Well then!" The salesman extended his hand toward Hank. "Happy birthday! I'm Miles. And your name is?"

"I'm Hank, and this is my friend, Douglas."

Miles shook Hank's hand but didn't offer one up to me. "Follow me, boys, for only I have the keys to the castle." With that, he pulled out some keys and jingled them proudly. Indeed, the sliding glass door leading to the high-end room was locked to keep the riff-raff out. I was sort of surprised that Miles was so amenable to letting us back there; usually the salespeople at Simon's kept a tight rein on who was allowed into the room, and for how long. If they suspected you were just a looky-loo and not serious about making a purchase, they'd cut you off after five or ten minutes or not even let you in at all. But I guess Miles figured the odds were high that Hank's parents were forking over a decent amount of bread for some high-end speakers for their son, so he might as well treat him as a serious customer. Besides, Labor Day sale or no Labor Day sale, there wasn't another soul in the store.

"Okay," Miles began, flicking on some equipment, "why don't you tell me about your system. What kind of equipment do you have now?"

"I've got a Marantz 2230 with some Acoustic Research 4x speakers and a Denon turntable," Hank said.

"Groovy," Miles said. "The Marantz is getting a bit long in the tooth and those basic ARs are now simply considered to be MOR speakers, but the Denon is high quality and in my opinion it's more important to have the best turntable you can afford, even if you have to go a bit basic on the receiver or amp."

"Yeah, my dad agrees. The entire system was his, and he gave it to me when he got a new one."

"Groovy," Miles repeated, stroking his beard and listening to Hank intently, or at least he appeared to be. "But you're right to want to replace those ARs. Your speakers are the heart and soul of your stereo system, and you could definitely use an upgrade. Was there any particular brand you were interested in?"

"Well, I was thinking either Advents or Bose."

"Right on!" the salesman said, smiling widely. "You have excellent taste, my man." And so began a forty-five-minute lecture on frequency response and tweeters and woofers and bass response. He stood there at a control panel like something straight out of *The Wizard of Oz*, his gold chains swaying around his neck as he moved up and down and right and left, flipping different switches and comparing several different sets of speakers against one another. When all was said and done, we were right back where we started: Hank had narrowed it down to the Advent speaker known simply as the "Large Advent" and the Bose 901s.

"Both are excellent, excellent choices, my man," Miles assured Hank. His level of enthusiasm had not waned the entire hour we had been in the store. If anything, he was more hyped up than when we'd first walked in. Perhaps it had something to do with the brief "bathroom break" he took about halfway through our listening session; when he returned, both Hank and I took note of his suddenly runny nose.

"Okay, I've saved the best for last!" Miles looked at us with excitement emanating from his eyes. Reaching for another key, he unlocked a lower cabinet beneath the wall of equipment. "This is where we keep the Japanese pressings," he said as he pulled out Supertramp's *Crime of the Century*. "This is still one of the primo albums to use when testing out speakers. The production is off the charts."

"Great!" Hank said, by now fully caught up in the salesman's elation. "We love Supertramp."

From the moment the album's opener, "School," had reached the point where the kids scream in the background and the bass and drums kick in, Hank was sold: "I'm going with the Advents," he told Miles.

"Far out!" Miles immediately hopped down off the table he had been casually sitting on and went to turn off the music.

"Can we listen to the rest of the side of the album?" Hank asked.

"Sure, my man. I'll just step out and prepare the paperwork." Miles rolled open the glass door and closed it behind him, leaving me and Hank alone in the room.

"What do you think?" Hank asked.

"I think they're great. You sure you can afford them?"

"Barely," Hank said. "But with the Labor Day sale, it's just within the budget my dad said I could spend."

"Cool. Ready to do it?"

"Bloody well right!" Hank laughed, mimicking the next song that had started playing throughout the room.

The hard part ended up being trying to fit Hank's new monster speakers into his Camaro. We somehow managed, though, by placing one speaker in his trunk and one in his back seat. When we got back to Hank's town-house—he was still at the Encino Royale, where I used to live when we first became friends—we hooked up his new speakers and, since his parents were nowhere to be found, headed out to the alley in back to smoke a joint, just like Weddy and Ronnie used to do.

"So," I asked, "what's the first record going to be?"

"I don't know," Hank said between hits. "What do you think? Miles already played Supertramp for us. The new Styx record has pretty amazing production. Same with the new REO Speedwagon record."

"Yeah, that's true. But I'm thinking we should reach back a bit. Maybe *Sgt. Pepper*? No! I got it!" My level of excitement was rising as the weed started to kick in. "Pink Floyd!"

"Great idea!" Hank said, taking the joint from me and inhaling deeply. Neither of us were huge Pink Floyd fans, but their records always sounded so amazing that they made even the most average stereo system sound like true audiophile.

When we went back inside the townhouse, we grabbed a couple of Cokes and some chips and went up to Hank's room, where we closed his shutters, put *Dark Side of the Moon* on his Denon, turned off the lights, and lay down on the floor, preparing to have our minds blown by both Pink Floyd and Hank's new pair of Advents. By the time "The Great Gig in the Sky" closed out side one, both Hank and I were flying, soaring with the crazy vocals, and then finally descending as the song quietly wound down to its conclusion. It's not often you get to take a journey like that, much less with your best friend lying there on the floor next to you. When it was over, Hank and I didn't say much; we just looked at each other and shook our heads in amazement at what we had just experienced.

The purchase of the Advent speakers was deemed a rousing success. Even Hank's Dad, a serious audiophile, gave Hank his stamp of approval when he came home later that afternoon and heard them for himself. From that moment forward, Hank and I would often laugh and talk about the time we took a trip to the "outer limits," courtesy of Pink Floyd and Hank's new pair of speakers.

The rest of the weekend flew by rather uneventfully. It was hotter than hell, so I mostly hung out at home, trying to psych myself up for my final year of high school. I wasn't all that excited about it, to be honest. They say your grades only really count the first semester, and since I already knew I was a shoo-in to go to San Diego State— just like my sister, most of my friends, and, frankly, most of Woodrow Wilson—I knew I could pretty much put it on cruise control. If I held a B-plus average, everything would be good. My dad had already told me he expected me to work twenty hours a week at his printing company during my second semester, when I'd only have three classes and be finished by noon. While I didn't mind earning some dough to bank for my college years, I wasn't exactly looking forward to the experience.

The one thing that *was* going to be cool about this year was that I was going to be writing for the *Woodrow Wilson Wire*, the school newspaper. I had taken Ms. Pearlstein's journalism class last year and did so well that she asked me if I'd like to join the paper during my senior year. I happily accepted her invitation, and talked Hank into joining, too. He'd be busy playing on the basketball team, but would contribute a weekly sports column about the

Torero varsity written from an insider's perspective. It was my idea, and it was an easy sell to both Hank and Ms. Pearlstein.

I was assigned to the city beat. What I really wanted to do was write for the Arts and Entertainment section, but everyone wanted to write for that section— after all, they got to go to free concerts, movies, plays, and even got free albums and books to review. But the Arts and Entertainment staff was filled with students who had been on the paper since the tenth grade, so it was hard news for me.

My first assignment was to write about Narconon, a new service in the Valley for families dealing with kids addicted to drugs. I felt a little hypocritical, since I smoked pot and drank alcohol, but I felt I could remain objective enough to do a good job on the story.

Aside from seeing each other occasionally at the paper—Hank wasn't required to go to after-school meetings, but he'd sometimes pop in to talk to Ms. Pearlstein at lunch and I'd often go with him—the only other class we had together was Trigonometry, which was going to be grueling. Both Hank and I had done well in Algebra 2, but everyone said Trig was on a whole other level. Fortunately, the teacher was Mr. Rhodes, who had us in tenth grade for Geometry. Hank and I both liked him and, more importantly, we believed Mr. Rhodes liked us as well. Only, that theory was momentarily thrown into doubt when we walked into class the first day of school, the Tuesday after Labor Day.

"Good morning, boys," Mr. Rhodes said rather gruffly when we walked in the door. The room was only about half full, and we still had a good seven minutes before class started, so both Hank and I thought Mr. Rhodes would've been a bit more friendly toward us, maybe even engage in some small talk. But evidently he was in one of his moods. Rhodes, a very large man with a thick walrus mustache who constantly had a hot rod magazine open on his desk, was known to sometimes lapse into bully mode—unfriendly, short, and very demanding. I remember one time back in tenth grade when he really got on Hank's case—who got an A- in the class, by the way, and was one of Rhodes' better students—for forgetting a simple formula he had aced on the test just a few days prior.

"You're like the guy who goes along like this in life," Rhodes lashed out, scribbling a bunch of nonsense in a line on the chalkboard with his right hand while holding an eraser a couple of feet behind and erasing his markings as he moved across the board. "You only remember what's in between the chalk and the eraser and you forget everything that came before. People," he turned and wagged a finger at the entire classroom, "cramming for tests and then forgetting the material immediately afterward is no way to achieve success—either in school or in life. You have to master the material, not simply memorize it for a couple of days."

Hank just sat there, stunned that Rhodes had made such a harsh example out of him, while the rest of the class went silent. The one good thing about Rhodes and his moods was that they didn't typically last long, and he certainly didn't stay mad at you. In fact, by the end of that year, Hank was probably Rhodes' favorite student.

My fears that Rhodes had either forgotten who we were or simply didn't care about us anymore ended up being groundless. At the end of that first day of class, as we were all packing up and rising to leave, he called out,

"Hank and Douglas, come see me, please, before you go."

Hank and I looked at each other. "What the fuck?" I whispered quizzically to Hank. We waited for the other kids to leave and then approached him together, both breathing a sigh of relief as a big smile spread across his chubby face.

"How are my two favorite math students?" he said warmly. "I was so happy to see you on my roster. I didn't see much of either of you last year and, to be honest, I was a little hurt that you never came to visit."

Came to visit? Was he serious? I mean, Hank and I both liked Rhodes, but we weren't in the habit of hanging out with teachers during our downtime.

"Oh, ah, sorry, Mr. Rhodes," Hank began. "Eleventh grade was a really, really busy year, and, you know, I had the basketball team and stuff."

"Yeah, yeah, yeah," Rhodes brushed him off with a wave of his hand. "And what's your excuse, Efron?" Rhodes was fond of using your last name when you were speaking privately with him.

"Well, like Hank said—"

"I'm just teasing you guys," Rhodes interjected before I could finish. "Listen, I wanted to talk to you about this year's Holiday Performance."

"What about it?" I asked. I couldn't imagine what Rhodes had to do with the Holiday show; that was the music and drama teachers' gig. And what the heck did he want from us? We weren't performers.

"I'm in charge of raising money for the event this year, and one of the main ways to accomplish that is by selling ads in the program that's handed out to everyone who attends. And when I thought of who would be crackerjack ad salespeople, the two of you came to mind."

"Us?" Hank asked, mimicking my thoughts exactly. "Why us?"

"Because the two of you are smart, you're hard workers, and I know both of your dads are smart businessmen. Besides, Douglas's father is printing the programs, and he was the one who suggested the two of you would be perfect for the job."

"Great," I muttered under my breath. "Thanks, Dad."

"What was that, Efron?" Rhodes asked.

"Oh, nothing, sir. We'd be happy to help out, wouldn't we, Hank?" I knew that with my dad behind this little enterprise, there was no way in hell I was going to get out of it, so if I was going to be forced into being an ad salesman, I was going to take Hank down with me.

"Well, I don't know," Hank said. "I mean, I might have to check with Coach."

"Oh, it won't take up that much of your time," Rhodes said. "All you need to sell is a dozen ads. A couple of afternoons spent visiting some of the local businesses in the area—you know, dry cleaners, liquor stores, markets—and you'll have the whole program sold out in no time." Rhodes' expression suddenly changed, and he grew more serious, maybe even a bit threatening. Sure, he was your classic "jolly fat guy," but his sheer size made him fairly intimidating. He looked at us intently and said, "What do you say, boys? Do I have my salesmen?"

"Sure," I said, knowing my dad had essentially left me with no choice.

"Yeah, I guess so," Hank said solemnly. He then quickly added, "But Douglas is the official ad salesman, and I'll just be his assistant."

"What?" I said in disbelief. "Why should all the responsibility fall on me?"

"Because your dad got us into this mess," Hank insisted.

"Whatever. You're still going on every sales call with me."

"I'm sure you boys will work it out. Now, I need these ads sold by the end of the month so that we can set our budget, and I want you to report to me once a week on how things are going between now and then. Understood?" He lifted his massive body out of his chair with a bit of effort and extended his hand.

"Deal," both Hank and I agreed, each taking a turn shaking his hand.

"Great. Now I have to get ready for my next group of students, and I'm sure you need to get off to your next class. I'll see you boys tomorrow."

"Thanks, Mr. Rhodes," Hank and I said in unison, adding, "See you tomorrow."

With that, Hank and I left the class with a new job and title: We were now officially in the advertising game. Maybe we weren't on the creative side like Darrin Stephens, but Larry Tate seemed to do all right for himself.

In the end, Hank and I only needed one afternoon—a Tuesday toward the end of September when Hank was able to get a day off from practice. We headed over to Corbin Plaza, a collection of shops right next to Corbin Bowl, where Hank, Weddy, Ronnie, and I used to bowl when we were in junior high. Every Saturday morning, the four of us, having spent the night at one of our houses, would head on over to the bowling alley, where we had our own team in a junior league.

We usually spent the night at either Weddy's house or my house; Ronnie's life at home was just too harsh and uncomfortable, and we all feared Hank's dad, a tough dude who worked as a key grip, whatever that was, in the film industry. Hank once explained that his dad helped to make sure all of the camera equipment was working correctly. Anyway, none of us liked sleeping over at Hank's townhouse because his dad would, after a few drinks, invariably challenge us to a round or three of "knuckles." We had no choice but to play this masochistic game in which Hank's dad would encourage us to slam our fists into his fist to see who could handle the most pain to their knuckles. Needless to say, it was brutal, and our hands would always hurt long into the night, sometimes even the next morning, which would end up affecting our bowling game. But no matter how much it hurt, the whole object of the game was to steel your nerves and show less emotion than Hank's dad, which was impossible because he was always stone-faced and seemingly impervious to pain.

Part of our Saturday morning bowling ritual was the game of APBA Baseball we'd have running simultaneously with the bowling match. We'd take turns in between our rolls, alternately throwing dice, then balls, then dice, then balls. I can still picture Hank, desperate for a come-from-behind win, shaking the dice in the bottom of the ninth while his best hitter, Darrell "Howdy Doody" Evans, was at the plate. "It's How . . . Deee . . . Doody time!" Hank would sing loudly as he furiously shook the dice out of the shaker and onto the table. I swear, more often than not, when Hank sang the Howdy Doody song, a pair of sixes would come up, signaling a home run, and Hank would be whooping and hollering all over that damn bowling alley.

"Maybe we should just go bowling instead," Hank said as we parked the car in the lot in front of the plaza, adjacent to Corbin Bowl.

"Now, now . . . come on, Hank. Let's get this thing done." Fortunately, a sales challenge like this was right up my alley. Back when I was a little kid in Northridge, I used to run my own car washing and dog poop scooping businesses around the neighborhood. I discovered early on that the best way to get customers was to let them know which of their neighbors had already signed up for my services. Not wanting to look like an unfriendly neighbor who refused to hire a local kid for a small job, or perhaps simply not wanting to look like a cheapskate, the mom or dad would gladly hire me.

"It's a snowball effect," my dad had explained to me. "Or maybe the 'odd man out' effect. People don't want to be the only one who isn't doing what their friends or neighbors or business rivals are doing. They're afraid of the consequences, and it's so much easier to say yes when others have already done it. That's why it's like a snowball; the list of customers just grows exponentially every time you add someone new. The challenge, of course, is landing that first customer. Getting the first customer to say yes isn't always so easy."

But I had a plan for that as well. "Hello, Sir," I said, walking into the liquor store in the middle of the small outdoor shopping mall. "My name is Douglas, and this is my associate, Hank. We are seniors at Woodrow Wilson High School, and we'd like to offer you the opportunity to place an ad in the program for our annual Holiday Celebration." The event was really called the Holiday Performance, but I thought "Celebration" sounded much better.

"Sorry, boys, not today," the man behind the counter said distractedly. Even though there wasn't another soul in the store, he had the *Racing Forum* open on the counter and was scribbling notes in pencil on the thin pages of newspaper.

"But, sir," I implored, ready to set my plan in motion to get that first sale. "I'm offering you the opportunity to be the first local business to purchase an ad in a program that will be viewed by hundreds and hundreds of local families. The ads sell out every year, and because you're going to be our first customer, I've been authorized to offer you a substantial discount." Hank gave me a what-the-fuck look, but I simply stepped on his toe, our regular signal to, well, to just shut up and watch.

"Discount? What kind of discount?" The man looked up from the *Forum* and took off his reading glasses. He had thinning gray hair and probably hadn't shaved in several days.

"Well, normally, a full-page ad goes for twenty-five dollars, but because you will be the first business to lend your support to our wonderful school, I can give you that ad for twenty dollars."

"No, no thanks," he said, taking his eyes off of me and returning to his paper once again. "Too expensive."

"Well, perhaps you'd like to consider a half-page ad? These normally go for fifteen dollars, but I can give it to you for ten dollars."

"Douglas, are you crazy? Mr. Rhodes would never go for that."

I stepped on his toe again. "Sir," I said, looking at the proprietor of the liquor store, "I can assure you that, in spite of my colleague's objection, I have been authorized to offer you that incredible discount on a one-time-only basis."

The combination of my offer and Hank's reaction had piqued the owner's interest. "Maybe. Let me think about it. Come back tomorrow."

I knew better than to let such a great prospect off the hook so easily; as my dad had always taught me, you have to strike while the iron is hot. "Sir, I'm afraid that if I walk out that door, I'm going to sell the first ad to your neighbor, Mr. Azarian the dry cleaner." In preparation for this day, I had called up several of the businesses in the plaza and gotten the owners' names. "And then Mr. Azarian will get the discount, and I will have to then charge you the full fifteen dollars for the ad."

The owner rubbed his stubbly chin and gave both Hank and me a good looking over, evidently trying to decide if we were on the level or just a couple of cons, a pair of hustlers looking to make a quick buck. "You have a sample of the program?" he asked gruffly.

I pulled out last year's program and explained how the Holiday Celebration had been going on at Woodrow Wilson for over twenty-five years and drew hundreds and hundreds of families every holiday season.

"How come nobody ever asked me before?" he wondered, opening his cash drawer and pulling out a ten-dollar bill. "I've been in business for over ten years."

"Well, I will personally make sure that going forward, you will be the first customer we call on so that you can get the special discount every time."

"Guaranteed?" he asked.

"Absolutely," I lied. I knew that after today, I would never be doing this again. He handed over the ten dollars.

"And if I could just get you to fill out this form and sign right here, we'll have everything we need to create the ad, and someone will contact you next month to show you the proof before the program goes to print."

After filling out the necessary paperwork, the man returned to his *Racing Forum* and didn't even raise his head to say goodbye as we walked out the door. "Why did you give that guy such a big discount, Douglas?" Hank asked after we were clearly out of listening range. "Rhodes is gonna kill us."

"No, he won't," I assured Hank, "because we're going to now sell out this whole program in the next couple of hours and he won't care about the five bucks. Watch and learn." We entered the dry cleaner next door.

"Hello," I said confidently to the woman at the desk. I was on a roll, and I knew it. "Is Mr. Azarian here?"

"You have an appointment?" the woman asked, her voice thick with an accent I didn't recognize.

"No ma'am, but I'm sure Mr. Azarian will be *very* interested in what I have to say."

She looked at me skeptically, but then called out, "Nishan!"

"What?" I heard a deep male voice yell from the back of the store.

"Come here. Someone to see you."

"Who?"

"Come here!" the woman yelled.

A heavy-set man with a full beard and dark, bushy eyebrows appeared from between the racks of clothes hanging in plastic bags. "Who are you?" he said to me warily.

"Hello, Mr. Arazian. My name is Douglas, and this is my associate, Hank. We are seniors at Woodrow Wilson

High School, and we'd like to offer you the opportunity to place an ad in the program for our annual Holiday Celebration."

"No. Not interested." He turned and began to walk away.

"But, sir," I implored, pulling out the form for the liquor store ad and waving it in the air. "Your neighbor at the liquor store just bought an ad, and your other neighbors will be buying ads, and you wouldn't want to be the only one in this whole plaza who isn't supporting the local high school, would you? I'm sure many of your customers have children at Woodrow Wilson, and what would they think if their dry cleaner was the only one who didn't support their children's school?"

Hank looked at me slack-jawed, amazed at my *chutzpah*. But my strategy seemed to be working as Mr. Azarian suddenly stopped and turned around, approaching me with an outstretched hand. "Let me see that," he insisted, reaching for the piece of paper.

I couldn't let him see the discounted price I had offered the owner of the liquor store, so I strategically placed my thumb over the price and held up the paper with both hands so that Mr. Azarian could confirm the liquor store's participation.

"How much?" he asked.

"Twenty-five dollars for a full page, fifteen dollars for a half page, and ten dollars for a quarter page." Mr. Rhodes had shrewdly priced the ads to incentivize businesses to go for the larger ads, which offered more space for the price. There was also a five-dollar option for a business-card-sized ad, but I saved those as the last resort, for when a customer was vaguely interested but didn't want to fork over even ten bucks for the quarter-page ad. "Your neighbor, of course, only went for the half-page ad, but for the greatest impact, I'd strongly recommend you take out a full-page ad. Remember, hundreds of local families will be seeing the ad in the program. You're guaranteed to get many new customers," I added in an attempt to sweeten the pot.

"Okay," he said to the woman at the desk. "Give him the money. Thank you, boys." And with that, he disappeared behind the rows of clothes to return to doing whatever it was that dry cleaners did all day. Clean clothes, I guess.

Needless to say, the snowball effect kicked in, and the more and more businesses in Corbin Plaza that signed up, the easier and easier it became to sell the ads. Just like I had planned, peer pressure did its job; nobody wanted to be the only business that wasn't supporting the school. Within a couple of hours we had filled every available spot.

We decided to celebrate with a snack at the nearby McDonald's. As we downed our Quarter Pounders with Cheese and fries, Hank shook his head. "I gotta hand it to you, man. You sure do know how to sell."

"Yeah, well, my dad was a pretty good teacher."

"Seriously, though, I didn't even need to say a word. You could've handled the whole thing yourself."

"Are you kidding?" I said, putting down my burger and taking a sip of Coke. "You were an integral part of the whole operation. You represent the all-American boy, the good-looking athlete who's everyone's fantasy of what a high school kid should look like. *You're* the kid they think they're supporting when they buy an ad. Don't sell yourself short, Hank," I said, looking at him with as much sincerity as I could muster. "You were extremely key to our success. It was all part of my master plan."

Hank shook his head and laughed. "Damn, you're good. *Really, really* good." We both smiled, and when Hank held up five fingers, we executed one of our patented Soul Brother handshakes that we'd been doing since junior high—version number #5, per Hank's request, which featured a nice crossover move—and returned to our burgers and fries, both knowing how lucky we were to have such a deep friendship. It didn't even require us to speak to know what we were both thinking, even though neither of us would ever openly admit that to anyone, much less to each other.

To say the least, Mr. Rhodes was more than thrilled with our efforts, and with the ad sales for the Holiday Performance program complete and off our plate, we could focus on all of the other things occupying our brains: girls, schoolwork, basketball for Hank, and my writing for the *Wire*.

I'd already learned a ton from Ms. Pearlstein. When I handed in the first draft of the Narconon story, I thought it was pretty solid. But Ms. Pearlstein sat down with me one day at lunch and went through the story line by line, teaching me so much about how the language of news reporting has to be so much more direct and to the point than other forms of writing.

"Like right here, Douglas," she said, tapping a sentence with her red pencil. See how much more effective it is if we take out these words? She drew a line through a handful of words and, just as she said, the sentence was much stronger, much clearer. "And why are you burying this wonderful quote from the girl in the program way down toward the bottom of your story?" she asked. "This is powerful material. You need to move it up. I'd suggest putting it here." Ms. Pearlstein drew an arrow to just below the second paragraph.

Suddenly, Genevieve Carlson burst into the room. Always a ball of fire, I'd known Genevieve since junior high, where she used to go by the name "Sandy." Apparently, when Genevieve was a toddler, she had blue eyes, blonde hair, and loved to play in the sand at the beach. One day, while covered in sand from head to foot as she stood in the bright sun at Will Rogers beach, her uncle called out, "Hey, Sandy, come over here!" And the name just stuck. Besides, at that young age neither she nor her toddler friends could pronounce "Genevieve," so Sandy was perfect. Eventually, though, her blonde hair faded to more of a light brown, and her blue eyes turned to green, and at the beginning of her junior year, after a summer trip to France to visit her French mother's relatives, she announced she was going back to her given name.

"Hi, Ms. Pearlstein. Hey Douglas," Genevieve said breathlessly. "Ms. Pearlstein, did you read that Op-Ed piece I wrote about nuclear power?" Genevieve had always been passionate about one cause or another. In eighth grade, she was in my filmmaking class and made not one but *two* films about the mistreatment of American Indians. She was always attending rallies on weekends, and hadn't eaten a grape in years in support of the farmworkers, even though the official boycott had ended long ago.

"Genevieve, can't you see I'm with Douglas?"

"It's okay, Ms. Pearlstein," I offered. "We're friends." While we didn't exactly hang out together, we'd known each other so long and been in so many classes together, I did consider Genevieve a friend of sorts. In fact, back in junior high, everyone always suspected that she had a crush on me, though I had never pursued anything with her. It wasn't that I wasn't attracted to her, it was just that there never seemed to be any spark between us. But I will say that I always felt comfortable around Genevieve, and whenever circumstances threw us together—we'd partnered on several class projects over the years—we always got along and worked well as a team. Even had fun doing it.

"Sorry, sorry," Genevieve said, still maintaining a rather frantic pace. "I just ran all the way over from the cafeteria and I'm really hoping you'll print the piece in the next edition of the *Wire*."

"We'll see," Ms. Pearlstein sighed. "It's very good, but I don't know yet if we have room."

"Pleeeeasssse, Ms. Pearlstein." Genevieve clasped her hands together, looked at Ms. Pearlstein, and batted her long eyelashes. We all shared a laugh at her theatrics.

"We'll see," Ms. Pearlstein said "I'll let you know next week. It's a very good piece, though."

"Thank you!" Genevieve smiled and winked at me. As she made her way back out the door, she called out, "Nuclear power is the most important issue of our generation. We've got to stop these plants!"

"She's a pistol, that one," Ms. Pearlstein laughed as Genevieve disappeared into the hallway.

"Yep. Always has been," I agreed.

Once I had taken all of Ms. Pearlstein's notes and rewritten the Narconon story, the article was published and was so strong that Narconon even asked permission to reprint it in their monthly newspaper, which made Ms.

Pearlstein—and my parents—really proud. I have to admit, I got a thrill from seeing my name and my writing in the school paper, and to know that Narconon was going to use it in their publication gave me a nice sense of pride as well. Who knew? Maybe my future was in journalism instead of marketing and sales. I even started checking out the SDSU catalog to see what kind of journalism classes were offered and what opportunities there were on their school newspaper, the *Daily Aztec*. I fantasized about how cool it would be to see my name in print *every single day of the week*. But when I brought up this new interest of mine to my dad, he was a little less enthusiastic.

"Look, Son," he began. Whenever he began a sentence with "Look, Son," I knew there was a lecture coming, and probably about something I was not going to be all that thrilled about. "I think it's wonderful that you've developed this new interest in journalism," he continued, "and I think it's great that you're writing for your school newspaper, but as far as college is concerned? Journalism is a tough way to make a living, and it's probably only going to get tougher. Stick with marketing and sales; that's where the big money is. Who knows? You play your cards right and maybe one day you and your brother will take over my business." He smiled broadly. "You gotta admit, it's done pretty well for me!" And then he laughed that infectious laugh of his, one that made you feel good about whatever it was he had just said, even if it wasn't exactly what you wanted to hear.

The late-September heat gave way to a more mild October as we headed further and further into fall. Of course, October brought its own challenges, namely Halloween and the anniversary of Weddy's death. I'm sure all of us—Hank, Andrew, Marco, Moose . . . hell, even Ronnie, wherever he was—were dealing with it in our own unique ways. We didn't talk a lot about Weddy anymore, not even Hank and I. It wasn't like he was forgotten or anything, I just think it was easier for us to avoid the topic, to avoid the pain.

One Saturday night in early October, the gang gathered at Moose's house. His parents were out for the evening, so we were free to do whatever we wanted to do. "You guys sure you don't want to go to Angela Sapphire's party?" Hank pleaded at the outset of the evening. "Since it's Angela we're talking about, you just know there's going to be a lot of hot chicks there."

Normally, I'd be up for going out with Hank to the party, but I had recently started getting friendly with a girl at school, Annie, and for some reason the thought of meeting girls at a party just didn't appeal to me at the moment. Could it be that I was seriously falling for my latest crush? Striking the thought from my mind, I focused instead on Hank. "Dude, I thought you were back together with Vicki?"

"Yeah, yeah," Hank said with a wave of his hand. He and Vicki had known each other since they were little kids, and had been dating off and on for several years. Vicki had pretty much always been in love with Hank, but my best friend had always been ambivalent about Vicki. "What does that have to do with going to a party?" he asked.

"Dude," Andrew spoke up. "I can't believe you're dating a girl who's still close friends with Douglas's ex." Andrew, of course, was referring to Natalia, the love of my life when I was in junior high.

"It's cool," I said in defense of my best friend. "That was a long time ago. I'm over her."

"Right," Andrew said skeptically. "And that's why you walked out of Licorice Pizza last week when we walked in and you saw her in there with Vicki."

It was true. Andrew and I had gone to Licorice Pizza late one afternoon to see if the new album by a new band I'd recently heard on the radio, Dire Straits, had come in yet. Andrew and I both dug their sound—the guitarist was killer—and their first record was supposed to be in stores any day. But when we walked in the door and saw Natalia and Vicki, something just made me turn and flee out of the store before either of them saw me. I don't know why I reacted that way; sure, it had been a long time, maybe even over a year, since I had last seen Natalia (it was at a party at the beginning of our junior year), but our conversation had been pleasant, and I really felt like I had nothing but good feelings about her. About us.

"Seriously?" Hank asked.

"No, that wasn't it at all," I lied, just as I had that day with Andrew. "I left because I realized I'd promised my mom I'd be home for an early dinner, and I didn't have time to screw around in the record store."

"I don't feel like going to any parties tonight," Marco said, thankfully taking the spotlight off me. "I partied way too hard last weekend at Matt Stoltz's party."

"Now *that* was a great party!" Hank acknowledged.

"Remember when Johnnie McArthur fell into the pool?" Andrew laughed, and we all cracked up with him. Well, everyone except for Moose.

"Moose," I said, "you should've seen it. Johnnie was talking to, like, three girls, acting all cool and everything, when suddenly he took a step back, lost his balance, and fell right into the water. It was classic!"

"Yeah, Moose," Marco said, tapping him hard on his chest. "Why the fuck didn't you come? I told you it was going to be a real shindig."

"I had a family thing I had to do," Moose said rather glumly. He spied Andrew slyly opening up Moose's parents' liquor cabinet. "Keep your hands off of my mom's liquor, Andrew! After the last time you guys were here, she actually drew lines on all of the bottles with a crayon to mark the alcohol level. She knows we've been drinking their booze. Especially you, fuckface." He nodded in Andrew's direction.

"Me?" Andrew said in disbelief. "Marco and Hank did way more damage to that bottle of rum."

"I had to fill that fucking thing with water after you guys left, but you'd drank so much that my mom immediately knew it was watered down the first time my stepdad made her a rum and Coke. I played dumb, of course, but that's when they started marking the bottles."

"It's all cool, my brothers," Marco said. Then, reaching inside the pocket of the army green canvas backpack he had brought over, he pulled out not one, but two bottles of rum. "You got any Coke in the house?"

"*Mais bien sur!*" Moose said gleefully. "Douglas, there's some bottles in the fridge in the garage. Why don't you go get those, and I'll run up to my room and grab my bong and my stepdad's weed and I'll meet you guys in the backyard. Feel free to get some glasses and ice from the kitchen. And remember—no smoking anywhere near the house. Go to the back of the yard. Otherwise, my stepdad will smell it and figure out we've been smoking his dope and there will be hell to pay."

I remember the first time Moose showed me where his stepdad kept his stash. There was a drawer in his closet, nondescript, sort of out of the way in the corner. The first thing you saw when you pulled open the drawer were a bunch of dirty magazines, and I'm not talking *Playboy* or *Penthouse*, but the hardcore stuff—*Screw* and *Hustler* and other shit I'd never seen or heard of before. I mean, they didn't even carry this stuff down at the newsstand on Ventura and Newcastle. And beneath the magazines were several baggies of pot. His dad didn't exactly have the greatest taste in weed—there was no Northern California Indica or Maui Wowie in his collection. Usually it was just your typical Columbian mersh, though every now and then he seemed to be able to score some Acapulco Gold that would just knock us completely on our asses.

We assembled in the back of Moose's yard. His house backed up to a small canyon; actually it was more like a ravine, with a concrete drainage ditch running just below the edge of the yard. We all sat there for at least a couple of hours, drinking rum and Coke and passing around the bong. Moose had recently bought a six-shooter, a metal device that fit over the normal bowl of the bong. It contained *six* bowls, and the idea was you could stuff them all with pot, light the first one, and when you had sucked that one down, you would turn the six-shooter to the next bowl and light that one and suck it down, and then turn to the next one and so on and so on. Try as we might, only Marco could make it through all six bowls before exhaling; he had an incredible set of lungs. Hank, being in top shape because of basketball, also had the lung capacity to get through all six bowls, but he was and always had been somewhat of a lightweight, so two, maybe three bowls was his max. I also stopped at three, while Andrew and Moose each made it to four bowls before erupting into a coughing fit that would go on for minutes at a time.

"Good, and good for you!" Moose would manage to say in between hacks, and we'd all laugh and raise our rum and Cokes and say in unison, "Good, and good for you!"

"Hey, did you guys hear the latest about Clark?" Andrew asked.

"No, what?" Hank said.

"I heard the dude has gone full white supremacist. Someone at school said they saw him at a Dodger game and the guy literally had a tattoo of a swastika on his neck and his head was totally shaved."

"What the fuck, Moose?" I asked. Moose and Clark had been best friends in junior high, but Clark ended up at Pershing High. The kids from Cabrillo generally went to either Pershing or Woodrow Wilson, depending on where they lived. Hank actually lived in Pershing's district, but an assistant coach at Woodrow Wilson had been working with Hank for quite a while—he'd even stuck with him when he went through that awful growth spurt that robbed him of much of his coordination for a couple of years—and managed to figure out a way to get Hank into the school. I think Hank's parents might have used Hank's uncle's address, which was in the Woodrow Wilson district, to get him enrolled.

"I don't know, man. It's been a while since I talked to that guy." Moose sounded a bit down, and just stared off into the distance. "I don't know what happened to him. He was never like that when I knew him. And I knew him really, really well. Or at least I thought I did. The last time

I saw Clark was about six months ago at Cal Jam II. We hadn't seen each other in a while and had decided to go to the festival together. But pretty early in the day, I was following him through the crowd to get closer to the stage for Black Sabbath, and I lost him, and I never saw him again. Didn't even know how he got home that night. I looked for him all during the show and waited forever in the parking lot afterward, but security finally forced me to leave. I later found out he met a group of these nutcases that day, and they'd given him a ride home. But it was almost like he got kidnapped by a cult. The last time I spoke to him on the phone, which was just, like, a month after the concert, all he kept railing about was how he and these new friends he had met at the festival were going to chase every last Mexican out of the Valley."

"Jesus," Hank said quietly. We all sat there in stunned silence.

All of us had suffered the loss of Weddy, but Moose had had it much worse. Toward the end of tenth grade, Moose's dad had suddenly dropped dead of a heart attack. He was forty-two years old, and while that seemed pretty old to all of us—I mean, he was the same age as Elvis when Elvis died later that same year, and we thought Elvis was old and fat by then—my mom and dad and Art all stressed how young Moose's dad actually was, and how that made his death all the more tragic.

Even worse for Moose was the fact that his mom started dating almost immediately after his dad died, and was remarried within a year. They stayed in the same house, with Moose's new stepdad slipping right into their lives as if nothing strange had occurred. And while he was a nice enough guy, Moose didn't feel bad at all about stealing his dope.

To make matters worse, it turned out that the same heart condition that killed his dad—something to do with a murmur, I think—had been passed on to Moose, and that meant he could no longer play football for Woodrow Wilson. Now, while Moose had been one of the more fearsome athletes in junior high—his sheer size had given him quite an advantage over the rest of us—he had essentially stopped growing by the time we got to ninth grade, while other kids, especially football players, continued to get bigger and stronger. By the time we reached our junior year, Moose was no longer such a, well, moose compared to everyone else. His freshman year playing football wasn't all that impressive, so who knows if he would've even gotten onto the field very much as a junior. But coming on top of his dad's death, finding out that he would no longer be able to play football—or any sport—competitively again made the whole situation that much worse for Moose.

"Well, at least I'll always have the memory of looking up from the ground as John Elway ran straight over me," a newly humble and softened Moose would joke. "I think his footprint is permanently tattooed on my chest," he'd laugh wearily. Moose was definitely a changed man. The death of Weddy, followed by the death of his father, and then the death of his football career, had turned him from an overbearing bully into a more sensitive, introspective person. On the positive side, I think the two of us became closer friends, as our friendship was no longer built on being athletic rivals, but on shared tragedies. Sure, we still went at each other like we'd always done, but there was now an undeniable depth to our friendship that had never existed before.

Everyone had grown quiet as we sat at the edge of Moose's yard. The strong scent of sage filled the air, with nothing but the darkness of the Santa Monica Mountains in front of us. Each of us was thinking about Weddy, or Moose's dad, or Clark, or any number of things. Suddenly, from out of nowhere, a coyote came dashing along the concrete drainage ditch just below us.

"Holy fuck!" Andrew shouted.

"Oh, don't be such a pussy," Marco teased. "He won't hurt you."

"I fucking hate coyotes," Andrew said glumly. It was true. He still pined away for his dog, Daisy, a fluffy white thing that had been snatched up by a coyote a couple of summers ago. I was thankful that L had so far survived our move to Stromness.

"Hey, *Saturday Night Live* is about to start," I said, trying to lighten the mood. "Why don't we go in and watch."

Andrew leaped to his feet. "Let's go!" He really did have a fear of coyotes.

We all laughed and, in a stoned, drunken haze, stumbled into Moose's den, flipped on the tube, and got ready for the season opener of *SNL*. The Stones were the special musical guest, and even though they were by now older than Hades and had recently gone disco, well, they were still the Stones. Of course they played "Miss You," which we all thought sucked, even live. *The Stones have gone disco*? I remember thinking the first time I heard the song. *What the fuck*?

Fortunately, they also played "When the Whip Comes Down," which I thought rocked pretty hard. The big news of the night, however, was "Weekend Update." Chevy Chase had quit the show after the previous season—he was planning on becoming a movie star instead—and this new guy named Bill Murray had taken his place as the host of the pseudo-newscast. Everyone was surprised that they were even going to continue with the skit.

"'Weekend Update' without Chevy?" Marco guffawed the first time we heard the news that someone else was going to step into Chevy's shoes. "Impossible!"

"I agree," Andrew said in a rare moment of collaboration with Marco. "Look how bad Aykroyd was when he tried to do it. If Aykroyd can't do it, nobody can. They should've just ended the skit."

When all was said and done, opinions were split: Hank and I thought Murray had done just fine, while Moose, Andrew, and Marco continued to profess their love for Chevy Chase. The show was just wrapping up when we heard Moose's garage door open.

"Shit!" Moose yelled in a sort of loud whisper. "They're home early! Everyone out the sliding door! Hurry!" Moose ran to the glass door that led out to the yard. From there, we could take the drainage ditch a hundred yards or so over to the street.

"I'm not fucking going out there," Andrew said. "No fucking way."

"Andrew," I pleaded as I followed Marco and Hank out to the yard, "the coyote's gone. And he wants nothing to do with us anyway."

"Get your ass out of here, now! *Sortez*! *Sortez*!" Moose hissed.

"Fuck!" Andrew said, snatching his cardigan—no matter the weather, Andrew always seemed to have a lightweight cardigan sweater with him—and finally joining us outside.

"See you guys later," Moose whispered before sliding the door shut behind us and undoubtedly scrambling to clean up the place as best he could.

"Thanks, Moose," each of us mumbled in response, hearing the door close before we could even get the words out of our collective mouths.

We got Andrew to his car safely with nary a coyote, roadrunner, snake, raccoon, or possum in sight, and said our goodbyes. I was happy I only had a short walk to make; the other guys all had to drive home fucked up, which was never fun. I slept the sleep of the dead that night, even though I couldn't quite get Charlie Watts' rhythmic drumbeat from "Miss You" out of my head.

Chapter Three

Annie was really my first girlfriend. Sure, my first love was Natalia, but I was a little kid then and it was more like a crush, although it did take me forever to get over her. But listen to enough music and smoke enough pot, and the pain eventually goes away. It's amazing how many songs have been written about breaking up; you don't even realize it until you actually experience a break-up. How many times did I cry to James Taylor after Natalia broke up with me? I'm embarrassed to say. I used to hear "Shower the People," and think, *But what do you do when they don't want to get wet*? And the next thing I'd know I'd be blubbering away like an idiot. Needless to say, I don't listen to much James Taylor anymore.

I first met Annie Thompson at the beginning of twelfth grade, in Mr. Mazursky's chemistry class. I sucked at science and didn't really care much about the subject, so I found myself spending lots of lab time just goofing around with Annie. She was hilarious.

"Don't be such a grinch!" she would laugh when I'd refuse to share an extra test tube or tease her over which beaker she wanted me to pass over to her.

"This one?" I'd say, pointing to a different beaker than the one she wanted.

"No, *that* one!" she'd laugh, pointing again to the other beaker.

"This one?" I'd tease again, picking up an entirely

different beaker, totally the wrong size.

"Douglas!" she'd scream.

We were a good fit together, body-wise anyway. It looked like my dreams of being a six-foot-four shooting guard in the NBA were going to be reduced to a five-foot-ten-on-a-good-day shooting guard at the local YMCA rec league. Annie, meanwhile, was petite like my mom, five-two tops, but with a curvy body, absolutely beautiful breasts, and a perfect, and I do mean perfect, ass. Lots of guys were after Annie in high school, and I was lucky—or unlucky—enough to be one of the ones who got her. At least for a while.

Annie had dark hair and dark eyes, and when she smiled, everything around her would just melt away until she was the only thing it was even possible to focus upon. The first time I saw her, she was standing at one of the lab tables waiting for class to start. I walked through the doorway, and it was like a laser; I was just immediately pulled toward her and nothing else mattered.

"Hey," I said as I approached her. "Anybody sharing this lab with you?"

"Nope," she smiled. "Just me, myself, and I. I'm Annie."

"I'm Douglas."

"Aren't you friends with Hank?"

"Yeah. You know Hank?" I was surprised, because even though I'd seen Annie around school a few times last year, Hank had never mentioned her, and she just hadn't ever come across my radar until that day in the new chemistry class.

"I'm friends with Tammy Goldblum, and her boyfriend, Mark Prince, plays basketball with Hank."

"Oh, okay. Yeah, I've met Mark before. But I don't

really know Tammy."

"She actually lives next door to my boyfriend, well, my ex-boyfriend, which actually gets a little awkward." She giggled in a cute, innocent way that I found to be immediately endearing. *How could any guy not love this girl?* She was the complete package.

"Who's your boyfriend?" I asked, trying to sound as casual as possible.

"Ex-boyfriend. Kenny Killian."

"Kenny the Killer?" I asked, wide-eyed.

"Yeah. You know him?"

"Only by reputation, thankfully!" I guffawed.

"Oh, don't believe everything you hear, silly," Annie insisted. "Kenny is very sweet. Anything that's happened has either been exaggerated or was somebody else's fault."

"Uh, okay, if you say so. Though I wonder what Jackie Lombardi would have to say about that." Jackie got his ass kicked last year by Kenny after Kenny accused him of scratching his car, a super hot Mustang that everyone knew not to fuck with. Jackie had parked a little too close to Kenny's car and not only dinged it when he opened his door, but banged into it with his metal lunchbox—yes, Jackie Lombardi still carried a metal lunchbox to high school. Kenny got pissed, one thing led to another, and Jackie took a serious beating.

"Jackie Lombardi is an idiot," Annie said. "Not only did he mess with Kenny's car, he was a complete jerk about the whole thing. *And* he threw the first punch. The first few punches, actually. He got what he deserved."

Annie's version of the event didn't match up to what I had heard, but she certainly seemed sure of herself and, hell, she was so damn cute that it was hard to resist believing her.

"So, how come you and Kenny broke up?"

"I caught him cheating on me, lying to me. I'm an honest person, Douglas." She placed her hand on top of mine and looked me directly in the eyes, her deep-black pupils staring right through to my heart. "I can't be with someone like that."

"I hear you," I said. "Life's too short to deal with people who can't be honest. I know I don't need friends like that in my life."

"Totally," Annie agreed, removing her hand and looking a little embarrassed. Her smile was so sweet and pure. "You have really beautiful hair," she said softly.

"Thanks." It wasn't the first time I had heard this. I had the perfect hair for the feathered Travolta look, and had gotten pretty good with the blow-dryer and a vented hairbrush. Girls were always complimenting me on it. Evidently there were good hair genes on my mom's side of the family.

I don't remember when I officially fell in love with Annie, but by the end of that first semester in twelfth grade, we were boyfriend and girlfriend. I was driving by now, so we were free to have a blast, especially on weekends. We'd go to the drive-in movies, out to dinner, to parties. By the time November rolled around we were going hot and heavy. The make-out sessions at the drive-in were legendary, and while we hadn't yet gone all the way, we were getting close. Annie had lost her virginity to Ricky Churchill, who was her boyfriend before Kenny Killian, during the summer between tenth and eleventh grade. Needless to say, she was a lot more experienced than I.

I was still a virgin until the Sunday night before

Thanksgiving. Annie and I were just hanging out at her house, in her bedroom, when I let out a long sigh. "What's the matter, baby?" she asked, stroking my cheek.

"Oh, you know, just stuff." I was feeling blue, as the third anniversary of Weddy's death had just passed this last Halloween. It seemed like everything had happened so long ago, but then again it also felt like Weddy was just here yesterday. I had, by that point, long stopped reaching for the phone to call him, but I still missed him deeply and thought about him all the time.

"You miss Weddy?" she asked. Annie was always so perceptive.

"Yeah. This will be the fourth Thanksgiving since he's been gone."

"I'm sorry, sweetie." She began kissing me softly, and soon the kissing became hotter and heavier. "Let's have sex tonight," she suddenly whispered. "I think I'm ready to do it with you."

"Really?" I said, surprised. Whenever we had reached this point in the past month or two, Annie always insisted she wasn't ready, that she needed more time and space between me and Kenny. "You sure? Here? With your mom in the other room?"

"Oh, she won't hear us. And she knows better than to come in here." Annie was beginning to unbuckle my belt and undo the buttons on my jeans. Her hand was rubbing my cock, and I was getting harder by the second.

"I don't know," I said, warily. "I mean, I don't want her walking in on us."

"Here," Annie said, jumping off her bed and proceeding to shove her dresser in front of the door. "How's that?" She laughed and jumped on top of me, making out with me like a mad woman. Over her shoulder, on the wall right next to her bed, was a small corkboard with some notes and photos and coupons and stuff pinned up. But one photo kept catching my eye: it was of Annie and Kenny. And the more I stared at it, the softer I felt my erection become.

"What's the matter, baby?" Annie asked, feeling my sudden deflation.

"I . . . I can't stand looking at that photo of you and Kenny up there," I said, pointing behind her.

"Oh, God," she said, and with a swat of her arm she knocked the corkboard off the wall and onto the floor below. "Better?" she asked. But before I could answer she was once again making out with me with reckless abandon and, well, within minutes I was no longer a virgin.

"Did you like that?" Annie asked.

"Yeah, of course," I answered. "That was great." I wasn't being entirely honest as the whole experience was also a bit awkward considering I was constantly worried about her mom busting through the door and, well, considering how fast I had cum.

"Next time try to hold off longer," Annie advised. "You'll have a much bigger explosion!"

"Okay," I said, trying my best not to look embarrassed. "I'll try to—"

I was interrupted by a sudden knock at the door. "Annie? Are you in there? Who's in there with you? Is that Kenny?"

"Mom!" Annie screamed. "Get out of here!"

"If that's Kenny in there, I'm gonna kill him," her mom threatened.

"Mom, it's not Kenny. It's Douglas. Douglas is in here with me."

"Who?"

"Douglas, Mom! You know who Douglas is."

"Hi, Mrs. Thompson," I piped up.

"Oh, yes. Hi Douglas." Mrs. Thompson's tone softened. "Sorry about that. How are you?"

"I'm fine, Mrs. Thompson. Thank you for asking."

"Mom! Can you please get out of here!"

"Okay, honey. Bye Douglas. Nice seeing you again."

"You, too, Mrs. Thompson."

"God, I hate her," Annie said, tears welling up in her eyes.

"Hey, hey," I said. "It's okay." I wiped away her tears and kissed her on the forehead. "At least she didn't force her way in," I joked.

"What did I do to deserve you?" Annie said, smiling weakly. "You're so kind and understanding. Promise you'll never break up with me."

"Break up with you? Why would I do that?"

"Just promise. Swear to me you'll never break up with me." Annie's tone was becoming more urgent.

"I promise," I said.

"Promise what?" Annie persisted, still pressing.

"I promise I'll never break up with you."

"Thank you." Annie closed her eyes and settled into me, her head resting against my bare chest. Within moments her breathing slowed, and she was soon fast asleep. I ran my hand through her soft hair, so long it nearly reached her waist in the back. Her skin was so smooth and perfect. I gently stroked her arm, reveling in her touch and feel, until I, too, drifted off to sleep.

When I woke an hour later it was dark, and I knew I should probably be getting home for dinner. I couldn't decide whether to wake Annie or not, but before I had an answer, I felt her hand reaching for my dick. Within moments we were once again making love. This time there was no picture of Kenny hanging on the wall, and I was no longer afraid of her mother, so we took our sweet, sweet time.

Even though it was a chilly night—definitely in the fifties and quite possibly in the high forties—I drove home from Annie's with the windows of my Honda Civic rolled down, the wind blowing back my hair that was already a mess from Annie's hands running through it.

"A little bit of heaven, ninety-four point seven. KMET—tweedle dee!" The KMET theme song ended, and the familiar voice of Jim Ladd came on the radio. "And now, let's explore a little bit of that darkness on the edge of town," he said, introducing the title track to Springsteen's most recent album. I cranked my Blaupunkt radio up high. "Well, they're still racing out at the Trestles," I sang at the top of my lungs.

All of us were infatuated with Bruce by this point. Back in June, he had played a special show at the Roxy after his show at the Forum, and they broadcast the concert on KMET. Hank, Marco, Andrew, Moose, and I had gathered at Marco's house to get wasted and listen to the show, and it was transcendent. That night, every one of us had instantly become a Springsteen devotee. Well, Andrew had passed out from the vodka Marco's mom had bought for us—she also happened to love Bruce—so he never did become quite as enamored with The Boss as the rest of us, but for Hank, Marco, Moose, and me, Springsteen would become *the* dominant musical force in our lives for our entire senior year. I don't think I'll ever forget the image of Marco and Moose holding the by-now empty Smirnoff bottle like a microphone, singing "Baby, we were born to run!" their lips almost touching as they shared the "mic." Meanwhile, Hank was tapping Marco's bong with a lone drumstick he had found lying around while I played air guitar. All of us were so high on pot, liquor, and adrenaline that our brains felt like they were going to explode from the sheer thrill and exhilaration the music had created. Bruce had definitely led us to the promised land.

Ladd followed up "Darkness" with "New Kid in Town," a cut from the Eagles' *Hotel California*. Evidently, the theme the DJ was exploring—Ladd was famous for creating sets around themes—had to do with "towns." Undoubtedly, Thin Lizzy's "The Boys are Back in Town," would appear somewhere in the set.

By the time I walked in the door, my mom, Art, and David—who seemed to be a semi-permanent fixture at our dinner table, even though he was living on his own now—were already sitting down to dinner. "Douglas? Is that you?"

"Yeah, Mom."

"You're late. Dinner's already on the table."

"Sorry, Mom," I said, walking into the kitchen. "I was helping Annie with her homework." They were all seated around the kitchen table, with a pile of lamb chops, a big salad, and some mashed potatoes sitting in the center.

"What subject?" David asked, chewing on the bone of a chop he'd just devoured.

"Huh?" I asked, settling into my seat at the wooden table next to him and across from my mom.

"You said you were helping Annie study. What subject?"

"Oh, ah, math," I lied.

"Yeah, I bet," David smirked.

"Oh, leave him alone, David," my mom directed.

"Hey, what's that on your neck?" David said, reaching over to tug the collar of my shirt down.

"What are you doing?" I yelped, trying to slip away.

"Ha! Douglas has a hickey! You sure all you were doing was studying with Annie?"

"Fuck off, David!" I hissed, stabbing his hand with my fork.

"Hey!" David shouted. "What the fuck?"

"All right, you two," my mom said. "Cut it out. Can't we just have a nice, quiet dinner without you two fighting?"

"How's Annie doing?" Art asked, trying to calm everyone down. "Things good between you two?"

"Evidently they're great!" David laughed, faking like he was going to pull my collar down again, but stopping just short as I clamped my neck with my hand. "Psych!" he teased.

"David, please!" Mom pleaded.

"Okay, okay," David said, tousling my hair. "I'm just messing with you." I hated it when he tousled my hair. "I just think it's great that the kid is finally getting laid."

I must have turned fifty shades of red.

"Ha!" David pointed at me with his knife. "He's so embarrassed it must be true!"

"Well, I hope you're using protection," my mom said, trying to look me in the eye.

Avoiding eye contact with anyone, I reached down to feed L a piece of lamb. "Can we talk about something else, please?" I begged.

"Don't give Lassie table scraps," Art insisted. "The vet

said it isn't good for her."

It was true that L had aged quite a bit in the past year or so. She was thrilled to no longer be cooped up in the townhouse in Encino. Once we had moved to Stromness and she had a yard to run around, she'd once again turned into a sweet dog with a wonderful disposition. But shelties didn't have a terribly long lifespan, and the years were starting to catch up to her.

I still had the piece of lamb in my hand, so I slowly moved my arm below the table and dropped it onto the floor. L immediately gobbled it up.

"I saw that," Art said.

"Douglas!" my mom admonished.

"I'm sorry, but I already had it in my hand," I said.

"I'm sorry, I already had it in my hand," David mimicked.

"You're pathetic," I muttered.

"Come on, guys," Art said. "Your mom made this lovely dinner. Can you show some appreciation and just behave yourselves for twenty minutes?"

"Sorry, Mom," David and I said in unison.

"Hey," David said. "I heard this new band from England you should check out. The Sex Pistols. They're amazing."

Ever since David had started seeing his girlfriend, Cameron, his musical tastes had dramatically shifted. Cameron had spent some time in the UK, where she was turned onto punk rock. David, who always seemed to take on the interests of whatever girl he was dating—with his last girlfriend, Jenna, it was disco—was now getting into punk. He had even gotten himself an earring, much to my father's dismay.

"You better take that thing out before you come to work in the morning," Dad had growled at David the first time he saw it, during one of our regular Sunday breakfasts. "Or everyone will think you're gay or something." David had been working full-time for my dad's printing business for almost two years now and was doing pretty well, having become one of their top salesmen.

And the first time David showed up at work wearing a leather jacket and pants with holes in them, my dad sent him home and told him to "put on some decent clothes and never walk through the doors of this office again dressed like a vagrant."

"But, Dad," David argued, "this is the fashion right now!"

"Oh yeah?" My dad raised his eyebrow. "What happened to those disco duds you were wearing last year?"

"Oh, I'm done with all that," David said with a wave of his hand.

"I've heard of the Sex Pistols," I said to David, "but I don't think I've heard their songs. Some friends are talking about going up to San Francisco in December to see Springsteen at someplace called the Winterland."

"You're not going to San Francisco," my mom insisted.

"Springsteen sucks," David said.

"Uh, yeah, right," I said. "He's only the greatest rock and roller of all time."

"The dude can't even play guitar!" David insisted.

"Are you kidding me? He's an incredible guitar player."

"Then why does he have a lead guitarist in his band? Why doesn't he just play the leads?"

"Because he's the singer, dumb-ass. And he does play his fair share of lead."

"Oh, bullshit. He can barely play rhythm guitar."

"You're an idiot," I muttered, finishing up the rest of my mashed potatoes.

"Fuck off, Douglas. You don't know what the fuck you're talking about."

"All right!" my mom finally exploded. "That's enough! David, go home. And the next time you come to dinner, you be nice to your brother or you're never coming back here again!"

"What did I do?" David whined. "You're always taking his side!" And with that, he slammed down his fork and knife and stormed out of the house.

Art, Mom, and I sat there in stunned silence.

"Well, at least we can finish our dinner in peace," Art joked.

My mom got up from the table and went upstairs.

"Aw, come on, honey. Don't do that. Come back!" Art called after her before rising from the table himself and following her upstairs.

"Well, L," I said, looking down at Lassie, who was still below the table hoping to get a few more scraps, "looks like it's just you and me, kid." I grabbed the last lamb chop on the plate and cut it up into small pieces, then fed them to her one by one. "Good girl," I repeated over and over. "Good girl."

Just then the phone rang. I waited a few rings to see if anybody else was going to answer, and when it became obvious that my mom and Art weren't going to pick up, I got up from the table and grabbed the kitchen phone hanging on the wall.

"Hello?"

"Hey, Douglas. It's Hank."

"Hey, Hank. What's up?"

"Not much. What are you doing?"

"Just finished dinner. Was hanging out with Annie a bit earlier."

"Oh yeah. How's everything going with you two?"

"Pretty good," I answered, my whole body swelling with pride. "Actually, *really* good."

"Oh yeah? Do tell."

"We went all the way today," I whispered proudly. I don't know why I was whispering, but it felt like the right thing to do.

"You're kidding! Way to go! That's my boy!" Hank had already lost his virginity to Darcy Cohen the last semester of eleventh grade. Darcy was a cheerleader, and everyone knew her primary goal at this stage of her life was to fuck each and every player on the varsity basketball team. Needless to say, Hank and Darcy did not end up in a long-term relationship.

In fact, Hank had never had a girlfriend. Being a stud basketball player with lots of girls after him, he preferred to play the field. This was actually a sticking point with Annie, who didn't like to double-date with Hank. "He always brings a different girl," she complained. "If he had a girlfriend that I could get to know, I'd be happy to do stuff with them. But I can't handle making small talk with someone I don't even know every time we go out with him. And remember that one time when he showed up with Jessica Farmer?" she said, rolling her eyes. Jessica Farmer was known to be the most stuck-up girl at Woodrow Wilson. Her father was super rich, and she always wore the finest clothes and accessories. Gucci purses, designer jeans . . . that sort of thing. I agreed with Annie on this one: Jessica was a total bitch. I don't know why Hank had dated her, but thankfully, like the others, it didn't last very long.

"Hey, Marco!" Hank said. "Douglas finally got laid!"

"Really? With who?" I could hear Marco in the background.

"Hank, please . . ." I pleaded.

"With Annie, you nitwit! Who else did you think it would be?"

"I don't know. Just asking. Jeez."

"Congratulations, Douglas!" Marco shouted. "You finally popped your cherry."

Marco had lost his virginity earlier than all of us, in the summer between tenth and eleventh grade. His family had traveled to Italy to visit relatives, and while he was there he met a girl, several years older than he as he told the story, who deflowered him on a beach in Sardinia in the middle of the night. "My dick got a bit sandy," he would boast to anyone who would listen, "but it sure was fun!"

"What's he doing over there?" I asked. "What are you guys up to?"

"He needed some help with our history assignment," Hank said. "We'll have to celebrate your deflowering next time we get together."

"Sure," I said, trying to be a good sport.

"Speaking of which, are you coming to the game on Friday?" The basketball team always opened the season the day after Thanksgiving with the annual Turkey Trot Tournament, which featured a bunch of the local high schools competing over the course of the three-day weekend. There was a long-standing 10K run on Saturday that was now held in conjunction with the competition, hence the "Turkey Trot" name. "We're all going to Jim Sutton's house after the game for a big blowout party to celebrate the start of the season," Hank said. Jim Sutton was Woodrow Wilson's star player, and it was already a forgone conclusion that he'd be playing for the University of Oregon after he graduated.

"Sounds fun," I said. "Who's hosting the tournament this year?"

"Junipero Serra."

"Seriously?" Junipero Serra was our arch-rival, and whenever a Woodrow Wilson Torero stepped onto their campus, danger lurked in the air.

"Yeah. I heard they're bringing in tons of security this year. Game starts at six o'clock."

"Cool. I'll be there."

"All right, buddy. See you at school tomorrow."

Since we only had a short, three-day week, my homework load was light that night. Unfortunately, Sunday TV wasn't all that great anymore; *All in the Family* was a bit long in the tooth, and while *The Jeffersons* was still good for some laughs, it had sort of settled into middle-of-the-road sitcom territory after a promising beginning. *Mary Tyler Moore* was off the air, and she was trying to get a variety show started, but it was a lame copycat of *The Carol Burnett Show*, which had ended the year before.

Fortunately, my mom and Art subscribed to Theta Cable, and even paid extra for the Z Channel. This was like having your own private movie theater in your house. Every week, the Z Channel featured a variety of movies, some old, some newer, though never anything that had been out in the last year or so. But the movies they showed were really cool, and David and I both killed a lot of time watching films—or at least parts of them because, really, you could pretty much turn the channel on any time of day or night and see something worth watching, even if it was just a part of the flick. The other great thing about the Z Channel was that if you liked a movie, you could watch it over and over all week, unless, of course, you only discovered it toward the end of its run, in which case you were bummed because it was really fun to watch a great film over and over; you often discovered things you missed the first time around.

I looked over at the clock on the wall above the kitchen sink and it read twenty to eight. Normally, they started the movies on the hour, but sometimes they began them on the quarter hour as well. I headed out of the kitchen and over to the big leather couch in the "conversation pit," a silly name for a small, step-down room right off the living room. It really should've been part of the already undersized living room, but an architect was a bit too clever for his own good. Anyway, I did enjoy watching TV in there when I was alone. The conversation pit was darker during the day and just somehow better suited for when I really wanted to concentrate on a film as opposed to just watching a show while doing homework, or talking with friends or my mom and Art during a fun movie, which was a better match for the vibe of the den.

I turned on the TV and picked up the *Z* magazine to see what was on. *Z* magazine was another perk of subscribing to the Z Channel. They gave you all kinds of write-ups on all of the films they were showing that month, complete with cast and credits so you knew who the actors were and learned about directors and even producers and cameramen. They had feature articles on various people, and it was always amazing to learn that the same director made three of your favorite films or that the same cameraman shot two totally different movies that you loved.

I was in luck. A movie called *Lenny* was starting 8:45. Perfect timing. I clicked the button for the Z Channel on the small brown box that was wired to the cable box on top of the television and settled into the couch, its soft, worn leather wrapping around me like a blanket. Since it was late November, and because the conversation pit was the lowest room in the house and located back in the corner adjacent to the yard, it was sort of cold, so I grabbed the orange and brown afghan my mom kept down there and threw it over me.

I knew that *Lenny* was about Lenny Bruce, but the only thing I knew about Lenny Bruce was that he was a famous comedian who got in trouble with the law and then OD'd. The yellow letters on the blue screen appeared on the set:

ENCORE

STARTING THE WEEK OF NOV. 17TH
ON THE "Z" CHANNEL

"LENNY"

STARRING: DUSTIN HOFFMAN AND
VALERIE PERRINE

SUN NOV 19—8:45
TUE NOV 21—9:15
THU NOV 23—7:00
THEATRICAL RATING. "R"
RUNNING TIME 1 HOUR 51 MINUTES

A UNITED ARTIST RELEASE

The next thing to appear on the screen was a message from the Z Channel. While holiday music played in the background, the yellow letter "z" started scrolling across the screen, eventually forming a gigantic "Z." Then, on top of that floated the following greeting:

THETA THE GODDESS OF TELEVISION
WISHES ALL "Z" SUSCRIBERS A JOYOUS
HOLIDAY SEASON AND A PROSPEROUS 1979!

After one final screen showing what was "coming soon"—I was excited to see that they'd be playing an encore of *Chinatown* at some point in the near future—*Lenny* started. As the movie played on, it became clear that Dustin Hoffman was going to be nominated for an Academy Award, as he was just chewing up the scenes. But for me, the true revelation was Valerie Perrine as "Honey." My God! Who was this beauty? She was the sexiest actress I'd ever seen. As Lenny says in the movie, a "Shiksa goddess!" By the time they got to the threesome scene, I had nearly lost my mind. I barely had to touch my dick, which had been hard for a while, before it exploded into my underwear. Honey, indeed. All in all, a pretty great movie.

The short school week flew by, and Thanksgiving arrived seemingly overnight. There was some tension surrounding the holiday this year, as David and I were scheduled to spend it with my dad and my stepmom, Cindy. Normally this wouldn't be that big of a deal—my mom and dad had long ago agreed to alternate Thanksgiving every year—but for some reason, my mom was having an especially hard time with it this year.

"This is the last time you'll be living at home over Thanksgiving," she lamented. "Next year you'll be in San Diego, and that'll be it." While none of us had received our acceptance letters yet, it was pretty much a forgone conclusion that me, Hank, and Moose were going to SDSU along with probably 50 percent of our high school. Andrew had his sights set on UCLA—law school had been preordained since his birth—and Marco was probably going to skip college altogether and go straight into working for his dad in the stunt-driving business. Unfortunately, Annie's grades weren't exactly stellar, and she'd be attending Pierce Junior College. At least we wouldn't be too far away from each other. "I can come down on weekends!" she enthused. I was a little nervous about how a long-distance relationship would work, but it was far enough down the line that I didn't really spend much time worrying about it. Still, I had heard my mom tell David to not bother with girls who were "GU," or "geographically undesirable," especially here in L.A. with all of the traffic. You can't get much more GU than living in separate cities, even if they were only 150 miles apart.

"But Mom," I tried to reassure her, "nothing will change. I'll still be spending every other Thanksgiving with you."

"No, you won't," she sobbed. "You'll meet a girl, and pretty soon you'll be spending Thanksgiving with her family." She dabbed her wet eyes with the ever-present Kleenex in her hand—my mom had terrible allergies, so a Kleenex was never too far away—and continued, "I know these things. This is how it works. Just look at your sister Julie! This is the second Thanksgiving in a row she's stayed down in San Diego because of some guy she's dating!" The tears started to flow even harder.

I sat down next to her on the couch. "Mom, come on," I said, wrapping my arm around her. "You know that's not true. Julie has to work on Fridays, so it's just tough for her to get up here right now. What is she supposed to do? Stay home alone? I promise that all of us will be here for you for years and years to come."

"I want you to stay here for Thanksgiving this year," she cried.

"Mom, you know I can't do that. It's tomorrow night, and Cindy's already in the middle of preparing a huge meal."

"I don't want to hear about that bitch!" Mom was really losing it.

Just then Art came into the den. "What's going on?" he said, the concern obvious on his face.

"Mom's upset that David and I are going to my dad's for Thanksgiving."

"Well," Art said, "I've told you many times that I think the best thing would be for everyone to bury the hatchet and spend the holidays together."

"I'm not spending Thanksgiving with *her*," my mom insisted. Art and I just looked at each other and raised our eyebrows. What could we say?

Art sat down on the couch on the other side of my mom. Now we both had our arms around her. "Look, honey," he said, "why don't I pick up the food from Gelson's earlier in the day, and the kids can join us for a Thanksgiving lunch?" Because Mom and Art would be alone for Thanksgiving— she had turned down every single invitation she'd received from her friends—my mom had decided she wasn't going to cook, and they would take out their Thanksgiving meal from the local supermarket. Art looked over at me. "Douglas, would that be okay with you?"

The pleading in his eyes gave me no choice but to answer, "Of course! Two Thanksgiving meals in one day? That'd be great!"

When told of the plan, David happily went along with the idea. "Double dipping for Thanksgiving?" he said. "Sounds awesome!" Of course, no one breathed a word of this to my dad or Cindy. I could just hear him now: "You'll have no appetite left for Cindy's dinner!"

So, the next day, Art grabbed the prepared Thanksgiving meal in the late morning while Mom happily set out her finest silver and china in the dining room. After David finally showed up—thirty minutes late (he said there was a lot of traffic)—we sat down a little before 1:00 for the first of our two Thanksgiving meals. Because it was lunchtime, both David and I made gigantic, warm turkey sandwiches on soft sourdough bread with cranberry sauce—"The good kind," David always joked, "straight out of the can"—and stuffing piled high. We could barely get our mouths around the towering sandwiches, but somehow we managed. My mom was happy, which was the most important thing about the whole affair.

"Thank you, boys," she said after what had actually been a fairly lively lunch, with Art regaling us with stories about shooting Germans during World War II. Art was actually shot in the leg—he still had a divot off to the side of his shin—and ferried back to America aboard the *Queen Mary*. His Purple Heart sat in a box with other war memorabilia.

After lunch, David and I turned on the TV and immediately went to channel 5 for the *Twilight Zone* marathon. Yeah, the Redskins and Cowboys game was on, but fuck the Cowboys. David and I both hated them, and even though we were Rams fans, we both actually had a soft spot for the Redskins (probably because of the George Allen connection), but the Cowboys were so good that year we knew they'd blow Washington off the field, which they did, winning 37–10.

First up was a classic *Twilight Zone* with the guy from *Kojak*. In this episode, he plays a mean stepdad whose wife buys her daughter a new doll, "Talky Tina." For some reason—I mean, he's a real shit to the little girl—he becomes extremely jealous of the doll his stepdaughter now loves, and takes it away from her. Talky Tina gets her revenge, however, by starting to fuck with his mind, changing her pre-recorded voice message from "I'm Talky Tina . . . and I love you" to "I'm Talky Tina . . . and I don't like you" among other nasty sayings. Tina eventually drives the *Kojak* guy crazy, and places herself on the stairs so that when he is walking down them late one night, he trips over the doll, tumbles hard down the stairs, and dies from his injuries. Talk about some freaky shit. Got to hand it to Rod, he sure did have a wild imagination, and he knew how to scare the hell out of us as well. Dude died way too young.

Both David and I alternately napped and watched pieces of episodes for the rest of the afternoon, as the huge turkey lunch went to work and did its thing. I remember catching bits of "A Stop at Willoughby," "I Sing the Body Electric," and "A Game of Pool." I woke David up for this last episode, because it was one of our favorites. We both played a lot of pool—mostly thanks to Art, who always insisted on having a pool table in the house and who taught us both how to play—and watching Jack Klugman from

The Odd Couple and the old comedian Jonathan Winters battle it out in a life or death match to see who is the greatest pool player of all time was just top-notch TV. In the annals of great stories with a "be careful what you wish for" theme, "A Game of Pool" has to be near or at the top of the list.

By the late afternoon, I knew it was time to go shower. Dad and Cindy had originally wanted us over there at 4:00, and that's when their friends and Cindy's family were going to arrive, but we knew that Mom would feel better if we spent as much of the afternoon as possible with her—even if David and I were stuck in the den watching the *Twilight Zone*—so we convinced Dad that 5:00 would be plenty early for us to arrive. Besides, it would give Cindy an hour or so to spend with her friends and family without the complications of having us around.

When we pulled up to my dad's house in David's Capri, we could already tell by the number of cars in the driveway and in the street around their house that the party was in full swing. As we approached the front door, the light drizzle that had accompanied David and me on the drive had turned into a steady rain—no surprise as the forecast was for thunderstorms pretty much all night long, though it would supposedly be clearing out not long after midnight. Tomorrow's Turkey Bowl—the annual tackle football game I played with my friends—would be epic, a mud-filled football fest.

The door was unlocked, and right as we walked in my dad greeted us in the front hallway with a big hug. "Hey, guys!" he said, smiling and holding what I was sure was a martini on the rocks, twist, no olive, in one hand, and wrapping his other arm around David and then me.

"Come on in!"

He was obviously in his entertaining mode and had probably already had a couple of drinks before the one in his hand. Letting David walk ahead, my dad hung back with me and then put his hand on my shoulder and grew closer as he whispered in my ear, "Thank God he dressed like a mensch." It was true, David knew better than to show up in the new punk rock garb that Cameron had him wearing, and so he had put on his work clothes to avoid a confrontation with my dad. Sure, he probably looked like he was just coming from the office, but the same could be said for half of the people at the party.

Assembled before us in the living room were a dozen or more guests. Compared to the small holiday dinners we always had with my mom, usually just the four of us, Dad and Cindy's celebrations were much larger, and tonight would be no exception. By the time Cindy's best friend's family arrived a few minutes after us, there were about twenty of us in all.

It was always a bit awkward when David and I went to parties like this at my dad's. Even though he was *our* dad, we felt like outsiders, and the fact that the other people at the party went *way* out of their way to make us feel included, to make us feel comfortable, only served to heighten our anxiety.

Cindy came over to give us a hug. "Hi David. Hi Douglas." She looked pretty tonight, and I still couldn't get over how much younger she seemed when compared to my mom. When my dad first started dating Cindy, she really wasn't all that much older than my sister Julie is now, which I think drove my mom sort of crazy. The fact that she'd had a baby a few years ago—my half-sister Rebecca, named after Cindy's grandmother—hadn't seemed to age her one bit, which drove my mom even more crazy, especially since she had proclaimed, "Once she starts popping out babies, she won't be looking so young and fresh, I can tell you that." In fact, Cindy was pregnant once again, and I noticed that her tummy was visibly larger than the last time I had seen her.

"Where's Becky?" Cindy called out to nobody in particular. From out of nowhere, my two-almost-three-going-on-fourteen-year-old half-sister came tearing at us. "Hi, Dougie!" she screamed when she saw me. She always called me "Dougie," which I actually hated, but she was so damn cute I couldn't bear to tell her to stop calling me that.

"Hi Rebecca," I said as she clamped onto my legs, her head only coming up to my knees. I still called her Rebecca, even though pretty much everyone else had settled on Becky; I don't know why, I just thought it was a more dignified name. I reached down and stroked her strawberry blonde hair, which she clearly got from Cindy's side of the family since every last person on our side of the family had brown or black hair. Well, except my mom, but she dyed her hair red. Her real color, which nobody but her hairdresser had seen for decades, was supposedly brown, confirmed by photos of her when she was a little girl.

"Can I get you boys anything to drink?" my dad offered. "Maybe a little white wine? I've got a fantastic Grgich Chardonnay."

"Sure, I'll have a glass," I responded enthusiastically. It wasn't often that my dad would offer me alcohol. Thanksgiving, Christmas, New Year's, and special occasions like weddings were the exception.

"Sounds good, Dad," David said, though I knew he'd

rather have a rum and coke.

Rebecca was still wrapped tight around my leg. "How are you?" I asked her.

"I have a new pony," she said.

"Oh, really?" I said, playing along. "Can I see it?" I assumed she would run to her toy box and pull out a new stuffed animal.

"You can't see him," she answered. "He's at the stable."

"Oh, I see," I said, still playing along. "What's his name?"

"Albert."

"Albert?" I laughed. "That's a funny name."

"Are you telling the boys about your new pony?" Cindy asked, coming up and pulling Rebecca up into her arms. "He's very handsome, isn't he?"

"Yes, he's brown with a big white patch on his nose. I love Albert."

"How did you come up with the name Albert?" David, who I had thought wasn't even paying attention, asked distractedly. I could tell he was homing in on an unfamiliar, yet very pretty girl sitting alone on the couch.

"That was mommy's horse, silly!" Rebecca laughed.

Cindy smiled. "When I was a child," she explained, "I had a horse named Albert that was the love of my life. We decided to honor Albert by giving Becky's new pony the same name. She's already started her riding lessons."

"Wait a second," David said. "Are we talking about a real horse?"

"Of course, silly!" Rebecca laughed again. Evidently, "silly" was her new favorite word.

"Didn't your dad tell you?" Cindy asked. "I'm surprised. We got him over a month ago." At that moment,

Dad came back from the bar with two glasses of wine in his hand. "Honey, you didn't tell the boys about Albert?"

"Oh gosh, I'm sorry. I've been crazy busy lately and it must've slipped my mind." As he handed us the wine, David and I glanced at each other. We both knew that Dad had probably just wanted to avoid telling us as long as possible. Back when we first got Lassie, it was a *huge* effort to convince my dad to let us get a dog.

"They're a ton of work!" he would yell when me, David, Julie, and my mom begged him to let us get a dog. "Who's going to feed it? Who's going to walk it? Who's going to train it? Dogs need a lot of attention."

"Don't worry, Dad," we'd say in unison, "we'll do all of that. You won't have to do a thing." In the end, Dad let us get Lassie and, of course, he ended up being the one who loved her the most. He was the one who trained her, never missing an opportunity to take her to obedience class. I know my dad loves his kids, but I gotta say, I think the thing that troubled him most about the divorce was having to give up L. But what could he do? He couldn't take her away from his kids, especially me, since I was so young and so attached to the dog. With the wreckage the divorce was going leave in its wake, he knew I'd need L to get me through it all.

"Wow," David responded with a tinge of anger, "I never pictured you as the horse type. They're a lot of work." Evidently I wasn't the only one remembering everything we went through to convince my dad to get a dog.

"Oh, it's not that much work," Cindy said, her pretty face and blue eyes lighting up. "And Albert is the cutest horse. He's a Shetland, and he's just adorable."

"Cindy rode as a kid and felt it would be a good thing

for Becky to experience as well. It builds confidence." Dad was doing his best to rationalize this rather extravagant purchase.

I looked over at David and could tell that the anger was building up inside of him. "Cool," I said, trying to diffuse the situation before it got out of hand, "I can't wait to meet him."

"You should come over to the stable tomorrow," Cindy suggested. "Becky has a lesson at ten o'clock."

"I'd love to," I feigned, "but we have our Turkey Bowl tomorrow morning." The Turkey Bowl had been going on for several years now and had earned the designation of being a "tradition" among my friends. We would all gather at Balboa Park the morning after Thanksgiving, no matter the weather, for a spirited game of tackle football. It was a great way to work off the huge meal from the night before, and this year I'd have *two* meals to work off.

"Isn't she a little young to be starting horseback riding lessons?" David asked, gritting his teeth.

"She'll be three years old soon, which is when I started," Cindy said rather defensively. She and David didn't really get along all that well, so even a perceived slight could turn into a real slight in an instant. "Right now she's just getting comfortable sitting on the horse and getting to know him more than anything else."

"I love Albert," Rebecca cooed.

"Oh, and he loves you, too, sweetheart," Cindy cooed right back, kissing Rebecca on her cheek.

"Hey, hon," my dad said, perhaps sensing that a change of subject was in order. "Everyone is here. Should we tell them the news?"

"Sure," Cindy smiled.

"Hey, Dad," David said, "who's that girl sitting on the couch?"

"Hang on a second, Son," my Dad responded. Then, clinking his wine glass with a stray fork someone had set down on the coffee table, he announced, "Hello everybody. Can I have your attention, please?" The room did not quiet down as quickly as he would've liked. "Excuse me!" he said a bit more loudly. "Your attention, please!"

"That's my niece, Marsha," Cindy whispered to David. "You should go say hello. She's a lovely girl."

"Cindy, please," my dad admonished.

"Sorry, honey."

"Cindy and I have a wonderful announcement to make." The room finally calmed down and Dad milked it until there was total silence. He was a master speaker, having taken a course to sharpen his skills. "We went to the OB-GYN yesterday, and we found out the baby is a boy!"

The room immediately burst into whoops and applause, with congratulations and mazel tovs shouted from every direction. "What's his name?" everyone wanted to know.

"Now, now," Cindy said, "we have to save some surprises for when the baby's born."

"I can tell you that, following the Efron family tradition, his name will begin with a 'D,'" my dad insisted. I looked over at Cindy, and it was tough to tell from her expression whether or not she was truly down with this plan. It was true, though: every male for generations on my dad's side had a name that started with a "D." The tradition dated back to my great-great-great-grandfather Donald, and continued down the line—Daniel, Dennis, Dov . . . hell, my cousin got the coolest "D" name of all: Dylan.

As people started to filter toward my dad and Cindy to congratulate them, I stepped back and watched as David walked over to Marsha. I could tell from his expression and body language that he was in full "puttin' on the moves" mode. Knowing David, he'd probably be fucking her by the end of the night.

Suddenly, from behind, I was wrapped in a big bear hug by Cindy's older brother, Pete, a sheriff who was currently working downtown at the county jail. Previously, he'd done everything from undercover drug and gang sting operations to regular traffic work.

"What's going on, Douglas? Long time, no see. You're looking good!"

I always liked Pete, and we often ended up hanging out together at these family gatherings. Sometimes he'd tell me some crazy shit about what goes on down at County, or things that happened to him back when he was working undercover. I appreciated his compliment, and I felt like I *was* looking good. I'd lost a lot of weight between tenth and eleventh grades, and by now had even added on a bit of muscle from the occasional weight workouts I'd do with Hank in his garage. Of course, I'd never be cut—it just wasn't in my genes—but having Annie as my girlfriend definitely incentivized me to at least keep the weight I'd lost last year off for good. Besides, she dug it when I wore tight pants. She said I had strong legs and a "nice ass," which of course made me feel pretty good about myself. I did have strong legs; it was how I could shoot twenty-five-footers with ease. People think shooting from long distance is all about the arms, but it's really all about the legs. That's where a great shooter's strength comes from. The hand, wrist, and arm are really only there to guide the shot.

"How you been, Pete? Still working County?"

"Yeah, but only for another three months."

"Really? Then what? Or are you not allowed to tell me?"

"No, no, I can tell. It's pretty cool, actually. I'm being transferred to the Malibu substation."

"Cool! I mean, that's a good thing, right?"

"Well," Pete said, smiling, "where would you rather work—County Jail in downtown L.A. or Malibu?"

We both laughed. Even better for Pete, as he explained, was that he and his wife had moved out to Calabasas only a year or so ago, so now instead having to make the slow crawl to downtown L.A. every day, he'd just cruise a few stops up the 101 and he'd be at work.

"Congratulations," I said, shaking his hand. "You've definitely earned it. I'm sure life will be much quieter out there than at County, or in South Central where you did all of that undercover work."

"For sure," he sighed. "Though now I'll have to deal with coked up Hollywood celebrities, and that's not always a picnic."

"Okay, people," Cindy announced. I had noticed that the caterer they had hired for the occasion had come out moments before and whispered something in her ear. "Dinner is served. Everybody into the den, please."

Because there were so many people, my dad and Cindy had decided to clear out the den—a room that was much larger than their dining room—and serve Thanksgiving dinner in there. As Cindy rather flamboyantly flung open the double doors leading into the room, we were treated to the sight of two big round tables decorated with orange-and-brown paper turkeys and enormous floral centerpieces. A fire raged in the tall brick fireplace. The tables and chairs, rented from Abbey Rents, were tastefully covered with crisp, white tablecloths and gold cloth chair covers, adding a "classy" feel to the whole affair. "We had to reserve them two months in advance!" my dad marveled, laughing. "I should've gone into the party rental business."

As if on cue, the light rain outside turned into a torrential downpour, complete with thunder. We had barely begun to take our seats when a huge crack of lightning seemed to flash right outside the two floor-to-ceiling paned glass windows that overlooked the backyard. And just like that, the electricity shut off. Sure, we had a roaring fire in the fireplace and plenty of candles, but my dad's kitchen was all electric.

"I *told* you we should've converted to gas!" I heard Cindy hiss at Dad behind the closed pantry door.

"But then it would've been a broken gas line at some point," my dad said, trying to calm her down. It didn't really work.

Even though we'd been asked to assemble for dinner and there were plenty of appetizers, not everything else was fully cooked. With the kitchen shut down, many of the other key dishes—ham, sweet potatoes, mashed potatoes, vegetables—weren't quite ready yet, so the meal basically came down to the turkey, some Swedish meatballs, bacon-wrapped dates, a hastily thrown together salad, and some pie for dessert that thankfully had been baked earlier in the day. We each got a bite of the stuffing from the bird, but there wasn't nearly enough for twenty hungry diners. I really did feel bad for Cindy; she was in tears and had disappeared upstairs to their bedroom before most of the guests had left.

The evening ended somewhat solemnly, though the electricity did finally come back on toward the end of the party, but the caterer was long gone by that point. The somewhat downer of a dinner evidently didn't exactly do wonders for David and Marsha. Even though he had rather cavalierly switched the place cards at the dinner table after the lights went out so that he ended up sitting next to Marsha, as the night wore on and the overall energy of the evening continued to drop, so did his prospects with her. She eventually excused herself in the middle of the meal, got up from the table, and simply never came back. David tried to put on a brave face, but I could tell he was hurt.

On the drive home he was pretty quiet, so I finally decided to ask him straight out, "What the heck did you say to Marsha that made her leave the party in the middle of dinner?"

Screeeeeeechhhhh! I grabbed the front dash of my brother's Capri as he slid to a stop next to the curb on an empty stretch of Ventura Boulevard.

"What the—" I yelled.

"Get the fuck out!" David said.

"What? What's the matter with you?"

"Get the fuck out of my car."

"Are you kidding?"

David leaned over me and pulled the handle of my door aggressively to open it, then started shoving me out of the car.

"David!" I shouted. "I'm sorry! I didn't mean anything!"

He continued to push me using both hands, picking up my butt with his left and grabbing my shoulder with his right and trying to toss me off the seat and out of the car. I clung to the frame of the door for dear life and placed my feet on the door, bracing myself against his strength.

"Come on, David!" I pleaded. "Stop it!"

Suddenly his grip lessened. He took his hands off of me, placed the gear in drive, and tore off, nearly throwing me from the car. "You fucking asshole!" I screamed as I somehow miraculously managed to swing my feet back inside *and* shut the door without flying out of the vehicle.

"You're the fucking asshole," David snarled.

"Jesus, David. I'm sorry. But I mean, seriously, what the fuck happened?"

"Fuck!" he screamed, pounding his steering wheel in frustration. "I have no idea, man!" After a few moments, his voice began to soften. "I have no idea. First Cameron tells me she met another guy and doesn't want to go out with me anymore. Then that bitch tonight gets up and walks out on me. I mean, what the fuck is wrong with me?" I was startled as he turned and looked searchingly into my eyes, as if I held the answer.

Of course, I had no idea what to say to him. "Damn," I sighed softly, "I'm sorry about Cameron. I didn't know."

We drove the rest of the way home in silence. At one point, Bruce Springsteen's "Thunder Road" came on the radio, and when I saw David's hand reach for the dial, I thought for sure he was going to change the station. Instead, he turned it up. To my further amazement, I saw his lips moving and heard him whisper, "The screen door slams, Mary's dress sways." By the time Bruce hit the line, "I just can't face myself alone again," tears were falling from David's eyes.

Chapter Four

I woke up early the next morning and started getting ready for the Turkey Bowl. I put on an already-ripped pair of jeans and the oldest pair of tennis shoes I could find, threw on my Merlin Olsen Rams jersey—number seventy-four, of course—and headed out the door.

"Douglas?" I heard my mom calling from the kitchen. "Is that you?"

"Yeah, Mom. Gotta run. Don't want to be late."

"Don't you want to eat anything?"

"No time, Mom."

I went out the front door and was walking to my car parked in front of the house when I heard my mom open the door.

"Douglas, here," she called, "I already made you a bagel and cream cheese. Take it with you."

I turned around and grabbed the warm bagel from her. "You're the best, Mom. Thanks. Love you!" I headed back to my car.

"Be careful! Don't get hurt!"

"Don't worry, Mom. I won't." It was true that injuries were a part of the Turkey Bowl tradition. That was the main reason Hank didn't play in the game; his coaches sat the whole team down and told them that if anyone was caught playing tackle football over Thanksgiving—there were a lot of games going on in yards and parks throughout the Valley—they'd be suspended from the team. Of course, there was really no way they could actually ever find out, but it was doubtful anyone on the team would be stupid enough to play tackle football with a bunch of scrubs the morning of the big rivalry game with Junipero Serra.

The bulk of the rain had fallen during the night, and there was just a barely perceptible morning drizzle coming from the sky as I drove my trusty Civic down the hills of Tarzana and toward Ventura Boulevard. I cranked my window open and inhaled the sweet, cool air; about the only time you could ever get air this pure in the Valley was after a rain. Sure, sometimes the high winds would clear out the air and the Valley would sparkle at night, but the morning after a rain you could literally taste the freshness. Even though my arm was getting a little damp from the open window, I loved to hear the sound of the tires as they rolled along the wet pavement.

I decided to skip the freeway and stayed on the surface streets, since Balboa Park wasn't all that far, and it was much easier to chow down my bagel while I was cruising on the street as opposed to speeding along the freeway. Heading down Ventura, I started getting myself psyched up for the big game. I wasn't a great football player, but as a decent athlete, I could hold my own. I usually played a fair amount of wide receiver; while I wasn't very fast, I had pretty good hands, so if the quarterback could put the ball anywhere near me, there was a good chance I would haul it in. On defense I usually played cornerback, though I also enjoyed—and was pretty good at—the free safety role.

By the time I pulled up to the designated spot in the park, the other players were starting to trickle in. We expected to have a solid showing this year, and sure enough, once everyone arrived we had sixteen guys, perfect for an eight-on-eight match. Moose and Mark Schiller, a guy we'd gone to Cabrillo with who was now at Pershing High, were the two captains, since they were the two best players. Even though Moose couldn't play sports competitively anymore, he was still allowed to play stuff recreationally, and we had actually seen his old competitive fire come to life here and there during PE at school as of late.

I was surprised when Schiller chose me with the second pick; I thought I'd probably go in the third or fourth round, which was when I was sure Moose was planning to grab me. Schiller was known to take the Turkey Bowl very seriously, and had probably thought through his draft order very carefully. He always showed up with a heavy knee brace that made him a difficult runner to bring down. Schiller was more of a rushing quarterback than a throwing quarterback, and when he was heading straight at you, knees pumping furiously high, you just knew that if you tried to hit him down low to take his legs out from under him, you'd get smacked by his metal brace and it would hurt like hell. Problem was, he was so solid and muscular up top that he'd generally slip through anyone who tried to tackle him from above the waist. Even though I liked playing with Moose, I was happy I wouldn't have to face Schiller and that damn brace.

Moose took Marco fairly early, with his second pick. Marco wasn't all that athletic, but he was strong and probably the best blocker out there, so Moose liked having him on his team for protection. Andrew, who wasn't a very good athlete, and was more of an annoying opponent than anything else, was picked last. Well, not really "picked"— he just ended up on Schiller's team since Moose had the first pick, which always pissed Andrew off.

"You guys are assholes," he said to both Moose and Schiller. "You're gonna regret it, Moose."

"Yeah, yeah," came Moose's reply. "Fuck you, Andrew. You suck."

Since Moose had first pick, we would receive. Sure enough, Schiller, knees pumping and knee brace glinting in the sunlight that occasionally peeked out from the puffy white-and-gray clouds, ran it back for the game's first touchdown.

"Fuck!" was probably repeated more than eight times by the guys on Moose's team as they went into finger-pointing mode about which one of them should've stopped Schiller.

Then, on Moose's first play from scrimmage, the inevitable happened. I had noticed Schiller and Andrew whispering to each other, and when we took our positions at the line of scrimmage, Schiller suddenly directed Andrew to move to the opposite side, away from Marco. With only little Dennis Martin trying to stop him, Andrew easily reached the backfield. An unsuspecting Moose, who was looking to throw deep but having trouble finding an open man, stood looking away from Andrew, who was charging ferociously toward him. With both arms raised high, Andrew flew at Moose and delivered a two-handed slap across Moose's face, bloodying his nose and sending him tumbling directly into a fairly large puddle of mud—one of many on the rain-soaked field.

"Yeah!" I heard Schiller scream. "Way to go, Andrew!"

"That's a fucking penalty, you asshole!" Moose cried out from the ground, rolling over and holding his hand up to his nose. We all gathered around him and could see the blood running down his face. "What the fuck do you think you're doing?"

"Sorry, Moose," Andrew said, trying to sound as sincere as possible, though we all knew he was full of shit. "I was just trying to deliver a clean hit."

"You're full of shit!" Moose rose up from the ground and charged at Andrew, but Schiller stepped into his path, protecting his teammate. Moose, not wanting to mess with Schiller, stopped and yelled "*Putain!*" before heading toward the sideline to grab his towel, which he'd probably brought along to wipe off mud—not blood. The old Moose would've undoubtedly kicked Andrew's ass right then and there, but the new Moose simply told his team he was done playing quarterback for the day, and would instead play the offensive and defensive line for the remainder of the game. Charlie Berger, Moose's first pick and probably just as good of a quarterback as Moose, took over throwing duties, though losing him as a receiver would undoubtedly hurt their team. Charlie had good hands and was fast, and their only other decent pass catcher, Jimmy Diamond, would now undoubtedly be facing double-teams the rest of the day.

"I told you he'd fold like a cheap tent if you delivered a big hit on the first play," Schiller laughed as he high-fived Andrew. I glared at both of them, but chose to hold my tongue.

Andrew, though, noticed the look on my face, and said, "Oh, come on, Douglas. He'll be fine. Besides, now that Moose isn't playing quarterback, we should win this thing easily."

"It was a dirty hit and you're an ass, Andrew," I responded.

"Whatever," Andrew replied, waving off my remarks, "you'll be singing a different tune when we're celebrating a Turkey Bowl victory."

"Let's not get ahead of ourselves, boys," Schiller spoke up, trying to place our focus back on the game. "Remember, Charlie is no slouch. He won't throw as deep as Moose, but he's probably just as accurate with his short passes, so let's tighten up our coverage."

Just as Andrew predicted, we controlled the game the rest of the way. A new kid from Cabrillo who'd never played in the Turkey Bowl actually kept things close by returning two kick-offs and one punt for touchdowns, and while Moose's team was only down by fourteen points early in the fourth quarter, they just didn't have enough firepower to compete down the stretch, and our team won by the rather wide margin of 63 to 42. These games were always high-scoring affairs, and when it was muddy like today, it was especially difficult to catch guys and bring them down. By the end of the morning, we were a ragged-looking group, muddy, sore, and exhausted.

Thankfully, Andrew and Moose made up when all was said and done; I think there was something in Moose that actually respected Andrew's hit, as it was certainly something the old Moose would've done in a heartbeat back in junior high, during our battles in the Boy's Afterschool Club leagues. "Next year," Moose promised, "I'm gonna see you coming, Andrew, and clock you with an elbow to the face just as you start to take your shot at me."

"That's *if* there's a next year," Schiller piped up. "Who knows where we'll all be."

It was true. By next Thanksgiving, most of us would be off at college. Sure, some of us would undoubtedly be home for the holiday, but would we ever really have enough guys to play the Turkey Bowl game again?

As we trudged off the field, and toward our cars parked in the muddy lot a few hundred yards off in the distance, we were mostly silent, each of us lost in our own reverie, enjoying both the pain that was starting to make itself apparent in various areas of our bodies—elbows, knees, bruises on the thighs—as well as the sweetness of the scent of the thick, soggy grass beneath our feet and the sight of the cherry trees throughout the park, their leaves now turned a fiery crimson in the cool dampness of a late autumn afternoon.

I mostly took it easy the rest of the day, lying on the couch with a couple of ice packs strategically placed on my right knee and inner thigh—well, my groin actually, which I'd strained diving for one of Schiller's longish passes. I hauled it in for a big gain, so I guess the pain I was now experiencing was worth it. Had I dropped the ball . . . not so much.

Tonight was the big basketball game versus Junipero Serra, which was sure to be a wild affair. As 5:00 rolled around, I started getting ready. Annie didn't live too far away from Junipero Serra—her house was across Ventura and straight up Winnetka near Oxnard—and I'd told her I would pick her up around 5:30. She was waiting outside when I pulled up, looking dazzling in a pretty yellow dress. But as she approached the car I noticed that her mascara was streaked, and it looked like she had been crying.

"Hey," I asked as she opened the door. "You okay? What's the matter?"

"Hi, baby," she cooed as she slipped into the front seat, wrapped her arms around my neck and gave me a long, wet kiss.

I wiped a bit of her mascara off with the tip of my finger. "What's going on?"

"Nothing. Just another fight with my mom."

"Sorry, sweetie."

"It's okay. I'm happy now that I'm with you." Annie curled up next to me as best she could across the armrest, and I shifted into first gear and pulled away from her house. She immediately reached for the radio and changed the station from KMET to KIIS, and then started dancing in her seat to "I Want to Kiss You All Over," while doing exactly that to my cheek, head, and neck. God I loved having a girlfriend.

There were already loads of people lined up to get into the gym when we pulled into the Junipero Serra parking lot; fortunately, we were able to get seats high up in the stands behind the Toreros' bench. I gave Hank the high sign when he turned around and saw us a few minutes before the game started. Hank was the team's sixth man, a valuable contributor off the bench who brought stability to the mix with his very deliberate, thoughtful approach to the game. He was also versatile, able to play both the power and small forward positions equally well. In a pinch, you could use him as a tall shooting guard, though he usually had trouble defending the opposing team's player at that position.

As promised, the game was heated and very, very tight. Hank was his usual solid self, chipping in eight points, five rebounds, two assists, and a steal. As the game headed into the final minutes, he found himself playing down the stretch, with Coach Warren obviously trusting him more than the hot-and-cold starter Jesse Robinson.

Junipero Serra was trailing by one point with a minute and half to go, when one of their players beat his man and drove to the basket for what looked like an easy lay-up. From out of nowhere, our star center, Timmy Green, flew down the lane and delivered a hard foul that sent the Junipero Serra player tumbling down to the ground and crashing into the padding behind the basket. The Junipero Serra fans went crazy, booing and even throwing popcorn and soda onto the court. They thought the play was dirty, that Timmy wasn't even trying to go for the ball but simply giving the other player a karate chop to the neck and shoulder area, and even perhaps catching part of his face.

Suddenly, a woman came racing onto the court from just next to the scorer's table. We would later find out that it was the Junipero Serra player's mom! Can you imagine how embarrassed this dude was? How would you like it if you were lying on the ground, having just been hammered by the other team's star player in the waning moments of a tight game, only to see your mom rushing onto the court? The player—number 22—woozily got to his feet, his arms outstretched as he cried, "No, Mom, no!" But it was too late to stop her; she had already come flying at Timmy Green, her two-inch nails extending from her outstretched hands like claws and scratching the hell out of poor Timmy's face before he even knew what hit him. The assistant coach for Junipero Serra was able to grab the enraged mom by her waist and pull her away from Timmy, but not before the damage to his face had been inflicted by this insane mama bear protecting her cub.

From that point on, things only got worse. Friends, family members, fellow students . . . scores of fans descended onto the court in what can only be described as an outright brawl. I grabbed Annie and, along with many others, headed for the safety of the exits. I later found out that Coach Warren and his assistants successfully navigated Timmy and Hank and the rest of the team off of the court and into the visitors' locker room, where they used benches to bar the door. It took about thirty minutes or so before the police, who were already on duty, were able to get some backup cops to come to the school and restore order.

When it came time for the Torero team to walk to the bus to go home, a phalanx of policemen had to escort them through what was still an angry mob of Junipero Serra fans, and as the bus drove away, Hank told me it was pelted with all manner of soda cans and even some beer bottles. As to the game, the referees ruled that Junipero Serra had forfeited because of the poor behavior of their fans, and Woodrow Wilson escaped with a big win, not to mention their lives.

A couple of weeks later—actually, it was the Saturday night before our last week of school prior to Christmas vacation starting—Annie, Hank, Vicki, and I decided to go out on a double date. It was a bit risky; while Annie and Vicki knew each other from school, they had never really hung out together. And Annie knew nothing about Vicki and Natalia's friendship. Hank and I talked about whether or not to tell Annie, but he felt the same way I did: let sleeping dogs lie. Hank would tell Vicki—who was totally cool with the situation because Natalia had given Vicki her blessing—not to bring up Natalia, at least not on our first double date as couples, and she agreed.

"It's no big deal," Vicki told Hank. "Natalia has nothing but positive feelings toward Douglas. She's now dating a boy who's in college." Obviously, I didn't need to hear that last part, and wished Hank had left it out when he was relaying the conversation to me, but I was glad to hear that Natalia still thought highly of me and that there were no hard feelings between us.

I picked up Annie, and we all met at Hank's town-house. Thankfully, Natalia had moved out of the Encino Royale a year or so before, so there was zero chance of running into her. Then we piled into Hank's '67 Camaro and headed off to the Griffith Park Observatory for a performance of Laserium. Hank and I loved Laserium. I had taken Annie once and though she liked it, I think she'd agreed to go again just to make me happy. As for Vicki, she had never been, but seemed excited to see it.

The back seat of Hank's car was ideal for cuddling, and Annie and I got right to it, kissing and lightly fondling each other while sliding all over Hank's perfectly Armor All-ed leather seats. Hank was the king of Armor All; the interior of his car, from the dash and seats to the doors, were all kept in mint condition. Of course, the outside of the cobalt-blue Camaro was always spotless and waxed to shiny perfection.

"Hey, what's going on back there?" Hank laughed. I looked up and saw his eyes reflected in the rearview mirror. Vicki turned around, and when she saw us with our arms around each other and lips close together, she rolled her eyes and turned back toward the front of the car. Oops. Maybe Vicki—and, by extension, Natalia—wasn't as okay with me and Annie as she claimed?

The rest of the drive out to the Observatory was on the quiet side. We listened to music and made some idle chit-chat, mostly about the basketball game the night before, which Vicki had been unable to attend because it was her mom's birthday. I pulled out a joint and Hank and I got high while Annie took a couple of small hits and Vicki passed altogether. After winding our way up through Griffith Park, we reached the top, parked the car, and got in the line, which was already wrapping around the building.

It was a beautiful night, cool and cloudless, the lights from the city below sparkling like they only seem to do in Los Angeles. Maybe it was simply the magic of Hollywood. I held Annie close. She had on a wool coat and a red beret. God, she was fine. In that moment I felt like the luckiest guy in the world. With my nose at the top of her head—she was a good seven or eight inches shorter than me—I inhaled deeply, reveling in the sandalwood scent of her long, freshly shampooed hair. Looking around, I noticed the usual mix of people at a Laserium show: music fans, science nerds, families with little kids, and a lot of stoners like us.

Hank and I had chosen to buy tickets for "The Best of Laserium," which had a bunch of great rock and roll songs. The highlights were obviously "Roundabout" by Yes and "Echoes" by Pink Floyd—each in their own unique way were just tailor-made for the Laserium experience—but Gary Wright's "Dream Weaver" was right up there with them and the evening's closer, Edgar Winter's funk masterpiece "Frankenstein," always brought the house down.

It was a typically great show, made even better by having Annie cuddled up next to me. When it was over, she was the first one to speak up. "I really liked that tonight," she said. "I thought it was better than the last show you took me to."

"Yeah, this one had more rock and roll than the one you saw," I pointed out. "That one was the original Laserium, and there was a lot more classical music."

"What'd you think, Vicki?" Hank asked.

"I didn't mind the music," she said somewhat coolly, "but to be honest I don't get all the laser stuff. It was like some psychedelic nut went on a trip! Just weird. I think I'd rather listen to the music and look at the planets and the constellations like they normally show inside the Planetarium. Maybe you need to be high. I don't know."

"Well, that's obviously not the case," Hank argued. "Just look at all the families with little kids who were there tonight."

"Yeah, I guess so," was all Vicki said as she increased her pace, now walking several steps in front of us.

Annie looked up at me, opened her eyes wide, and whispered, "What a grinch," and then laughed.

The rest of the evening didn't go much better. While Hank, Annie, and I were up for getting some late-night Thai food, Vicki insisted on being driven home. Needless to say, the drive on the way back was even quieter than the drive on the way to Griffith Park, and you could feel the tension inside the Camaro. When we were finally back alone in the calm of my Civic, Annie and I breathed a sigh of relief.

"Well, that was fun—not!" Annie joked.

"I'm sorry," I said. "She's usually not like that. I don't know what's up. Maybe her and Hank aren't getting along these days."

"Did he say anything to you?"

"No, that's what's weird. I'll talk to him tomorrow. I'm sure Vicki is giving him an earful about something right now."

"So, what do you want to do?" Annie asked, a twinkle

in her eye.

"I don't know. Are you still hungry?"

"Hungry for you," she purred, placing her hand on my dick and stroking it with her fingers through my tight jeans. "Why don't we go find someplace to park?"

And that's exactly what we did, up on a quiet stretch of Mulholland, in a pull-out overlooking the Valley, its lights glistening even stronger than the lights of L.A. we had been admiring earlier in the evening. Just moments after we had parked and I had shut off the engine, I pushed my seat as far back as it could go and Annie got on top of me, kissing me furiously. Cynthia Fox was talking on the radio and then somehow, miraculously, Seger's "Night Moves" started to play. My pants were unzipped and my underwear was pulled down, and I was just about to go inside of Annie. Could life possibly get any better than this?

Unfortunately, it could not. The sound of tires squealing and the flashing of blue-and-red lights ended my little bit of heaven. A cop had pulled in behind us.

"Shit," Annie said, scrambling to get off of me and pull herself together as I did the same, zipping up my pants and wiping Annie's lipstick off of my face.

"Can you roll down your window, please?" The voice startled me; I hadn't seen the officer walk up to my door. I immediately did as he asked.

"Good evening, kids. How we doing tonight?" Once he moved his flashlight from me to Annie, I could make out that the officer was an older guy, with a fairly large paunch. He seemed like he'd be better suited to busting kids for making out on Mulholland than chasing down real criminals.

"Um, we're fine, officer," I stammered. "Real good."

"You know," he said, shining his flashlight over at Annie, "we've been getting a lot of complaints from some of the homeowners up here lately about kids parking their cars, having sex, drinking alcohol, smoking pot . . . now, you haven't been doing any of that, have you?"

"No sir," Annie spoke up, smiling that adorable smile of hers. "We're just enjoying the view. It's a beautiful evening." I had to hand it to Annie, she could bullshit and lie with the best of them. I'd seen her do it over and over again with her mom. It was a trait I didn't share; I was too much of an open book. Sure, I could handle delivering the occasional white lie, but anything more serious was just beyond my capabilities. I simply couldn't pull off the major con.

"Uh-huh," the officer replied. "Can I see your license and registration, please?" I immediately handed over both and the officer trudged back to his car.

"Do you have any more pot on you?" Annie whispered, concerned. "What if they search the car?"

"Don't worry," I said. "I only brought the one joint, and we already smoked it in Hank's car."

"Can they bust us for having sex?" Annie asked.

"Hell if I know," I said. "Is it illegal to do it in your own car?" I really had no idea.

It seemed like an eternity before he came back. "Okay, kids," the officer said, giving my documents back to me and then writing something down on a pad. "I'm going to let you off with a warning this time." He tore off a pink slip of paper and handed it to me. "I don't know exactly what you were doing in here, but you know it's illegal to have sex in your car in a public place, don't you?"

"But we weren't—"

"Save it, mister," he said pointedly. "Just be thankful I'm letting you off with a warning."

"Yes, sir," I replied obediently.

"Now I want you to take this pretty young lady home and then get yourself home and in bed. It's getting pretty late for you young kids to be out and about."

"Yes, officer," Annie replied. "And thank you, sir."

On the way home, Annie helped ease my jittery nerves. "Well, I've never had *that* happen before!" she laughed.

"Jesus," I said, finally breathing a sigh of relief. "Can you believe it?"

"What were the odds?"

"I'm just glad he let me off with a warning. Can you imagine if he'd given me a ticket? How would I have explained that one to my mom?"

I drove Annie straight home as the cop had demanded, kissed her goodnight, and made my way back to my house. The double date hadn't exactly gone as planned—nor had my time with Annie between the date and the end of the evening—but I was feeling good about my girlfriend. We were definitely on solid ground. After several years of simply being the male friend and shoulder for girls to cry on when their boyfriends were causing them grief, I finally had an L.A. woman to call my own.

Christmas vacation couldn't come soon enough, and when it finally did arrive, my friends and I were ready to celebrate. We had all agreed to meet at Marco's house, since his mom was totally mellow about kids partying in her home. It turned out that Marco's mom and stepdad had gone to Vegas for the weekend, so he and his older stepbrother, Craig, had the house to themselves. Originally, I didn't think I was going to be able to make it because

I'd already made plans with Annie, but she canceled at the last minute—something about an aunt and uncle being in town—so I was free to join the gang on what would turn out to be a wild Saturday night and a crazy way to start our holiday break.

"So what's on tap for tonight?" Andrew asked as he took a bong hit and passed it over to Hank. Marco had two single beds in his bedroom. Andrew and Hank sat on one of them while Moose and I sat across from them on the edge of the other bed. Marco was standing the whole time; his nervous energy was off the charts.

"My stepbrother turned me on to something pretty cool recently," Marco said.

"Oh yeah?" I asked. "What's that?"

"You guys want to go to a porno theater?"

"What, you mean like the Corbin Theater?" Moose asked.

"No, no," Marco replied, "they don't take fake ID's and Andrew will never pass for eighteen."

"Fuck you, Marco," Andrew replied. "Prick." It was true, though. Andrew had a baby face; he even had trouble getting into R-rated movies.

"This is a little theater in Hollywood," Marco continued. "And as long as one of us has a fake ID, the guy will let all of us in."

"I don't know," Hank said dubiously. "It's a long way to drive just to be turned away."

"I went there a couple of weeks ago with my stepbrother," Marco insisted.

"Yeah, but Craig's over eighteen," I pointed out.

"Exactly," Marco said. "Once he showed his ID, the rest of us just walked right in. No ID required."

"But that still doesn't solve the problem of one of us having a fake ID, you idiot," Andrew said, laughing. He was obviously already stoned.

"Ta-da!" Marco said, pulling what looked like a California driver's license out of his back pocket with a flourish. "Courtesy of Craig."

He passed around his newly minted fake ID, and we all had to admit that it looked like the real deal.

"Amazing," Hank said. "It looks just like a regular driver's license."

"Hang on, hang on," Moose's voice rose above the excited din in the room. "This says you were born in June of 1957. That would make you twenty-one."

"Of course," Marco said. "Why would I get a fake ID that didn't make me twenty-one? That's the whole point, dumbshit."

"Oh, right," Moose said, still staring at the fake ID. "Damn. I'd like to have one of these. Can you get them for us?"

"I'll have to talk to my stepbrother. We had to drive down to some crummy photo studio in La Habra to get it."

"La Habra?" Andrew challenged. "Why La Habra?"

"I don't know, fuckface, that's just where the guy does his business," Marco said, irritated as always with Andrew's questions. He looked around at each of us. "What do you guys think? You down for a little Hollywood porno action?"

"Sure," Moose and Andrew said in unison.

"Hank? Douglas?" Marco looked over at us.

"I'm game," Hank answered.

"Yeah, sounds like a grand adventure," I laughed.

"I'll drive," Andrew volunteered.

"Fuck that," Marco shot back. "I ain't riding in that death trap." Andrew owned a Pinto, and there had been all kinds of lawsuits and recalls on his model and year because of a problem with exploding gas tanks.

"Well, I ain't driving with you, maniac. The last time I did that, I almost got arrested for leaving the scene of a crime." We all broke up laughing, and even Marco couldn't resist.

"I'll drive, I'll drive," Hank said, and with that, we headed out the door.

"Shotgun!" Andrew yelled.

"No chance," Marco insisted.

"We gotta go rock-paper-scissors," I suggested. "Winners split the ride there and the ride back."

I challenged Moose, and Andrew and Marco went at it. Marco and I won, and he climbed into the front seat for the ride to Hollywood.

"Both of you guys get the middle when you're not in front," Andrew demanded.

Marco and I reluctantly agreed, because we knew it was only fair for each of us to suffer in the back seat, squished between Moose and Andrew, in exchange for the pleasure of driving in the front for one of the lengths of the trip. Only, the difference between Hank's style of driving and Marco's style of driving was so vast that I don't think Marco was actually enjoying his time in the front seat.

"Why the fuck are you slowing down?" Marco whined to Hank once we had been driving for a few minutes.

"Because that light up ahead is going to turn red."

"But if you speed up you might make it."

"Gas mileage, my friend," Hank said with a smug smile on his face. "It's all about saving gas."

It was Hank's theory that one should never speed up when approaching a light but do the opposite instead: slow down and coast so that you didn't waste one precious drop of fuel speeding up to make a light, only to have to slam on the brakes when you realized you weren't going to make it. And, of course, while coasting toward the light you were using exactly zero fuel. Thus, in Hank's mind, you saved gas by not speeding up, and you saved gas by coasting whenever you were approaching a light. With gas prices recently breaking through the seventy-cent barrier, everyone was trying to save fuel, but Hank took it to an extreme.

"You're an idiot." Marco just shook his head and stared out the window.

"When the price of gas goes over a buck," Hank continued to defend himself, "you'll be coasting up to lights, too."

"Over a buck?" Moose said incredulously. "You're out of your mind."

"Mark my words," Hank responded with absolute confidence.

"He thinks Mr. Watts is a genius," Andrew explained. "The other day Watts told us gas prices would be over a dollar by the end of '79." Andrew and Hank had economics together this year, and Watts, whose real job was as the VP of marketing and sales for a local pool supply company, was the teacher. He actually volunteered to help out the school and teach the class; his son had gone to Woodrow Wilson many years before. Hank thought Mr. Watts was super cool, and he was now thinking of majoring in business or marketing when he went to San Diego State.

Once we were on the freeway, the argument about

slowing down for lights faded away, and we all settled into a nice, friendly groove, passing doobies around and around as we listened to Hank's stellar car stereo: a Pioneer KP-500 under-dash cassette receiver. It was probably the most popular car stereo on the market; everybody wanted one. The best feature, besides the ease of mounting it to the bottom of your dash, was what Pioneer called their "Supertuner," a large dial, like the face of a clock, that you'd spin to tune into your favorite station. Hank, however, had stuck a cassette into the player by a new band called Toto. The reviews in the car were mixed.

"I dig it," Marco said. "Listen to those drums!"

"For once I agree with you, Marco," Andrew said. "These guys can play. I heard they all grew up in the Valley."

"I don't know." I paused, blowing out yet another cloud of smoke. "It's a little mersh for my tastes. What do you think, Hank?"

"Yeah, I get the mersh vibe, too," my buddy replied. "But I'll admit the tunes are catchy and the guys are the real deal. I read they're all, like, famous session musicians or something."

"Hey!" Marco turned and looked at me. "Quit bogarting that joint, dude."

"Oh," I said sheepishly, handing the joint to him. "Sorry, man."

We cruised along, windows cracked to release the smoke and let the cool night air enter the car, and made our way through the Hollywood Split and up toward the Cahuenga Pass. All was mellow until Hank's propensity to steer with one finger on the wheel began to drive Marco crazy.

"Will you please put at least one hand on the wheel?" Marco pleaded. "How the fuck can you drive down the freeway at fifty-five miles an hour with only one fucking finger on the wheel?"

Hank just laughed and continued with his index finger placed directly at the bottom center of the wheel, occasionally making a slight adjustment to stay in his lane. Sure, if Hank needed to change lanes, he'd grab the wheel with his hands; he didn't have a death wish or anything. But he rarely made lane changes—again, he believed lane changes just wasted gas—and he was perfectly happy cruising along with his one finger perched on the bottom of the wheel.

"For fuck's sake," Marco continued. "Dude gets a killer automobile passed down from his dad, and he drives it like a sissy."

"Let's see," Hank shot back whimsically, "how many accidents and tickets have I had?" He paused for effect. "The answer would be none. And how many accidents and tickets have you had, Marco?"

"I'm in training, asshole."

"Yeah, I'm sure your dad loves paying those speeding tickets and your sky-high insurance," Andrew zinged.

"Those are write-offs, fuckface," Marco said. "They're tax deductions, expenses related to my training as a stunt driver."

"What are you, a fucking accountant now?" Moose chimed in.

Marco ignored the jab. "Just drive and get off at Highland," he directed Hank. "We can check out the Bowl and get a good look at all the loonies on Hollywood Boulevard on the way there."

The theater sat directly on Hollywood, but down on the scummy east side, way past Gower, even. Hank wasn't comfortable parking on a side street, and the rest of us—seeing the bars on the windows of the houses and apartment buildings in the surrounding neighborhood—didn't blame him, so we all offered to pitch in the fifty cents it cost to park in the one lot we found that looked relatively safe in that part of town.

As we approached the theater—if you could actually call it a theater, for it was really just a converted storefront—we all laughed at their attempt at a marquee. It was a poorly hand-painted slab of wood nailed into the stucco above a door that read, not "XXX Movies" as one would expect, but "XXXX Movies," with "Hot Adult Action" painted below on the second line in slightly smaller letters.

"Quadruple X!" Andrew yelled, laughing hysterically. We were all stoned, but none, it appeared, more so than Andrew. "What the fuck does that even mean?"

"Well," I surmised, "it means their films are obviously a cut above your typical triple X flick."

"Okay, guys," Marco directed. "Just stand in a line behind me. I'll pay for all of us, and once the dude lets me in, just follow right behind me and look straight ahead like you belong there. Don't even make eye contact with the guy at the door."

As we approached the entrance to the theater, I could see a slight, balding man perched on a metal stool at a bright green door that sat at the end of a short, narrow passageway. Just as Marco promised, his fake ID and twenty-dollar bill were accepted—at four bucks a pop, this was one expensive movie—and we followed behind our fearless leader. I was bringing up the rear with Andrew in front of me, and the idiot couldn't resist taking a glance at the guy at the door as he walked past.

"Wait a minute," the doorman said, grabbing Andrew by his arm. "Are you twenty-one?"

Andrew started to stammer, so I decided to take the bull by the horns and take control of the situation. "Yeah, yeah, he's twenty-one," I said coolly, not even looking at the bald guy while pushing Andrew hard in the back, surging him forward and forcing the man to release his hand from Andrew's arm. I quickly walked past him without so much as a glance. The combination of the weed and the thrill of seeing what existed beyond the green door had puffed up my confidence. Besides, the dude had already taken Marco's twenty bucks.

I honestly don't remember much of what we saw that night, just a bunch of penises and vaginas and people fucking in all different kinds of positions. There was even a Chinese lady on a swing at one point. The movie wasn't really a movie, but rather an endless series of short films without any plot and very little dialogue, featuring a lot of sucking and screwing.

The thing that probably stuck out the most that night was the sticky floors—our tennis shoes felt like they were constantly stepping on gum, but we all knew there was no gum on the floor. The seats were actually broken wooden chairs. When we entered, the shadows of our heads and shoulders appeared on the screen, as we were backlit from one of the two 16-millimeter projectors set up on a small platform at the back of the room. There were only three other people in the theater, and even though it was fairly dark in there, I swear they were all wearing overcoats.

When we had all finally had our fill, we got up and left, our shadows once again appearing on the screen. Upon walking back out onto Hollywood Boulevard, we were shocked to discover that it was now approaching midnight.

"Jesus!" Andrew said, looking at his watch. "It's after eleven thirty! We were in there for over three hours!"

"Time flies when you're having fun," Moose dead-panned.

"You boys enjoy that?" Marco asked.

"I don't know," Hank said, somewhat solemnly. "I sorta felt bad for some of those girls. You think they like doing that?"

"Are you fucking kidding me?" Marco said. "They *love* it! Don't be a pussy, Hank."

"I'm with Hank," I said. "I'm glad we went, because I always wondered what these movies were like. But I just sort of feel sad for all of the people involved."

"You guys have been listening to too much James Taylor and Jackson Browne. You need to grow some *cojones*." Marco turned to Moose and Andrew. "What about you two?"

"My stepdad has a huge collection of this shit," Moose replied. "Ain't nothing in there I haven't seen before."

"Moose, you been holding out on me?" Andrew said, surprised to hear this news.

"What, I'm going to invite you over to watch porn with me? *Certainement pas!*" Moose laughed.

"You two can jerk off together," Marco teased.

"That's not what I meant!" Andrew cried.

"Well, I'm not hearing much love for my putting together this little excursion tonight," Marco complained.

"It was an experience I'll never forget," Hank said.

"Thanks, Marco." And the rest of us thanked Marco in kind.

Once we got back to Hank's car—which was thankfully still sitting safely in the parking lot a block or two from the theater—we lit a joint and discussed what to do next.

"I'm hungry," said Moose. "Anyone up for Ben Frank's?"

"I had a huge dinner before we got together tonight," Hank said.

"Me, too," agreed Andrew, who was super skinny and never ate that much anyway.

Before I could respond, Marco put forth another idea: "A few weekends ago, my brother took me up to this cool spot in a canyon above Beverly Hills. We can cruise down Sunset, and then head up the canyon and eventually make our way to Mulholland and over to the San Diego Freeway."

"Sounds like a plan, Stan," Hank said as we all piled into the car. My buddy, now next to me since I'd won the right to the front seat on the way home, started up the Camaro and pulled out of the lot. The Boulevard was still packed, especially with the police presence slowing everyone down, so we cut down Bronson to Sunset, which wasn't nearly as crowded. Sure, it didn't have the freak show like Hollywood did, but it was still fun cruising past the Palladium, the Cinerama Dome, and, of course, Carney's, where we made a quick pit stop for a dog, in spite of Andrew's protests. He insisted that Pink's wasn't that far out of the way and was much better.

"Fuck it, I'm not wasting the gas," Hank said, putting an end to the brief skirmish. "Besides, Pink's is only better than Carney's when it comes to the chili dog, and the only time I'll eat a chili dog at midnight is when I'm drunk."

"Speaking of which," Marco said, leaning forward from the center seat, "after we hit Carney's, why don't we make a quick pit stop at the liquor store just past The Whiskey so we can pick up a six-pack?"

"I don't know, man," Hank spoke up immediately. "I don't want any open containers in the car."

"That's fine," Marco agreed. "We'll drink 'em up where I'm taking you."

By the time we ate our hot dogs and were sitting outside the liquor store on Sunset, waiting to see if Marco's fake ID woud work once again, a little bit of apathy was beginning to fill the inside of the Camaro's cabin. Andrew was the first to yawn loudly. "I'm tired," he complained. "You sure we want to do this?"

"I'm with Andrew on this one," Moose piped up. "I say let's go home."

"Well, he's already bought the beer," I pointed out as soon as I saw Marco emerge from the store. "He'll be pissed if we tell him we don't want to go."

"Well then, light another doobie," Moose suggested. "That'll wake us up."

"Hello, boys," Marco smiled as he opened the door and thrust a six-pack of Foster's into my face. "The ID worked like a charm. Now, everyone get out so I can get in."

We played our version of musical chairs—Moose and I both had to get out so Marco could climb into the middle of the back seat—and then set off down the road.

"Why the fuck did you get Foster's?" Andrew complained.

"Because it's great beer, dickwad."

"Everyone knows Australians don't know shit about

beer," Andrew said with authority. "Gotta go Bavarian."

"Listen to this clown." Marco laughed, punching Andrew in the arm. "*Bavarian*," he mocked. "Mr. Bigshot attorney can't even say 'German.'"

Andrew gave Marco an elbow to the ribs in retaliation. Ever since Ronnie used to throw him in the trash can, Andrew had vowed that he would always fight back, even if the opponent were bigger and stronger, and I think Marco actually appreciated his pluckiness. "You'll be thankful for my intelligence once you get sued for killing somebody while doing a stunt, or better yet, when you need to sue someone else because you got hurt doing a stunt. I've decided I'm going to become a personal injury attorney."

"An ambulance chaser?" I asked, surprised. I'd heard my dad call them that. He hated PI attorneys. He said they were always looking for someone who got hurt to see if there was anyone they could sue.

"Fuck you, Douglas. You don't even know what you're talking about. I'm going to help people who need the help the most."

"Yeah, while lining your pockets with money," Moose laughed. "My uncle's a PI attorney. He lives in Beverly Hills. 'Nuff said."

"So? What's wrong with making money? Your dad's a fucking stockbroker, for Christ's sake!"

"Was," Moose said flatly. A brief silence enveloped the car.

"Oh, uh, sorry, dude," Andrew apologized.

"Turn right at the second light up ahead," Marco instructed after a few moments, thankfully changing the subject.

We headed deep into one of the lesser-known canyons. We were Valley boys, and while we knew how to get around the city fairly well, we usually stuck to either Beverly Glen or Laurel Canyon, depending on how far west or east in the city we were going. Once we got up high enough, the houses began to thin until there were only a few here or there on the rim of what appeared to be a large canyon.

"Slow down," Marco told Hank. "Turn up here on the left."

"The dirt road?" Hank complained. "I just washed my car today!"

"Turn left," Marco ordered.

"Fuck!" Hank complained as he turned onto the dirt road, only to hear his beloved Camaro bottom out.

"It's not my fault!" Marco insisted. "Tell Moose here to lose some weight."

"Fuck off, Marco."

"It's just up ahead," Marco said. "You'll be fine."

Hank crawled along for another couple of hundred feet.

"This is good," Marco said.

"Where, right here?" Hank asked in disbelief.

"Just pull off to the side a little bit. You'll be fine. Trust me, no one else is coming up here tonight."

Hank pulled over to the right as much as he could without putting the car into the small ditch that ran alongside the dirt road, and we all stepped out of the car. There was a full moon up in the nighttime sky, so the visibility wasn't bad. Marco led us up a trail that climbed a small hill. There was a cool rock outcropping on top, with a ledge that seemed to stick out at least five or six feet over what appeared to be a decent drop of at least twenty feet, maybe even more on the backside; I couldn't really see from where we were standing.

Marco popped open some beers and passed them around. Within what seemed like seconds, he had chugged his whole huge can of Foster's and grabbed a second one. "You don't mind, right boys? I figure there's only five of us and six of them, so I might as well get the extra one since I bought them. By the way, anything each of you assholes can chip in would be much appreciated," he said, slightly swaying as he smiled hazily.

About halfway through his second beer, and in spite of our protestations, Marco climbed up onto the outcropping and stood on the very edge.

"Come on, Marco," Andrew said. "Really?"

"You've made your point, Marco," Moose said, clearly irritated.

"Shhhhhhhhh," Marco ordered, putting his finger to his lips. "I'm going to tell you a little story, a little story about a nice little family." He let his words linger in the by-now damp night air. A bit of fog had appeared at the bottom of the canyon that sat below us, the lights of a few houses dotting the hills. "You've undoubtedly heard of the Manson family, right?"

"Sure," we muttered. Hell, Spahn Ranch wasn't that far from where I had grown up in Northridge.

"And do you know about what happened to Sharon Tate and her friends?"

"They slaughtered them," Moose said sadly.

"And scrawled 'pig' on the door in blood," Andrew added.

An owl hooted in the distance, momentarily startling us. I thought I heard something rustling in the bushes. I could feel the hairs on the back of my neck stand up on end.

"Look straight down there," Marco ordered. We all turned our attention in the direction of where he was pointing. "See the two-story house with the lights on upstairs? See it?" He wanted to make sure we all knew where to look, so he waited until we'd all confirmed we had spotted the target. "Just beyond that house, you can see the outline of a ranch-style house with a long drive-way leading up to it. See it?"

Once again, Marco waited until we all could spot it, even though Moose would later claim he could never quite pinpoint the house.

"That's where the Manson family killed Sharon Tate, her baby, and her friends."

"Jesus," Hank murmured. We all stared down the canyon toward the ranch house in quiet, creeped-out disbelief.

Marco chugged the rest of his second beer and suddenly, for no reason, he began to howl, and I mean howl like a werewolf. He was freaking us all out.

"What the fuck is wrong with you?" Andrew said, while the rest of us just looked at this lunatic, howling in the light of a full moon not far from the site of one of the worst murders in the history of Los Angeles. Marco ignored him and kept inching closer and closer to the edge furthest away from us, where I suspected the drop was significant.

"Hey, asshole!" Hank yelled. "You're a stunt *driver*. Not a stunt*man*. Get the fuck off of that rock before you hurt yourself."

The next thing we knew, Marco leaped off the back

edge of the outcropping, disappearing from our view. "Fuck!" Hank shouted, leading a charge up the hill to the top of the rock, the rest of us following closely behind. When we reached the top where Marco had been standing, we looked down the other side only to see him standing on a wide ledge about eight feet below.

"You guys are such pussies," he laughed. "Did you shit your pants, Andrew?"

Hank and I actually thought the gag was pretty funny, but Andrew and Moose were not amused. "Asshole," Andrew spat. "Just remember what happened to the boy who cried wolf. You're gonna need me one day, and if you keep pulling shit like this I won't be there for you."

Marco wasn't listening. "Hey!" he said gleefully. "Check out what my stepbrother taught me." With that, he very loudly hawked a big loogie up from his throat and into his mouth. He titled his head as far back as it would go, until his mouth was nearly parallel to the ground, pursed his lips, and fired a round loogie bullet high into the air above him—easily fifteen feet, maybe more—and caught the damn thing in his mouth as it fell from the sky. We were suitably impressed and gave him a standing ovation as we looked down on him.

"Okay," Hank announced. "It's getting late. Thanks for the show, Marco, but I want to get out of here before the cops show up. Everyone finish their beers and ditch your cans before you get back in the car."

On the drive back, Marco tried to force Hank to play *Frampton Comes Alive*, pulling out a cassette from the jacket of his pocket and attempting to shove it into the Pioneer deck from the back seat. He was drunk and high and obviously feeling good after his performance in the canyon, but we were all sick of the record and Frampton had sucked in the horrible *Sgt. Pepper* movie that had come out last summer, so Marco was universally shut down by everyone in the car. Instead, Hank threw Springsteen's little-known first album into the cassette player.

When we pulled up to Marco's house, it was well past 2:00 a.m., and we were surprised to see activity through the windows. "Huh," Marco peered out the front windshield. "I guess Craig has some people over. Anyone want to come in for nightcap bong hit?"

By now we were all so tired and slap-happy, we couldn't make a rational decision.

"I gotta go," Andrew finally insisted. "I have a shitload of homework to do tomorrow."

"Yeah, I should probably do the same," Moose agreed.

"Oh, come on, you pussies. What's ten more minutes? You guys worry about school too much."

"That's because we want to get into a good college and have a successful life, you nitwit," Andrew fired back. "Besides, not all of us have a dad who's a famous stunt driver."

"Yeah, whatever," Marco waved him off.

Hank was peering over Andrew's shoulders toward the house, where he could see a bunch of people in the kitchen that overlooked the front of the house. "There do seem to be some pretty hot girls in there," he remarked.

"It's my stepbrother. What do you expect? I guarantee there's nothing but foxes in there."

"All right, ten minutes, guys," I said authoritatively, and everyone fell in line. None of us could say no to an opportunity to meet a cute girl.

"When do your parents get back?" Andrew asked hesitantly.

"Tomorrow night," Marco assured us. "We're cool."

As we walked in the door, Marco's stepbrother Craig was coming down the stairs wearing a pair of sweatpants and a shirt that was unbuttoned, revealing his washboard stomach. Craig was a pole vaulter for a local junior college's track team, and he'd been something of a star in high school. He also had one of the most beautiful girl-friends in the world: Susie Montgomery was a legend at Woodrow Wilson, where she was not only the captain of the cheerleading team, but the homecoming queen as well. She'd claimed the "foxiest female" title in the year-book all three years she had attended our high school.

"Hey, fellas," Craig said, smiling. "What bad deeds have you been up to tonight?"

"I took them to the porno theater in Hollywood," Marco smiled proudly.

"No shit?" Craig was obviously impressed, both with Marco for taking us, but also with himself for introducing the theater to Marco and, by extension, to all of us. He continued down the stairs toward us, and as he reached the bottom step he stopped and beckoned us to gather around him. "Come here for a second. Ready? Smell my fingers." He moved his hand quickly in a semi-circle beneath each of our noses before we could even react. We all stood there like idiots and sniffed away.

"Oh, man!" Moose laughed, as he was the first one to get a whiff.

"What that fuck is that?" Andrew asked, scrunching his nose.

"Susie's pussy juices. She's upstairs, and I just fucked the shit out of her."

"You're beyond disgusting, Craig," Marco said.

"What?" Craig said, feigning ignorance. "You guys just spent hours in a porno theater . . . I thought you might like to experience a taste of the real thing."

"Sorry, guys," Marco said to us, obviously embarrassed.

None of us knew Craig all that well—he was several years older than we were, and we'd only met him in passing a handful of times—so we remained silent and just followed Marco through the entry and down a hallway that was lined with photos of Marco's dad pulling off all kinds of famous stunts in a variety of unbelievably cool cars. I glanced behind us to see Craig still standing on the bottom stair, smiling smugly. Upon meeting my gaze, he brought his fingers up to his nose and inhaled with exaggerated gusto. "Like fresh roses from the garden," he cackled.

We walked through another door and into the kitchen, where we were greeted by the sight of a handful of people sitting around a large wooden table that was absolutely trashed with empty beer and liquor bottles, half-drunk glasses of alcohol, and ashtrays filled with roaches. An elaborate glass bong sat in the middle of the table.

"Hey Marco, come on in, man." An extremely large dude stood up a little unsteadily and reached out to shake Marco's hand. "Hey everybody, this is Craig's stepbrother, Marco."

"Hey," Marco said, glancing around the room at what was a slightly older crowd, a mix of guys and girls. "These are my friends, Andrew, Moose, Hank, and Douglas over there."

Pleasantries were exchanged, and then Marco added, "Guys, this is Joe. He's the shot-putter on Craig's team."

"Actually, Craig's the pole vaulter on *my* team," Joe joked, and everyone laughed. "You guys want some bong hits?"

"You read my mind, Joe," Marco smiled. "I promised these guys a nightcap, and it looks like I can deliver."

"Help yourself." A beautiful blonde wearing a black velvet top hat and glitter on her eyelids thrust the bong at Hank.

"Oh, thanks," Hank said, slightly startled.

"Don't worry, honey," she cooed. "I won't bite."

Hank wasn't sure what to say, so he just took the bong and lit the bowl and did his thing in silence.

"What's the matter, Hank?" Andrew piped up. "Cat got your tongue?" Always the smartass.

Hank gestured meekly to the bong and then launched into a coughing fit that had everyone laughing. He passed the bong to me, and so it went down the line. Just as it reached Marco, Joe picked up a little leather bag, almost like something you'd put your toothbrush and stuff into if you were going on a trip. He unzipped it and took out a glass vial and what appeared to be a needle. He pulled his loose sweatpants all the way up to the top of his thigh. After spending a moment preparing the needle with whatever was in the vial, without warning he forcefully jabbed the needle right into his thigh and pushed down on the plunger. We all watched in amazed curiosity as the medicine or whatever it was flowed into his body.

Joe looked up at our wondering eyes. "Time to bulk up," he smiled. But then, after he had pulled the needle out and set it down on top of his bag, he suddenly started convulsing, all 250 pounds of his muscular body shaking so badly that he collapsed out of his chair and onto the floor, and we watched in horror as his eyes literally rolled back into his head. I had heard of that happening, but had actually never seen it.

"Oh my God! Oh my God!" the girl with the glittery eyelids started screaming. The rest of Joe's friends leaped to their feet as calls of "Craig! Craig!" rang out from the kitchen.

Craig rushed into the room and saw Joe lying on the floor, still having full-on convulsions. "Shit! What happened?"

"I don't know," said another guy, probably another track athlete judging by his solid build. "He took a shot and almost immediately started convulsing."

"Get a pencil!" Craig shouted to Marco, who immediately opened a drawer beneath the house telephone and pulled one out. He handed it to Craig, who was by now kneeling beside Joe. Craig shoved the pencil across Joe's mouth, in what I determined was an effort to keep Joe from swallowing his own tongue. I remembered seeing a teacher do this to an epileptic classmate in the second grade.

"I'm calling an ambulance!" Miss Glitter shrieked hysterically, scrambling toward the phone next to Marco.

"No!" Craig shouted. "No fucking way. Joe will get busted for steroids, and we'll all be fucked."

"He looks like he's gonna die!" Andrew yelled.

"He'll be fine. Just give him a moment. Someone get me some water." It seemed like Craig had been through this before, so everyone followed his lead. No phone calls were made and, sure enough, after a few more minutes, Joe started to come around.

"I don't get it," Craig said. "We went to the same place in Tijuana we always go to. I guess this time we got a bad batch."

"You guys are fucking nuts," Andrew said. "I'm out of here." With that, he turned and headed for the exits. Andrew took his future law career seriously, so the last thing he wanted to be associated with was a drug bust involving steroids smuggled in from across the border.

"I think I'm going to take off, too," Moose said, following Andrew. We all eventually did the same, with Marco trailing behind. As I left the kitchen, I could hear Craig finally getting through to Joe. "You all right, buddy?" he asked. We were out the door before we heard Joe answer.

"Well, that was certainly an interesting way to end the evening," Hank joked.

"I only try to provide the best in homegrown entertainment," Marco laughed as we stood in the driveway. "Sorry if that freaked you out, guys. I didn't know that was what was going to greet us when we walked into the house."

"Yeah, that and Susie Montgomery's pussy juices!" Andrew cracked up, and we all started laughing, harder and harder until tears were running down our faces.

"I'll be telling that story for a long time to come," Moose promised. We all shook our heads in agreement. It was true; between the porno theater, the canyon excursion, and the activities inside Marco's house, tonight had been one for the ages.

The rest of Christmas vacation sped by quickly. In spite of the fact that Annie had gone out of town to visit relatives for part of the break, we still managed to see each other a couple of times, including the night we went and checked out the new *Superman* flick. I wasn't much of a comic book guy, and while I admit the movie was fun to watch, it was basically just pure fluff. However, I knew that Valerie Perrine was in it, and she, as always, looked hotter than hot and was definitely worth the price of admission. Whenever she appeared on the screen, I found myself cuddling even closer with Annie, who by the end of the movie had figured out my obsession with the actress.

"You really like that Miss Teschmacher, don't you?" Annie said as we were walking to my car after the movie had ended.

"Wha-what do you mean?" I stammered, more than slightly embarrassed.

"Oh, come on, silly," Annie teased. "Don't play dumb with me, mister. Every time she came on the screen I could see your dick getting hard beneath those tight jeans of yours."

I was busted, and I had no comeback.

"Oh, don't be so embarrassed," Annie said, pulling me close. "I don't care. I find it sexy."

"Really?" I asked, wide-eyed.

"Well, it's not like you're ever going to date her. She's a movie star, for Christ's sake."

Annie had a good point there. Why should she be jealous? After all, if she told me she had the hots for Christopher Reeve, I wouldn't be upset or anything. So I had a crush on Valerie Perrine. Big deal. I breathed a sigh of relief; compared to how Natalia used to react to other girls, Annie was once again proving to be the coolest girlfriend in the world. Bonus points: The night ended well as we headed back to Annie's house, barred the door to her bedroom with her bureau, and made sweet love.

As I was kissing her goodnight in front of her house later that night, I brought up New Year's Eve, which was just a couple of nights away. A kid in our grade named Jimmy Taylor was having a huge open party that the whole school seemed to be going to. He was a rich kid with a big house and a tennis court, where he had supposedly set up a small stage for the event and was having not one but two bands play that night. The over-under on the cops breaking up the party was 12:30 AM.

"I'm looking forward to spending New Year's with you," I said, kissing her lightly. "I'll pick you up at eight thirty and then we'll head on over to the party, okay?"

Annie looked away silently.

"What's the matter?" I asked. I could tell something was wrong.

"Listen, Douglas," Annie said, turning back to me and searching my eyes, evidently preparing me for what was about to come. "I can't see you on New Year's."

"What do you mean? Why not? Is something wrong?"

"No, no, nothing like that. I just . . ." She was having trouble getting the words out.

"What is it?"

"My dad made reservations for me and my sister to join him and my stepmom at some fancy restaurant."

"What?" I said, incredulous.

"I know, I know. But he insisted. Said it might be the last time he could get his 'two little girls' to spend New Year's Eve with him." She seemed genuinely despondent, perhaps even more so than I was.

"Dang. That's harsh. Doesn't he know you have a boyfriend?"

Annie didn't respond.

I caressed her arms and held her tight, trying to soothe her, though it was probably me that needed the soothing. I looked up at the large maple tree in front of Annie's house. Its leaves were mostly brown and dead, and the branches were nearly empty.

"I'm sorry, Douglas," Annie purred into my chest.

I stroked her hair. "It's okay," I lied. I was pissed at her dad, but I knew he ruled Annie's family, even after the divorce, with an iron fist.

We said our goodbyes, and I drove home in silence; I didn't even turn the radio on, instead rolling down the window and turning the heat up high to counteract the cold December air. It began to drizzle, but I kept the window down in spite of the fact that it was making the left sleeve of my jacket damp.

"Fuck," I murmured to myself. I was definitely feeling down and disappointed. This would've been my first New Year's Eve with a girlfriend. The party just didn't seem as exciting now that I knew I'd be going stag.

Fortunately, the next morning, Hank called bright and early with good news.

"Hey buddy," he said sounding chipper.

"What's up?" I asked, much less enthusiastically.

"What's the matter with you?" Hank could sense I was down right from the get-go.

"Annie and I went out last night, had a great date, and then at the end of the night she told me she couldn't see me on New Year's Eve."

"That's perfect!" Hank shouted gleefully.

"Huh? No, it sucks, actually."

"Listen to me, my friend. My cousin called me about an hour ago and offered his tickets for Soft White Underbelly at the Starwood on New Year's Eve."

"Soft White Underbelly?" I asked, unimpressed.

"Never heard of them."

"That's the thing," Hank said excitedly. "It's actually Blue Oyster Cult! They're performing under a fake name. It's a secret show. They never play places as small as the Starwood."

"Wow. Seriously? Wait, why aren't you taking Vicki?"

"Seriously, dude? I haven't spoken to her since that night at Laserium."

"Oh right, forgot about that."

"Yeah, I've been trying to forget about that night, too!" Hank laughed. "What do you say, buddy?"

"Sounds good to me," I responded, trying to drum up as much enthusiasm as I could. "Although, what about Jimmy Taylor's party?"

"Jimmy Taylor's party? Come on, Douglas! This is going to be amazing! Blue Oyster Cult at the Starwood! I mean, dude, when they were here last August they played the fucking Forum. And now we're going to get to see them in a tiny club. They'll be playing 'Don't Fear the Reaper' like ten feet away from us."

"Sorry, it sounds great, man. It's going to be an awesome show. Thanks for scoring the tickets and inviting me." I was actually starting to turn the corner and get genuinely excited about the concert. I was still bummed about not seeing Annie, but spending New Year's Eve with Hank and seeing Blue Oyster Cult in such a small venue sounded like a lot of fun.

"That's more like it, my man. Hey—can you drive? My dad wants the Camaro that night."

"Sure. What time should I get you?"

"Why don't you pick me up at six thirty. The show doesn't start until eight, but I'm sure people will be lining up early for this one."

"Sounds like a plan, Stan," I said.

"Okay, dude. See you tomorrow night. Gotta run. Coach called for an 'unofficial' scrimmage today." The team wasn't allowed to practice over the holidays, but all the high school coaches had figured out various ways around this LAUSD regulation, including Coach Warren.

The line went dead before I could even respond. I hung up the phone and went downstairs, where I found my mom cooking in the kitchen, L lying at her feet in her eternal quest for scraps.

"Good morning, honey. Want some breakfast? I'm making scrambled eggs, bacon, and bagels."

"Sure," I said. L slowly got up from the floor and waddled over to me. She had definitely aged in the past year or so. I bent down to pet her and scratch her chin. "Hey, happy girl," I cooed.

"How was your date last night with Annie?" Mom asked.

"Okay, I guess. But she canceled our plans for New Year's Eve."

"What? But that's tomorrow night! Why?"

"She said her dad was insisting on spending the night with her and her sister."

My mom just rolled her eyes and shook her head. "Annie the whammy," she said in a singsong voice. "You better watch out for that girl."

It was a line I had heard her speak more than once. While Mom liked Annie, for some reason that even she couldn't explain—"Just call it good old-fashioned intuition," she'd say—she didn't completely trust her. Like any caring mother, she was worried that Annie was going to break my heart. I always assured her that there was nothing to be concerned about; while Annie could certainly fib with the best of them, I was certain that she'd never deliberately lie to me. Well, pretty certain, anyway. Besides, my early experience with Natalia had toughened me up when it came to girls. Still, Mom remained steadfast in her belief that all would not end well with my first really serious girlfriend.

"Come here," she soothed, pulling me in tight for a long hug, the two of us standing in the center of the kitchen, embracing each other lovingly. "I'm sorry, honey. I'm sure you're disappointed."

"Thanks, Mom." I looked away, not wanting her to see the tears welling up in my eyes. "Anyway, Hank scored tickets to see Blue Oyster Cult at the Starwood. It's a really special show. So, we're going to go out and have fun."

"Terrific! Well, it all worked out for the best, then," she chirped, turning back to the bacon in the frying pan, which had just started to burn slightly while we had been talking. No matter: The whole family liked their bacon extra crisp. The same with our bagels. There was only one way to cook a bagel in the Efron household. Even Art, set in his ways by the time we came into his life, was an early and easy convert. First of all, the bagel has to be frozen. And only bagels from Western Bagel down on Beverly near the Original Tommy's would do. You needed to set the oven at 425 and bake the frozen bagel for eight to ten minutes. The result? A beautifully crisp bagel on the outside, and then the unexpected joy of the Soft White Underbelly on the inside. Dough that was warm, moist, and just melted in your mouth, perfectly complementing the crispy outside. Plain, sesame, onion . . . pick your poison.

It was all good.

"Good morning!" Art walked in the door, happy as a clam. He'd taken the week off from work and had been playing a ton of golf. Apparently, by the way he was dressed—colorful plaid pants and a tight gold shirt that showed off his still-amazing physique—he would be golfing once again today.

"What time do you tee off?" I asked.

"What? Oh no, I'm not golfing today."

"Oh, I thought those were your golfing clothes."

"They are," Art said, looking quizzically at me and then shrugging his shoulders. "What's everybody doing today?" he asked, pouring himself a cup of coffee. It was probably his third or fourth already that morning. Art loved his Yuban.

"I'm meeting the guys over at school. The gym is open this afternoon, and we're gonna play some ball."

"I sure wish you'd get out on the course with me once in a while instead of spending so much time playing basketball," Art sighed. "Golf is a sport you can play the rest of your life. Basketball is a young man's game, and you'll pay for it later in life with busted-up hips, knees, and ankles."

"Oh," I defended myself, "like golf isn't hard on your back and your knees? Who's the one who has to get a shot of cortisone in his knee every three months?"

"Yeah," Art laughed, "let's see how your body is doing when you turn sixty."

"Seriously, I'd love to play with you, but I just don't think I'd enjoy the game. I need the adrenaline rush that basketball gives me."

"Believe me," Art insisted, "you can get that same rush playing golf."

"Maybe when I get older and I'm done with basketball," I promised.

"But if you start now, you'll be a good player for life."

"Sorry, Art. Maybe at some point, but it's just not for me right now." I knew Art really wanted to play golf with me so we could develop a tighter bond, which was cool, but I just couldn't do it. Golf was an old man's game.

Suddenly, without any warning or explanation, Art reached into a drawer in the wood hutch behind the kitchen table and pulled out a little box with a red bow tied around it. "Happy New Year, kid," Art said, holding the present out to me.

"What?" My mom smiled broadly. "What's this about, Art? Is it something to do with golf?"

"Just watch." Art actually giggled, he was so thrilled with himself.

"Mom?" I said, looking at her searchingly.

She threw her arms in the air, one of her hands holding a spatula. "I don't know anything about this!"

"Open it!" Art urged.

I untied the ribbon and opened the lid. Inside was some tissue paper neatly folded over. I lifted the tissue to reveal a Mobil credit card with my name on it. "A gas card?" I gasped. "You're giving me a gas card?"

"You're a good kid, Douglas. Enjoy. I'll pay the bill every month while you're in high school and college."

"Wow! Thanks, Art!"

My mom had a couple of small tears rolling down her face as she went over and gave Art the second long hug the center of the kitchen had hosted in the past few minutes. It was important to her that Art liked her kids, and that her kids liked Art, me especially since I was the only one living at home.

"Now, how about some breakfast?" Art asked. "I'm starving."

We all sat down and enjoyed our eggs, bacon, and bagels. My mom made some small talk while we ate, but there really wasn't all that much that needed to be said: The three of us were simply basking in the warm, loving glow that enveloped the kitchen at that moment in time. Art didn't even seem to mind when I slipped L—sitting patiently by my side—a few pieces of bacon here and there.

I tried calling Annie that night; I wanted to tell her about the concert I was going to with Hank on New Year's Eve. If I was perfectly honest with myself, I guess I wanted to let her know that I was totally fine with not seeing her and had found something super cool to do instead. Unfortunately, I was only able to reach her answering machine, and by the time New Year's Eve rolled around, I still hadn't heard back from her. Maybe her mom had picked up the message and erased it without telling Annie, I rationalized.

"What's up, dude?" Hank bounded down the brick walkway in front of his ranch-style house and opened the door to my car. "You ready for a crazy New Year's Eve?" We exchanged a Soul Brother #1 Handshake. We had seven different Soul Brother handshakes and knew them so well that once one of us started the motion, the other understood immediately what to do.

"Yeah, man, this should be fun." I popped in a cassette of *Some Enchanted Evening*, a live album the band had released a few months back.

"Is this the new BOC live album?" Hank asked excitedly. "Killer!"

"Yeah, I picked it up today at the Wherehouse especially for tonight."

The album began with some crowd noise as the band noodled around onstage. Then an announcer introduced the group, and they launched into "R. U. Ready 2 Rock."

"Are you ready to rock?" Hank sang out loud.

I joined in for the response: "Yes, I am!"

Hank rolled down the window and screamed, "God, I love rock and roll!"

"Listen to Buck Dharma," I said. "What a great guitar player."

Hank pulled out a doobie and held it aloft. "Shall we?" he smiled.

"The night's not getting any younger," I enthused.

We drove along the Ventura Freeway and exited at Laurel Canyon, which would eventually turn into Crescent Heights and take us straight to the Starwood, sitting on a funky triangle of land at the intersection of Crescent Heights and Santa Monica Boulevard. As we hit the canyon, Hank lit a second joint.

"Another one?" I asked.

"Hey, it's New Year's Eve. Why not?"

He had a point there. Besides, the pot Hank got from an older kid in his neighborhood was mostly shake with almost no buds: easy to roll, but not all that powerful. Or smooth. I pulled over for a second when I had a coughing fit a few minutes later.

"Good, and good for you!" Hank laughed.

As we drifted through the canyon, the band launched into "Kick Out the Jams" through my car speakers.

"Hey," Hank looked confused. "I've heard this song before. This isn't a Blue Oyster Cult song, is it?"

"MC5," I managed to say, my throat still recovering from my coughing fit. "It's a cover."

"Oh, right," Hank said distractedly as he looked up into the hills above us. "There sure are some cool houses in here."

"A lot of famous musicians live in here," I remarked. "Or at least they used to."

When we reached the Starwood, we could immediately see that a fairly long line had already formed; we were lucky to find a parking spot a block or two away on Laurel, a quiet side street. I shut off the car and the music, and we hustled back to the club to get in line. Sitting in the middle of what was widely known as "Boys Town," the Starwood was a bit of an anomaly, with hordes of rock and rollers invading on show nights, looking out of place with their long hair and leather jackets in the middle of a boulevard filled mostly with gay guys with short hair, tight jeans, and red or blue bandanas stuck into either their left or right back pockets. My brother told me these were signals telling other guys whether you liked to be on top or on the bottom. Even though we could feel some of the guys checking us out as we passed them on the sidewalk, Hank and I just avoided making eye contact and headed straight for the club.

We got in line behind two girls about our age, or maybe a year or two older. Hank immediately started talking to them.

"Hello, ladies," he said in his suavest voice. Hank could totally turn on the charm whenever he felt so inclined. "How we doing tonight? Looking forward to the show?"

The girls turned around and smiled; they were even cuter than I had originally thought. "Yeah, man, we can't wait. We drove all the way from San Bernardino for this."

"Wow!" Hank responded with enough enthusiasm to knock over an elephant. "You must really like Blue Oyster Cult."

"To be able to see them in a small club like this?" The girl with the blonde hair turned to her friend, who had darker hair, and executed an intricate double high-five. "Hell yeah!"

"Hey, that was pretty cool," Hank said. "We have a special handshake, too. Actually, several of them." And with that, he turned to me and we executed Soul Brother #3, much to the girls' delight.

"Cool!" they said in unison.

"I'm Renee," the blonde girl introduced herself. "And this is my friend, Carrie."

"Hey, Renee, hey, Carrie. I'm Hank, and this is Douglas."

"Nice to meet you," I bowed formally.

"Well, it's nice to meet such a nice pair of gentlemen," Renee smiled, obviously enchanted by my bow. "You guys want to sit together? I think all of the tables are for four." She looked past us at the other people in line. "We don't want to get stuck with any creeps."

"And you trust us because . . . ?" Hank teased.

Renee looked at me with her large blue eyes. "Something just tells me you guys are all right, that's all."

"And check it out," Carrie said, pulling what appeared to be a very large jug of wine partway out of her oversized purse. "I'm gonna sneak this Boone's Farm into the show."

"Nice!" Hank said. "They won't check your bag?"

"Nah," Carrie replied. "Renee's got one, too."

Renee patted her purse with her hand, smiling

smugly. "It's the fucking Starwood. They don't give a shit. I've done it a million times."

"Maybe even two million," Renee enthused. They laughed and exchanged another double high five.

I knew all about Boone's Farm. It was awful stuff, super sweet, almost as bad as the Manischewitz we drank on Passover. My brother and sister used to drink Boone's Farm all the time when they were in high school, and each of them had gotten sick more than once on the stuff. Amazingly, it was still pretty popular among high schoolers, although kegs of beer were more likely to be found at the parties the kids at our school threw.

Carrie was right; the doorman didn't even bother to look in her bag, especially when she and Renee started flirting with him while we were waiting for him to let us into the club. "Enjoy the show, girls," he smiled, revealing several missing teeth. Turning to Hank and me, his tone grew much more severe. "You with them?" he snarled.

"Yeah, we're all together," Hank responded without missing a beat.

"All right," he said, stamping the backs of our hands lethargically as he must have done to a thousand hands before. "Go on in."

We followed the girls and were able to get a table toward the back of the tiny club, but in the center. We would have a great view of the band.

"I'm so excited!" Renee exclaimed.

"So, where are you boys from?" Carrie asked, already unscrewing the cap of the strawberry wine and taking a quick, furtive swig before handing it over to Renee.

"The Valley," I said proudly.

"Ohhhhh." Renee smiled. "A couple of Valley boys,

eh?"

"Yep," Hank said, equally proud of his Valley roots.

Renee handed the bottle to Hank under the table. "So do you Valley boys go to college out there or what?"

"Us?" I asked. "No, we're still in high school."

Hank shot me a what-the-fuck look; he obviously wished I had lied.

"High school?" Carrie said incredulously, turning to Renee. "Jailbait!" they said in unison, once again executing a double high five.

"But we're seniors," Hank said in our defense. "And we'll be off to college next year."

"What about you two?" I inquired. "Are you in college?"

"Nah," Carrie answered. "We're not really college types. I work at an insurance company, and Renee here works for a construction company."

"Oh, cool," I said with as much enthusiasm as I could muster. By now Hank had taken a swig of the Boone's Farm and passed the bottle to me. Even though I couldn't stand the stuff, I didn't want to be the lone man out, so I took a large gulp and handed the bottle back to Carrie. "Do you like your jobs?"

"Huh?" Renee asked. "Who the fuck likes their job? No, dude, I'm just waiting for that special guy to come along, sweep me off my feet, and support me so that I can quit working."

"Here's to marrying a rich dude!" Carrie concurred, and the two girlfriends executed yet another double high five. At least Hank and I had the good sense to have a variety of Soul Brother handshakes so that we weren't always repeating the same one. Plus we knew not to overdo it, but to pick our spots and not give them too much exposure.

These girls seemed to have no such restraint.

By the time the show started, Hank and I were already feeling the effects of the wine, and about halfway through the show, the four of us were basically shit-faced. The girls, who really weren't our type, were getting a bit sloppy, leaning into us and rubbing our thighs with their hands while drunkenly trying to talk *over* the music. Hank and I were more interested in the concert and tried our best to watch the band. By the time they closed with a monster combination of "Godzilla," a cover of "Born to Be Wild," and "Don't Fear the Reaper," we were all on our feet, arms wrapped around each other as we sang the lyrics at the top of our lungs in a drunken revelry. While Blue Oyster Cult typically ended their shows with "Reaper," we were in for a special treat as the band brought up Doors legend Robby Krieger for an extra tune, a cover of "Roadhouse Blues." Sure, it wasn't Morrison on vocals, but watching Krieger and Dharma and Bloom trade guitar licks was worth the price of admission.

As the four of us stumbled to the door, the girls told us to wait outside for them while they went to the bathroom. "What do you think?" Hank asked as we walked out, our sweaty bodies meeting the cool, late-night air. "Should we wait for them?"

"I don't know, man," I said. "I don't know if I really want to hang out with them."

"I agree," Hank said. "They're sorta trashy."

"You think?" I laughed. "Besides, did you see the line for the girl's bathroom? They'll be in there forever."

"Let's split," Hank agreed. And with that, we high-tailed it out of there, disappearing down Santa Monica and up Laurel to our car before the girls had probably even exited the club. "You cool to drive?" Hank asked.

"Yeah, but I could probably use a couple of hits to sober up. You got another doobie in that pocket of yours?"

Hank reached into his jacket and pulled out a joint. "You betcha!"

"What do you want to listen to?" I asked as I simultaneously pulled out of the parking space and pulled on the jay.

"I don't know, something mellow maybe," Hank suggested. "My ears are ringing."

"Me, too. How about some Neil. I think I have a tape with *Harvest* on one side and *After the Gold Rush* on the other. Why don't you pop it into the deck." Hank reached into my small faux-leather carrying case, located the tape, and did as I instructed. As "Tell Me Why" started to play on the stereo, Hank and I settled into a mellow drive home through Laurel Canyon.

"Hey," Hank said in between tokes. "Didn't Neil live in Laurel Canyon at some point?"

"I don't know," I said. "I think Neil was more of a Topanga guy."

"Yeah, I think you're right."

We had just passed the Canyon Country Store when I hit a series of curves, pretty much the sharpest curves in the whole canyon. While the pot had definitely settled me down, I was still pretty drunk, and as I came around the second of the three nasty curves, I found myself on the other side of the road.

"Oh, fuck!"

In that instant, I finally understood what it was like to see your life flash before your eyes; had there been another car coming around the curve from the other direction—a DWP truck, for example—we'd have been toast. My little Honda would've been crushed, ditto Hank and me along with it. At the very least, a trip to the emergency room would have definitely been in order, which would've meant police and most likely a DUI. Thankfully, it was so late that traffic in the canyon was almost non-existent, and I was able to yank the car back onto our side of the road before disaster struck.

Hank, who was singing along to "Southern Man," his eyes closed tight and his voice loud and loose, hadn't even noticed. When a Pontiac Firebird came rumbling past us as we rounded the next curve, I could literally feel myself shaking. Had we met the Firebird on the previous curve, we might've been dead.

For the rest of the drive home, I kept thinking about how any slight delay could've ended our lives. What if Blue Oyster Cult had taken one more bow? What if I'd taken a bit more time pulling out of our parking spot? Or hadn't made the light at Sunset? It was amazing how life could turn on the tiniest twist of fate. You decide to take a certain class in school and end up meeting your future girlfriend or even your wife. Or you decide to go to a party even though you don't want to go, and you wind up meeting a kid from another school who becomes a good friend. That night, I decided that life was essentially a crapshoot; there was only so much you could control. Sure, your decisions were your decisions, and they ultimately decided your fate, but how could you possibly survive and live a long life when you were constantly making decisions, even the tiniest of choices, on literally a minute-by-minute basis, that could determine how you would live the rest of your life? It was almost too much to comprehend.

Or maybe I was just stoned.

As we got out of the Canyon and I prepared to hit the Ventura Freeway, I looked over at Hank, hoping to share my thoughts and hear what he had to say about such weighty matters, but he was passed out, snoring softly, his head against the window. I turned the radio down a notch to let Hank sleep and listened as Neil cautioned me to don't let it bring me down.

The next morning, as I struggled to wake up, my head aching from the Boone's Farm I had consumed the night before, flashes from the evening began to hit me: Carrie and Renee, the infamous Laurel Canyon curve where I ended up in the opposite lane, Neil Young . . . and then I seemed to recall hitting a curb, yet I couldn't quite place where or when it had happened. I threw on some sweats and went outside. Was my car okay?

The brown Civic was out front, parked at the end of the long curb that ran in front of our neighbor's house to just before our driveway. Everything appeared to be fine, and I breathed a sigh of relief. But as I came around toward the back of the car, I saw exactly what I had been struggling to remember upon waking up: a thirty-foot streak of black that ran from the beginning of the curb all the way down to where my car was parked. Evidently, I had pulled into the curb to park, and then drove along it for quite some time, my tire rubbing along the cement the whole way until I finally came to a stop.

"Damn," I muttered to myself, checking out my front right tire, which was a bit worse for the wear. Shaking my head incredulously, I made my way back into the house, vowing that I would never drive that drunk again.

Chapter Five

Our "nutrition" get-togethers during our first week back at school after Christmas vacation were mostly spent recapping the highlights of everyone's holiday break. Andrew was telling everyone and anyone who would listen about the night we paid a visit to the porno theater, which went over really well considering most of the other kids were mostly complaining to each other about long plane rides to visit nearly dead relatives living in very cold places. Gregg Svenson, who we all just called "Sven," was wearing his ski jacket with a phalanx of ski-lift tickets hanging from the bottom zipper on a daily basis, telegraphing to everyone what he had been doing over the holidays.

Mammoth was having record snowfall, which was great news for skiers since the previous few years had been pretty dry as a result of the drought we had gone through. But the days of "If it's yellow, it's mellow," draining swimming pools, and other water-saving measures were over as California, which had suffered its driest year in history in '77, had been hit fairly hard this winter by large storm after large storm, especially in the Sierra Nevadas, where we needed the snowpack the most. This, of course, made the skiing conditions incredible.

"Cornice was awesome!" Sven marveled, and we all shook our heads as if we cared, even though we didn't since none of us skied. "And the powder on Scotty's was up to my waist. For once, Sierra cement was actually fluffy and light."

"Nothing compares to Vail," Andrew spoke up. He had only skied once in his life, but it was at Vail, so, being Andrew, he figured that entitled him to speak like an expert.

"Shut up, Andrew," Marco said. "You don't ski."

"I'm an intermediate," Andrew insisted.

We all laughed, none harder than Sven. "Yeah, I'd like to see you come down the face of three," he challenged, referring to a run at Mammoth. I only knew this because Annie had told me her mom once broke her leg skiing down the face of three.

"I was skiing blue runs by the time we left Vail," Andrew doubled down. "You guys don't know what the fuck you're talking about."

The bell ending nutrition sounded, and we all finished our drinks and snacks and headed off to class. Most of us had either English or History, and our classes were right next door to each other. When we arrived, we saw Hank, who hadn't been with us at nutrition, standing at the door to our history class.

"Hey Hank," I called out. "Why weren't you at nutrition?"

"Shhhhhh!" Hank admonished, signaling for all of us—me, Andrew, Moose, Marco, and Sven—to gather around him quietly. As we did, Hank crouched down, and we peered over his shoulder and saw that only a few kids were already sitting at their desks. One of them was Jerry Malinowski, who was sitting by himself in the back corner of the room. "Check out my desk," Hank whispered. We could see a small package of some sort sitting on his desk, which was right next to where Malinowski sat.

"What is it?" I asked.

"They look like cookies," Hank laughed softly. "But they're really dog biscuits."

"No way!" Marco said gleefully.

"God, I wish Weddy were here to see this action," I said. "He would've loved it."

"You got that right," Marco smiled.

"Shhhhhh!" Hank admonished once again. "A buck says he sneaks a cookie off my desk."

"He's not that stupid," Moose insisted quietly.

"I don't know about that," Andrew whispered, seriously considering whether or not to take the action.

"I'll take that bet," Sven said confidently in a low voice. "Malinowski is stupid, but at least he can read. It's gotta say something about dogs on the package, right Hank?"

"It does, indeed," Hank assured him out of the side of his mouth, not daring to take his eyes off of Malinowski. "We on?"

"Yeah." Sven reached down and shook Hank's hand, which he held up above his head. "We're on for a buck."

Not five seconds later, Malinowski glanced around him, made sure no one was looking, and reached over and snuck a cookie out of the package. He quickly shoved it into his mouth and chewed it quickly, seeming to enjoy the snack wholeheartedly.

We almost pissed ourselves right there in the hallway, we were laughing so hard. By the time Malinowski had figured out Hank's ruse—once he saw us falling out about the place, he checked the package carefully and a look of horror spread across his face—it was much too late; the cookie was well on its way to his digestive system.

"Fuck!" Sven said in disgust, reaching into his pocket

and slapping a crumbled dollar bill into Hank's hand. "You idiot!" he shouted at Malinowski. "You just cost me a dollar!" Sven and Malinowski, who remained rooted to his seat, his head buried in his hand, embarrassed beyond all hell, were actually pretty good friends.

Just then, Annie walked up behind me and squeezed my ass. "Hey, babe!"

I turned, saw it was her, and leaned in for a quick kiss as she walked by, obviously late for class. "Meet you at lunch?" I called after her.

"Sure!" she said over her shoulder, smiling that gorgeous smile of hers before turning away, her tight ass looking incredible tucked into jeans that showed off every last curve.

"Wait a second," Sven said. "You're still together?"

"Yeah, of course," I shrugged. While Annie and I hadn't spent New Year's Eve together, we'd seen each other several times since then and all seemed to be going well. Sven appeared to be a bit tongue-tied. "Why do you ask?" I said, suddenly sensing I should be worried about something.

"Um, well," he obviously didn't want to tell me what he was going to tell me.

"Come on, spit it out," Marco demanded.

"It's just that, while I was up in Mammoth, I saw Annie together with Kenny the Killer."

"What?" I was flabbergasted, like someone had just punched me in the gut. "That's impossible."

"I-I'm sorry, Douglas, but I saw them. I was standing right behind them in a lift line on New Year's Day for like twenty minutes."

"What the fuck, dude?" Hank looked at me, concerned.

"Are you sure, Sven? I mean, weren't they wearing

hats and goggles and shit? You sure it was her?"

"I'm positive, Douglas. Besides, it was a sunny day so we all just had sunglasses on and she wasn't even wearing a hat. And, I mean, you can't miss that ass."

"Fuck you!" I exploded, shoving Sven straight in the chest.

"Hey, man!" Sven said, putting his arms up in front of his face, afraid I might try to punch him. "Don't take it out on me. I'm just the messenger."

By then, Hank had wisely stepped between me and Sven. "Let's take a walk," he advised, putting his arm around my shoulder and leading me away. "Calm down, Douglas. I'm sure there's an explanation."

"Fuck!" I said, breathing heavily. "What could possibly be the explanation? Sven was certain he saw her up there with him."

"Look," Hank said, "just assume it was a mistake and give it a rest until lunch, and then you can talk to her."

The bell rang and we needed to hustle into class. "Okay, okay," I said, "you're right. No sense getting upset about it until I talk to her."

History class seemed like an eternity; it felt like the teacher covered about a hundred years, instead of just the Roaring '20s. When it finally ended, I trudged off to English, my mind still obsessed with visions of Annie and Kenny the Killer hitting the ski slopes together.

"Mr. Efron? Hello? Earth to Douglas." I looked up from my desk only to discover Miss Duncan standing just a few feet away, and the rest of the class looking at me with knowing smiles on their faces. We'd all been there—either sleepy or hungover or just plain disinterested. Or, like me, lost in other thoughts. The teacher called on you once, twice. Then, irritated, she started walking down the aisle in a further bid to get your attention. And it was even worse for kids who were smart, the ones who she expected to be ready with an answer, no matter the question. I was one of Miss Duncan's top students, not only in our class, but in all of her classes.

"I'm sorry, I didn't sleep well," I lied. Again, every kid in class knew that line was your best and only shot at getting out of trouble for not paying attention. That, or a death in the family—or of a beloved pet, even—but that was a tough fib to pull off more than once or twice a year. Sort of up there with "The dog ate my homework."

"Did you do the required reading, Douglas?"

"Yeah, of course," I answered. Miss Duncan was a Henry James freak. She had written some kind of thesis on him and felt it was her mission in life to expose high school kids to "the master of the psychological novel." *The Turn of the Screw* was a particular favorite, although in a bid to go against the grain, instead of having us read another accepted James classic like *The Portrait of a Lady*, she made us read *The Tragic Muse*, one of James' little-known works, a convoluted tale of art and politics set in late-nineteenth-century Britain.

"Okay then," she continued, "please tell us one of the main differences between *The Tragic Muse* and *The Turn of the Screw*. And skip the part about the latter being essentially a ghost story; I'm sure we're all aware of that." She glanced smugly around the room at her students.

"Well, this book," I said holding my copy of *The Tragic Muse* up in the air, "has like fifty different characters. It's worse than *As the World Turns!*" With that I got a rousing laugh, not only from the whole class, but from Miss

Duncan as well. She bopped me on the head with her copy of the book, turned, and began speaking over the laughter as she walked back up to the front of the room.

"You're exactly right, Douglas. In *The Tragic Muse*, James offers us a plethora of characters, which I actually think is quite apt, given that it's also a book about the theater." She pronounced "theater" like some British actor: "Theeeeatah."

Just then the bell rang and a frown appeared on Miss Duncan's face; she truly did love to teach. "We'll resume this discussion tomorrow. I want you to read chapters thirty-four, five, and six tonight."

A loud, collective groan rose up in the room. "But Miss Duncan," complained Lucy Clopton, a cheerleader, "that's too many chapters!"

"I'm taking out my violin," Miss Duncan teased, pretending to play the world's tiniest violin with her fingers while mock sobbing.

"See you tomorrow," I said as I walked by the teacher.

"Douglas?" she asked. "Is everything okay?"

"Um, yeah. Sure. Just a bit distracted today, I guess."

"All right. You take care of yourself. See you tomorrow," she smiled.

I adjusted the heavy backpack bursting with books that was straining my shoulders. "Bye," I said.

Walking out the door, a sense of dread and foreboding sank into my stomach. I headed toward the cafeteria, feeling like my entire future was about to be decided. Was this one of those life-altering moments, like the one on New Year's Eve, that I had come to expect to pop up entirely at random over the course of the rest of my existence?

Annie was already standing by "our" tree, a ficus just

across the path from the lunch tables that were the furthest away from the actual food lines. She stood with her
back to the tree, her left foot resting behind her against
its thick trunk. Lost in the shade of the large canopy, she
was beautiful even in silhouette, her long hair tumbling
over her shoulders, down her back, almost to her waist. It
would be tragic to lose her.

Her eyes were cast down toward her right hand, which
was half-closed and facing up at her. She appeared to be
checking her nails, making sure her French tips were still
looking good. When Annie looked up and saw me coming,
a wide smile spread across her face. "Hi, Douglas!" she
called out. She came running toward me and wrapped her
arms around me. Looking up into my eyes, she purred,
"I've been thinking about you all morning."

"Me, too," I said, flatly.

"Oh yeah?" Annie said, reaching up to give me a kiss.
"Whatcha been thinking about, mister?"

I separated from her and, holding her in front of me
with my hands on her shoulders, I took a deep breath and
dove right into the treacherous waters. "I heard you were
skiing with Kenny Killian over New Year's." I was trying
with all my might not to shake, not to yell, not to cry.

"What?" Annie gasped. "Who told you that?"

"Gregg Svenson swore he was behind the two of you
in a lift line on New Year's Day." I could feel the intensity
in my voice; my nerve endings across my whole body felt
like they were on fire.

"No way!" she insisted. "I told you, Douglas, my dad
took me and my sister out to dinner on New Year's Eve.
In fact—" Annie ran back over to the tree and dug through
her backpack, which was lying on the ground, and then

ran back to me, a box of matches in her hand, "it's from L'Orangerie, the fancy French restaurant we went to. I thought you'd like them."

She handed me the box, a very classy set of matches as befitted one of the most acclaimed restaurants in Los Angeles. "Your dad took you to L'Orangerie on New Year's?" I had read about the place in one of my mom's magazines—*People*, I think—and knew that it was a very, very expensive restaurant.

"Yeah, silly. I told you we were going out. So, you see? That couldn't have been me that Gregg saw up in Mammoth on New Year's Day."

"But he was so certain," I said, not sure what to believe. "And your dad does have a condo up there..."

"So that makes me guilty?" Annie said, with what seemed to be a bit of anger in her voice. "Come on, Douglas." Her tone was softer now, and she stroked my cheek.

I so badly wanted to believe Annie. But Gregg seemed so certain, and he was generally a reliable kind of guy. And what did giving me matches from L'Orangerie really prove? The fact that Annie's dad had a place up in Mammoth and that Annie did grow up skiing made the whole situation that much more complicated. But when I looked down at Annie's smiling, soothing face, I decided I had to give her the benefit of the doubt; Gregg must've been wrong. A simple case of mistaken identity. He didn't mean anything malicious. I would be sure to apologize to him for my outburst.

"Are we good?" Annie asked. "Want to get some lunch, baby?"

"Yeah, yeah," I replied. "We're good. Let's grab something to eat." Annie picked her backpack up off the ground and we made our way over to the food lines. My stomach was feeling a little queasy, so I probably wouldn't eat much, but overall I was starting to settle down, my arm wrapped around Annie as we walked side by side, our bodies fitting together like an old pair of shoes. I guess this wouldn't be one of those days where life turned on a dime after all. I felt myself take a deep breath, and a huge weight drifted off my shoulders as I look upward and exhaled into the sky above.

The next couple of weeks crawled by as our first semester of senior year slowly came to an end. It would really be our last semester, since our final term wouldn't really count toward college. Besides, I had an extremely light load next semester and would be getting out of school at noon every day. Unfortunately, my dad insisted that, before I go off to college, I spend the upcoming months working part-time at his printing company. That meant that as of Monday, February fifth, I'd be slaving away from 1:00 to 5:00 every afternoon after I finished at school.

While I couldn't say I was looking forward to it, it would be good to bank some dough before I headed off to San Diego in August. My dad was going to take care of college expenses like tuition, books, and room and board in the dorm at SDSU, but if I wanted money for any sort of extracurricular activities—concerts, movies, alcohol, pot, records—I would have to earn it myself. It was the same arrangement he had made with David and my sister Julie, who had both held down part-time jobs throughout college. It seemed to work out well for them.

A few days before the end of the semester, Hank and I were heading to Trig when he said, "I'm really nervous about getting this math final back."

"Oh, I'm sure you did fine," I assured Hank.

"Yeah, I know. But if I don't get an A, I think I'll end up with an A- in the class."

"So?" I shrugged. "Nothing wrong with that. I think I'm pretty locked in for a B+, and I'm happy with that. Trig is hard, man."

"I know, I know," Hank said. "But Coach Warren said there have been a couple of inquiries about me from local colleges."

I stopped dead in my tracks. "Huh? What do you mean? I thought we were both locked into San Diego State."

"I am, I am," Hank assured me. We had already agreed to be roommates once we hit SDSU. "But if I can get a scholarship, even a partial scholarship, somewhere else, my dad says I have to at least consider it."

"What schools are we talking about?"

"Apparently Cal State Northridge has talked to Coach Warren about me."

"Cal State Northridge?" I said dubiously. "That's a big-time Division II school! I mean, you know . . ."

"Gee, thanks," Hank rolled his eyes.

"Come on, man. I know you've had a good year, but do you think you can hang with Division II players?"

"I don't know. Maybe," Hank shrugged.

"Anyway, what does this have to do with your grade in math?"

"Because the other school interested in me is Occidental, but you need really good grades to get in there, even if you're an athlete."

"Occidental?" I asked. "Where is that? In Pasadena or something?"

"Sort of. More like Glendale or Eagle Rock. And it's

Division III, which Coach thinks I can play, no problem."

"But why would you want to go to school in Eagle Rock? Don't you want to get away?" I could feel myself getting upset. The whole plan was for Hank and me to room together in the dorms at SDSU; he had never once even mentioned the possibility of going to another school. "Jesus," I said, stopping just short of the classroom, "this is really throwing me for a loop, Hank."

"I know, man, I've been meaning to tell you . . ." his voice trailed off.

"Occidental?" I repeated, disbelievingly.

"It's a really good school, Douglas. Lots of famous politicians have gone there. You know that congressman, Jack Kemp? The guy who was a star quarterback in the old AFL?"

"Yeah, I think so," I replied.

"We've been learning about him lately in Economics," Hank muttered. "Anyway, my dad says I can't pass up an opportunity like Oxy if they offer me something. Sorry, dude."

"Fuck. What's so great about Occidental? I mean, are you planning on going into politics?"

"Well, I'll tell you this much," Hank joked, though it felt more like a punch to my gut, "I'm more likely to be president with a degree from Occidental than SDSU!"

"What the fuck is wrong with SDSU?" Now I was getting irritated.

Hank quickly backtracked. By the look on his face, he was now realizing what a dick he was being. "Nothing, nothing at all," he insisted. "It's just, I don't know, Oxy is supposed to be a better school, that's all. And, yeah, I am actually interested in politics."

"Well, that's news to me," I said, brushing past him and entering the classroom.

"Come on, Douglas, don't be like this," Hank said, following me. "Besides, it's probably not gonna happen anyway."

"What's not gonna happen?" Mr. Rhodes, who had his back to us while scribbling formulas on the chalkboard, had evidently overheard the last bits of our conversation.

"I might have a shot at getting a scholarship offer from Occidental," Hank said.

"Really?" Mr. Rhodes replied. "It's a great school. Congratulations."

"Well, it's still a long shot," Hank admitted. "But, of course, getting an A in Trig would really help my GPA, which would increase my chances of getting in. Are we getting our final back today?"

"Sorry, boys," Mr. Rhodes said, stroking his thick walrus mustache while looking over our shoulders at the seats in the classroom, "I didn't quite finish grading them. I should have them done by tomorrow."

Hank didn't hide his disappointment. "Aw, you're killing me, Mr. Rhodes!"

"What can I tell you? You know, I have a life, too. They'll be done tomorrow. I promise."

I took my seat without saying another word, but I was seething. How could Hank do this to me? To us? I could barely concentrate as Mr. Rhodes launched into a new section on cotangents, which seemed like the least important thing in the world right now. When the bell finally rang, ending the class, Mr. Rhodes called out from the front of the room, "Hank? Douglas? Would you please stay a moment after class? I need to talk to you about something." I made eye contact with Hank for the first time since class started, and he shrugged his shoulders. Great, I thought, did we both fail the final? Well, at least it might end Hank's chances of getting into Occidental. I knew it wasn't fair to think that way, but I couldn't help myself.

"Boys," Mr. Rhodes began once everyone had packed up and left the room, leaving the three of us alone, "you remember how thankful I was when you sold out the ads for the Holiday Performance program?"

"Yeah?" Hank and I both responded.

"Well," he said, reaching into his desk drawer and pulling out what appeared to be our math finals. "I actually finished grading your finals last night." He handed us our papers, and I could see Hank's face fall. He had received an A-, which meant he would fall short of what he needed to get an A in the class. I was happy with my expected B+.

"Your final grades happen to match the grades you've earned in the class," Mr. Rhodes said. "Congratulations. Trig is a tough course, and you've both done very well."

"Thanks, Mr. Rhodes," Hank and I said in unison, though Hank was much more downbeat in his response.

Mr. Rhodes sat down in his chair behind his desk. Unlike most teachers, who kept either a regular wooden chair like you'd sit on at your kitchen table, or maybe even just a stool, Mr. Rhodes had an oversized leather swivel chair, like something you'd see behind the desk of the CEO of GM. Leaning back, his large frame now settled into the "Corinthian vinyl," as he liked to joke. He looked at us and said, "However, to show my appreciation for your tremendous salesmanship, and because you were both sooooo close to the next grade level"—he held up his thumb and forefinger to demonstrate just how close we were to getting an A and an A-, respectively—"I'm going to use my prerogative as your teacher to bump you up to an A for Hank, and an A- for you, Douglas."

"Yes!" Hank yelled enthusiastically. "Thank you so much!"

"Thanks, Mr. Rhodes, that's great," I joined in, though perhaps not quite as effusively as Hank.

"Thank *you*," Mr. Rhodes laughed, leaning so far back in his chair that the only thing stopping him from going over was the wall behind him. "You guys saved my ass. You don't even know the half of it!"

While we didn't completely understand how selling a handful of ads had saved Mr. Rhodes ass, we didn't ask any questions and accepted his generosity. We shook his hand and thanked him again. As we were walking toward the door, I said to Hank, "Well, I guess this will help your chances for getting into Occidental."

Once we were out in the hallway, Hank stopped and grabbed my shoulder. "Look, Douglas, even with an A in Trig, Oxy is still a long shot. I haven't said anything to you because I figured it wasn't even worth mentioning."

"Then why now?" I asked, wishing that Hank had just kept me in the dark.

"Because Coach Warren told me the other day that once the playoffs start, they're sending a scout to watch me play. And CSUN will be there, too, though more for Randolph and a couple of other guys than for me."

"God," I said, "it seems sorta late for colleges to still be looking for players to recruit."

"No, not at all. Sure, they've been recruiting our stars for a long time, but for guys like me, and for small colleges like Oxy, this is when they do it. Anyway, that's what

Coach told me. I don't know what to believe. The whole situation is sorta crazy. I never thought in a million years anyone would be interested in me."

"Well, you've definitely come a long way from when you suddenly became a total spaz." I was starting to calm down, and even chuckled as I recalled the period in ninth and tenth grade when Hank had a huge growth spurt that robbed him of his coordination for a couple of years.

"I know. Fuck, can you believe it? It's been a long road back." We were silent for a bit as we made our way out of the long hallway and into the bright January sun. This was always one of the best months for weather in Los Angeles. In fact, they say that the Rose Bowl and Rose Parade are responsible for all of the people who move out to California every year from other parts of the country. I guess if I was freezing my ass off in Chicago in December and I saw clear skies and seventy-degree weather in L.A. every New Year's Day, I'd want to get the hell out of Dodge and make my way to a paradise filled with orange and lemon groves as soon as possible.

"I promise I'll let you know the second I hear anything, *anything* at all," Hank assured me. "One way or another, it'll all work out. The most likely scenario is that nothing will happen, and we'll head down to San Diego as we planned. And if some really good school comes along and offers me a scholarship, then we'll just have to adjust. It won't affect our friendship. And you can always room with Moose. He doesn't have a roommate yet, right?"

"Room with Moose?" I laughed. "I think Moose needs a room to himself. Those dorm rooms are *tiny*." I mimicked Mr. Rhodes' thumb and forefinger demonstration.

"Yeah, I guess," Hank laughed along with me. "Can

you imagine Moose climbing into the top bunk above you? Now *that* would be a sight to behold."

"I don't even want to go there. I'm not going to put that image into my head." It was true. For now, I was determined not to worry about how this was all going to play out. What could I do about it, anyway? Intentionally injure Hank so that his basketball season would come to an end? I couldn't believe that thought had even entered my head. And it wasn't like I was going to start rooting for my best friend to start playing poorly. No, I would be a mensch about it. I'd cheer for Hank and support him wholeheartedly and then just hope for the best. Once again, life seemed to be turning on a dime. And I was just going to have to wait to see if that dime would turn up heads or tails—San Diego State or Oxy.

Later that day, Hank and I met up with Ms. Pearlstein. Things had been going really well at the *Wire*, for both Hank and me. Hank's columns that he wrote up after games weren't long, but they were insightful, and the kids and parents who were fans of the team loved them. Even Coach Warren had complimented Hank on the great job he was doing.

Before we even stepped through the door into the classroom, we could hear Genevieve passionately arguing with Ms. Pearlstein. "But this country's dependence on foreign oil is ruining our economy, Ms. Pearlstein. And this is something that affects every single student at this school."

"I just think it's a little out of the wheelhouse of the editorial pages of the *Wire*, Genevieve," Ms. Pearlstein was calmly explaining as we entered the room. "I ran your piece on nuclear power, but I just can't turn our paper into the *New York Times*. We have to stay focused on topics that affect our local community, though I'm happy to occasionally give attention to larger issues as well. Just not in this instance, I'm afraid."

"Ughhh!" Genevieve exclaimed. "Douglas, maybe you can talk some sense into her," she said as she stormed out of the room.

"Like you said, Ms. Pearlstein," I joked after Genevieve had left. "She's a pistol!"

"You can say that again!" she laughed.

I was there to speak to Ms. Pearlstein about the latest story assignment she had given me, a feature on a new tennis coach at the school, Mrs. Livingstone. "It's a profile piece, Douglas," Ms. Pearlstein advised. "She has a fascinating background, and not just as a tennis player. Dive into where she grew up, and what her dad did for a living." She handed me a manila folder with a few pieces of paper inside. I opened it up and discovered a photocopy of an article about an Admiral Livingstone and his adventures in Antarctica.

"Wow," I said, "is this her dad? Did she really get to live in Antarctica?"

"All interesting questions, Douglas. I'm sure Mrs. Livingstone will provide you with a wealth of material. Now get to work," she smiled. "Both of you. I'm expecting another wonderful column from you after tonight's game, Hank."

"Done," he assured her.

"Thanks, Ms. Pearlstein," I added as Hank and I headed for the door.

"She's the coolest," I said to Hank once we were in the hallway.

"Yeah, I really like her," Hank agreed. "And boy, did you get lucky!"

"What do you mean?"

"Have you seen Mrs. Livingstone?" he asked, wide-eyed.

"I-I don't know. I don't think so. Why?"

"Holy guacamole! She is one foxy mama!"

"Seriously?"

"Ha! Just you wait, my man, just you wait. Gotta get to the gym! See you later!" And with that, Hank took off, hustling down the hallway and through the doors that led out to the playground and the gym.

"See ya!" I called out, but he was already gone. I watched through the glass panes of the doors as he high-fived a couple of tenth graders who seemed so excited by the act, you'd think they had just slapped hands with Dr. J.

That Friday night, Woodrow Wilson was opening up the first round of the City playoffs at home against Reseda, so a bunch of the guys and I went to cheer on our buddy. Reseda wasn't very good that year, but had somehow managed to sneak into the playoffs. They were almost always better in football than basketball, though Greg Lee, the great UCLA Bruin, had attended the school way back when.

True to form, the game was a blowout, so Coach Warren was able to give the starters a rest. That meant Hank got to play about thirty minutes, which was about ten above normal. He responded with his best effort of the season, scoring sixteen points, grabbing eight rebounds, dishing out four assists, and chipping in a steal and *four* blocks. Plus, not one, but two of Reseda's forwards fouled out trying to guard him. I wondered if any Occidental scouts were in attendance that night; if so, Hank was a shoo-in for Oxy. At one point during the game I glanced over at Moose, who was working his way through a giant tub of popcorn—solo—the bits of popcorn kernels and debris all over his face, chest, and lap, and wondered aloud, "Could I really live with this guy?"

"What was that?" Andrew asked.

"Oh, sorry," I said, shaken out of my daydream. "I said, 'Hank is killing this guy.'" Fortunately, the noise of the boisterous Woodrow Wilson crowd made it difficult to hear in the crowded gym.

After the game, we met up with Hank outside the locker room in the back of the building. "Nice game, buddy," I said, giving him our original Soul Brother #1 Handshake.

"Thanks," he said, humble as usual, but obviously proud of himself.

"Great game, man," Moose chimed in. "You were awesome."

"You destroyed that number 33," Andrew said a bit too loudly. "He should be embarrassed to be wearing Kareem's number after what you did to him tonight."

"Yeah, and he was a pretty strange dude." Hank lowered his voice. "Early on in the game, he kept telling me what he was going to do me. He'd literally get the ball and describe his move, as if I couldn't stop him even with that information. At first, I thought he was playing games with me, going to go the opposite way, whatever, so I just ignored him and played D. Then I started listening to him and I stopped him cold. Really weird."

"I think you blocked three of his shots," I marveled.

"So what's up?" Moose asked. "You guys want to grab something to eat?"

"I'm starving," Hank said. "I have to say hi to my parents out front. And Kelly Burnside is having a party later on. You guys wanna go?"

"I've already been invited to Tammy Goodrich's party," Andrew said proudly.

"Yeah, I heard about that one, too," Hank added. Tammy and Kelly were both cheerleaders, but parties that got too big would attract the attention of neighbors and cops, so it wasn't that uncommon for there to be multiple parties every weekend hosted by cheerleaders, athletes, music freaks, and druggies. Everyone had their crowd, and fortunately for myself and my friends, we had access one way or another to pretty much every scene. The theater kids and the surfers were probably the only ones we didn't hang out with. The former were mostly gay guys and the cute—though overly dramatic and emotional—girls who liked to hang out with them, and the latter usually just wanted to beat the shit out of us for using their beaches up in Malibu and Zuma.

We all met at Bob's Big Boy just a few miles up Ventura, each of us driving our own cars so everyone could do their own thing from there. The place was packed with kids and families, many of them streaming in after the game. We ate our burgers and fries, slurped our milkshakes, and argued over who was the better player: Magic Johnson or Larry Bird.

"Just wait until the tournament next month," Andrew assured everyone at the table with the confidence of a future attorney. "Bird and Indiana State will run the table, even if it means beating Magic and Michigan State along the way."

"How great would it be if the seeding ends up working

out so that they face each other in the final?"

"I'm sure the NCAA will figure out a way to make it happen," Moose laughed.

"I'm a Magic guy," Hank pronounced. "Take nothing away from Larry, he's an amazing player, but how can you not love Magic? If the Lakers end up with him, it'll be amazing."

"I'm with Hank: Magic all the way," I insisted. "Can you imagine him and Kareem together? They'll be unstoppable."

"And don't forget Jamaal and Nixon," Hank chipped in.

Andrew, who was always a pessimist and just plain enjoyed playing devil's advocate, sometimes rooting for other teams like the Reds in baseball or the Supersonics in basketball—he was the ultimate fair-weather fan—stayed true to form. "I don't think Magic and Kareem could ever play together. They both need the ball in their hands."

"And this, Andrew," Moose raised the index finger of his right hand high in the air, "is why God himself thinks that when it comes to sports, you are the biggest *imbecile* on the face of the planet."

"Agreed!" Hank and I chimed in.

"Fuck you all," Andrew looked down and ate a fry. "Marco isn't even here and I'm still getting shit."

Marco usually spent Friday nights working on cars with his dad; we could never really tell if he enjoyed it. "He usually ends up yelling at me for screwing something up," he'd often joke. He was never available to do anything with us on Fridays, which was sort of a drag for him.

"Andrew, let me explain it to you," I said. "Magic tosses the ball to Kareem down low, Kareem shoots a skyhook.

Basket and assist. It's a simple game, my friend."

"Yeah, yeah," Andrew waved me off. "The Lakers will probably end up taking David Greenwood anyway."

"Like I said," Moose repeated. "*Imbecile.*"

"What do you know Moose?" Andrew spat. "You're a fucking hockey fan."

It was true. Nobody we knew gave a shit about hockey except for Moose. He even had an autographed hockey stick from Rogie Vachon, the former Kings legend. Moose relished saying "Vachon" with his French accent, always drawing out the last syllable for as long as he possibly could.

"You guys want to head out to the party at Kelly's with me?" Hank offered in an attempt to lighten the mood.

"I'm in," I said.

"I'm going to stick with Tammy's get-together," Andrew asserted. "Moose? You going home to jerk off or what?"

"No, dildo, I think I'll go with you just to torture you. Besides, in second grade, Kelly Burnside told me I was fat and ugly, and I don't think I've ever forgiven her."

"Well," I suggested, "if you come with us, maybe she'll compliment you and tell you what a fine, good-looking young man you've become."

"No thanks," Moose laughed. "I think I'll stick with Tammy's party. And it wouldn't be fair to leave poor Andrew here all alone."

"Awww," Andrew mocked, "aren't you sweet."

We split up the bill and then got into our cars, going our separate ways. As I drove along behind Hank, I thought about Annie. We were supposed to go bowling together tomorrow night with a friend of hers and her boyfriend, and I was looking forward to it. Things had been fantastic between us ever since the Mammoth misunderstanding, and I was beginning to think about how much I actually was going to miss her when I went away to SDSU.

As we wound our way up in the hills south of the Boulevard and east of Reseda, we passed by an unassuming house. I stopped dead in my tracks and silently mouthed the words, "What the fuck?" I couldn't believe what I was seeing: Kenny Killian's unmistakable red convertible Mustang was parked in the driveway of the house, and there, parked on the street right in front of the same home, was Annie's green Toyota Corona. I mean, Coronas were common cars, but how many green ones could there be? And who else with a green Corona would be parked in front of what appeared to be Kenny the Killer's house?

I felt sick to my stomach. My head was spinning, and I wasn't sure what to do. Should I go knock on the door? No, that would be stupid. Kenny would chop me up into a thousand pieces. I didn't want to lose Hank, as I wasn't exactly sure where Kelly lived, so I floored it, my tires screeching as I took off and raced up the hill to catch up to him. As we were nearing the top of the hills by the western edge of the Encino Reservoir, on a cul-de-sac off Alonzo, the quiet lull of the suburban neighborhood gave way to the raucous sounds of a bunch of teenagers getting in and out of cars and playing music on their stereos, the crushing of beer cans beneath feet and the laughter of kids getting high.

Hank passed the cul-de-sac and parked around the corner where there was plenty of room, and I followed suit. Upon exiting our cars, Hank could immediately tell something was wrong.

"Jeez, what's wrong with you? You look like you've

seen a ghost."

"I think I did," I replied glumly.

"What's the matter?"

"Do you know if Kenny Killian lives around here?"

"No idea," Hank replied. "Why?"

"I think we just passed by his house. I saw his Mustang in the driveway."

"Yeah, so?"

"Annie's car was parked in front," I deadpanned.

"What? No way. You sure?"

"I mean, it was a green Corona. Who else could it be?" I was clearly devastated.

"Fuck. Sorry, Douglas. That's harsh." Hank wrapped his arm around my shoulder. "Come on. Let's go in and grab a beer."

"I'm gonna need more than that tonight." I tried to laugh, but it was a dismal effort. "I'm glad David laid some joints on me earlier today. I was completely out."

"The night is young, my friend," Hank pronounced, trying to lighten the mood. "Let's party!"

We approached the crowded area at the front door where Kelly herself was presiding, refusing entry to some, and recognizing others and rushing them inside. "Will you guys please go somewhere else to party?" she begged those who didn't make it past her but continued to linger in her front yard and in the street, extending the party into the neighborhood—which was the very last thing she wanted to happen. "You guys are going to ruin everything by bringing out the cops!"

"Then let us in!" someone yelled from the darkness of the street.

"I can only fit so many people!" Kelly cried. "The house

isn't that big!" Then, recognizing Hank from the handful of individuals directly in front of her, her mood changed into that of a chipper hostess. "Hey, Hank! Come on in!" I followed Hank inside, but Kelly completely ignored me. "Great game, Hank!" she said as we walked by.

The party, as Kelly had told everyone out front, was packed. The soundtrack from *Saturday Night Fever* was blasting, as it would continue to do all night long, over and over again. People were dancing in the dimly lit living room and partying in the yard near the roaring gas firepit, and the bedrooms off the hall were being used for a variety of illicit actions, mostly involving sex or drugs. Or both.

At one point, on my way to the bathroom I passed an open door and saw several people gathered around a mirror with what I guessed was a small pile of cocaine in front of them. While all of us knew about coke by then—I mean, Clapton even had a hit song about it—as far as I knew, none of my friends had ever seen it or used it. Sure, Marco claimed to have "done plenty of blow," but you never knew what to believe with that guy. Then again, with Craig as his stepbrother, anything was possible.

Within an hour, after repeated visits to the multiple kegs set up by the barbecue—especially by yours truly, as Hank was trying to be mellow with the City playoffs in full swing—I was thoroughly blitzed. Even Hank had had a couple of beers and took a few hits from the joints I smoked, and as the night wore on, we found ourselves in the den with two girls who went to Reseda High, Linda and Lorie. They were friends with some cheerleaders who, in turn, were friends with Kelly, so they had tagged along with their girlfriends just as I had tagged along with Hank. While they weren't quite as pretty as their cheerleader friends who knew Kelly, they were still very cute all the same. I was pissed off at Annie and had a righteous buzz on, so I was more than a little receptive to the advances Linda was bestowing upon me while Lorie was showering Hank with praise and affection.

"You were awesome out there tonight, Hank," Lorie flattered, freely tossing her loyalty to her school out the window. She was sitting on Hank's lap, running her fingers through his hair and occasionally kissing him. My stud friend just sat back, cool and calm as could be, enjoying the attention.

Hank's brilliance must've somehow made me more attractive, because Linda was being equally generous with her overt friendliness toward me. In spite of my protestations, she had convinced herself that I, too, played basketball for Woodrow Wilson, which seemed to only increase her attraction to me. In fact, at some point later in the evening, we found ourselves in the living room, holding each other close while the Bee Gees' "How Deep Is Your Love" played for the umpteenth time that night. I was exhausted from the stress of seeing Annie's car parked in front of Kenny's house, and felt like I was leaning into the arms of this stranger more out of desperation than anything else.

When the song ended, we wandered down the hall toward a back bedroom. My walk was so unsteady from all the beers I had drunk that I bounced off the walls of the hallway like a pinball. Linda and I laughed the silly laugh of high school kids who've had too much pot and beer.

Just like the night of the porno movie, I don't remember much of what happened next. I know I was alone with Linda in a dark bedroom, and that we ended up on top of the bed, but I don't even think my dick made it out of my pants that night, though I do remember removing Linda's bra. At some point, Lorie came bursting into the room and dragged her friend out of there, all the while making crude accusations toward me. Linda smiled and waved back at me as her friend led her out the door. Hank walked in shortly thereafter.

"Hey, buddy. I think it's time to go."

"Okay," I slurred.

Seeing me struggle to get off the bed and onto my feet, Hank laughed and said, "Maybe I should drive you home."

Flashing back to my drunken attempt at driving in Laurel Canyon, I wasn't about to put up a fight. "Okay," I simply repeated. I finally managed to roll off the bed and wobble unsteadily onto my feet, feeling the need to brush off my clothes. "Can you give me a ride tomorrow morning to come back and pick up my car?" I squinted at Hank, who was backlit from the light in the hallway.

"Sure thing, buddy."

"You're a pal, Hank," I said as I threw my arm around his shoulder and leaned my drunken body into him. Hank held me upright as we made our way through the by-now dwindling party and out the door to his car. "You're a real pal," I repeated over and over again.

And Hank was a true pal. Not only did he drive me home that night and back to Kelly's house the next morning to fetch my car, he didn't even get mad when I threw up out the window as we drove away from the party, my chunks of vomit steaking the passenger side of his beloved Camaro.

The following day, I was determined not to confront Annie over the phone. I decided I would just pick her up for our bowling double date at 6:30 as planned and have it out in person. If it meant we had to cancel on her friends at the last minute, so be it.

I nursed my hangover with plenty of water and even forced myself to head off to the gym to play some ball in an attempt to sweat out all of the crap I'd ingested the night before. Like always, it worked like a charm. Moose, Andrew, and Marco showed up and the four of us, plus a tenth grader who we didn't know—we never even got his name and instead just called him "rookie" the whole time—held the court for five straight games. I was hot the whole day, hitting my patented fall-aways from the baseline like there was no tomorrow. Moose actually made a couple of lay-ups, and while Andrew had too many turnovers as usual, he didn't hurt us all that much. Marco, whose offensive skills were extremely limited, played his stellar defense and rebounded the ball like a madman. And the rookie, while young, hit a bunch of big shots for us, including a game-winner. I had two winners myself, and we only lost the last game when Moose's lay-up woes came back to haunt him, and he missed two crucial absolute gimmees down the stretch.

No matter; by the time we lost game six, we were all wiped out. My hangover was long gone, and I had that incredible high you get after playing full-court basketball for over two hours. My white T-shirt was so drenched, I had to take it off and wring it out before putting it back on and getting into my car to drive home, or else my seat would've been soaked in sweat.

Driving over to Annie's that night, I rehearsed what I was going to say over and over again. My plan was to play it cool at first, testing her and watching her expression closely, but I was already so tense, I could feel my armpits getting wet with perspiration. When I pulled up to Annie's house, she was waiting in front for me, looking as beautiful as ever. In anticipation of our bowling excursion, she was wearing her dad's vintage bowling shirt, a colorful job with "The Turkeys"—a reference to getting three strikes in a row, no doubt—printed in large letters on the back. It was so big, it fit Annie like a mini-dress, and she wore yellow hot pants over a pair of orange leggings to complete the outfit. I stepped out of the car before she had a chance to open the passenger door.

"Are you coming to open the door for me?" Annie asked sweetly. "You're such a gentleman, Douglas. That's why I love you so much." She threw out her arms and attempted to put them around me as I approached, but I stopped short and put my hands out in front of me.

"Actually, I need to talk to you," I said ominously, my anger welling my eyes with tears.

"What's the matter, baby?" Annie said, looking concerned. "Is something wrong?"

"Yeah, something's wrong!" I blurted out. "I fucking saw your car in front of Kenny Killian's house last night!"

"What?" Annie was flabbergasted. "No, you didn't! I was home last night."

"Bullshit! I saw your car. I know you were over there."

"I swear, Douglas, it wasn't me! Do you want to go ask my mom?" Annie insisted. "She can tell you I was here all last night. Come on." With that, she turned on her heels and strode toward her front door.

"Annie, I don't want to bring your mom into this." Annie stopped in her tracks, her back to me. I could only imagine what was going through her head. When she turned around, I could see tears in her eyes.

"Douglas, why do you do this to me? You're always accusing me of cheating on you with Kenny."

"Annie, how many other green Coronas could possibly be parked in front of Kenny's house?"

"I don't know . . . millions?" She paused, and we were both silent for a moment. "Besides, you don't even know where he lives!"

"I saw his Mustang in the driveway. Nobody else around here drives a car like that."

"This green Toyota," Annie continued, ignoring my response, "did it have a bumper sticker?" She pointed over to her car parked in front of her garage; sure enough, the bumper had a sticker that read, "Hang Loose" with a shaka hand sign and "Hawaii" printed below. I had never seen— or noticed, anyway—the sticker before, and it was true that Annie's dad had taken her and her sister to Hawaii in the past. *Had* the green Corona in front of Kenny the Killer's house had a bumper sticker? I tried to replay what I'd seen that night in my head, but honestly, I wasn't sure.

"Well, did it?" Annie repeated after I didn't respond.

"I-I don't know," I said, confused, my head spinning.

"Baby," Annie purred as she walked back over to me, "I found that sticker in my drawer over Christmas vacation. I had forgotten that I'd bought it the last time my dad took me to Hawaii. It's been on my car for over a month."

"Really? How come I never noticed it before?"

"I don't know, silly," Annie laughed. "Maybe you should be more observant." She put her arms around me and kissed me on the lips. Looking into my eyes, she swore, "You know I love you, Douglas. I would never hurt you."

Annie felt so good as I held her tight, I didn't know what to believe. Of course, the easiest thing to do was to forget the whole thing and just chalk it up to nothing more than a weird coincidence. I inhaled her woody perfume; she was wearing the Opium I had bought her for Christmas. It was probably the most expensive present I had ever given anybody, and my mom had chipped in to help me pay for it, in spite of her mixed feelings about Annie.

"You smell good," I said, calming down.

"It's your perfume," Annie smiled. "The most beautiful gift anyone's ever given me." She kissed me again and I could feel my anger melting completely away. I still didn't know what to believe, but the bumper sticker had definitely given me pause. I really didn't remember seeing it on the green Corona that night, and there was no way Annie could have possibly anticipated this scenario and put the sticker on her car today.

"Are we good?" Annie asked. "Should we go meet Jennifer and Jack at the alley?"

"Yeah, sure," I said, not completely believing my own words. "We're good. Let's go. It'll be fun."

And it *was* fun. Jennifer and Jack, who I only knew in passing, turned out to be really nice, and we all had a good time that night. We bowled a few games and then hit the salad bar at Marie Callender's, which left plenty of room for each of us to cap the night off with our own large slice of pie—fresh berry for me, pecan for Annie, and banana cream for Jennifer and Jack.

When I dropped Annie off at the end of the night, we spent a good twenty minutes making out in the car. "I'd invite you in," Annie said with a devilish look in her eye, "but I know my mom is going to wake up as soon as I walk in that door."

"That's okay," I said. "Next time." We kissed for a little

while longer and, just as she was getting out of the car, Annie turned to me and said, "You know I would never hurt you, right, Douglas?" Her deep, dark eyes were so seductive.

"Yeah, I know," I said. But did I really believe her?

On the way home that night, I fired up Jackson Browne's *Late for the Sky* and wondered: Was Annie my fountain of light, or my fountain of sorrow?

When I arrived home, I found my mom crying in the kitchen, with Art trying to console her. Even L was cuddled up at her feet. "Hi Mom," I said softly when I walked in and discovered her with a tissue wadded up in her hand, dabbing at her mascara-streaked eyes. "What's the matter?"

"Your mom's upset about Julie."

"What happened to Julie?" I asked, concerned.

"Nothing happened to Julie," my mom shot back angrily. "And even if something had happened, do you think she would tell *me*?"

It turns out that Mom was upset because ever since Julie had started seeing some new guy she'd met, she'd barely called my mom. "Is it too much to ask your oldest daughter to call every once in a while? Even if it's just to tell me that she's alive? I haven't heard from her in over *three* weeks. You boys would never do that."

While I couldn't speak for David, I made a mental note to myself to make sure and call Mom at least once a week after I moved to San Diego. Just then, Art stood up from the kitchen table and gestured to my mom. "Come here," he insisted, holding his arms out.

"Why?" my mom questioned.

"Just get up and come here," Art insisted once again.

My mom slowly got up from her chair, and Art took her in his arms. He held her for a few moments and then started to dance with her right there in the center of the kitchen. I could hear him singing the Carpenters' "Close to You" into Mom's ear, and watched as a smile slowly spread across Mom's face.

Wanting to give my mom and Art some space, I picked L up off the floor and backed out of the kitchen without saying another word, the sound of Art's calming voice singing about sprinkling moon dust in my mom's hair trailing behind me. I left the room with L peacefully resting in my arms, her mellow vibe providing me with some much-needed solace as well.

Chapter Six

The last semester of high school began, and I had a pretty easy load, finishing each day at noon. As planned, I started working for my dad at the beginning of February. He decided that it was a good time for me to get some experience in sales and marketing, so he put me in an office with two of his employees, Glen and Larry, where I would assist them with everything from sales projections to cold calls. What I probably enjoyed the most, though, was helping put together flyers and advertisements for the company; it was where I could best put my creativity to use.

Glen and Larry were real characters, and I learned *a lot* about working in an office from them. Glen was Larry's boss, even though Larry was a good fifteen or twenty years older than Larry. Both of them were addicted to coffee and cigarettes; Glen drank a solid three pots of coffee a day just by himself, and they each smoked at least a pack a day. Larry had once been an air traffic controller but had quit because of the stress, not to mention the addiction to speed. "Every single one of those guys in those towers across the country is hyped up on something, I can guarantee you that," Larry insisted. "How else are you supposed to stay that focused for that long? It can't be done without some form of artificial stimulation." He seemed to make a valid point, though I suspected he was still addicted to some sort of amphetamines based on his day-in and day-out high level of energy, which at times bordered on manic.

Larry kept a goalie's hockey mask next to his desk and, without warning, he would yell, "Rubber band fight!" He'd then slip on the mask and begin firing rubber bands at me and Glen. We'd both dive beneath our desks, using them as barriers from Larry's missiles while we armed ourselves with the abundant stash of rubber bands we all kept in our desk drawers. Trudy from accounting was always questioning why we ordered so many rubber bands every month on the office supply request form, and Glen would just tell her it was for a secret project we were working on for my dad, so secret that she wasn't allowed to ask my dad anything about it.

It was amazing how much goofing off went on at the office. Sure, everyone worked hard and got their jobs done, but I found the inefficiency to be astounding. I would sit in meetings for an hour that consisted of a lot of shooting the shit, company gossip, and one of the blowhards from the executive offices giving us his opinion about something irrelevant to the subject at hand, followed by ten minutes of conversation about what we really needed to do.

Even though I didn't start work until 1:00—and despite the fact that the office was way over in an industrial part of Van Nuys due to the large warehouse and printing presses my dad required—I would often race from school to try and meet my fellow co-workers at a restaurant near the office for lunch, as it seemed like they were celebrating some birthday, work anniversary, or accomplishment once or even twice a week. Free lunch? Check. Get back to work at 1:30 or 2:00 even though I would write 1:00 on my timecard? Check. Who wouldn't want to join them whenever possible?

And then there were Yvonne and Nicole. The closest Sparkletts bottle to my office was down the hall and in the office where Yvonne and a couple of the other "girls," as my dad would say, did whatever it was that my dad's "girls" did. Which was actually all of the bookkeeping, which meant they took care of the money, which meant my dad trusted them implicitly. Yvonne was the low woman on the totem pole, but she was still obviously a pretty smart cookie. Unfortunately, she had suffered from polio as a child, one of the last of her generation to do so, and now walked with a severe limp that at times required her to use a cane. An enormous rock and roll fan, she was said to have been inconsolable when the news broke that Keith Moon died last September, crying hysterically in the office and repeating over and over a story about the time she had met him at the Rainbow and how nice he had been to her. The heavy mascara she wore was streaked all the way down her face by the time Nicole drove her home early from work that day.

Nicole didn't work in bookkeeping; she worked in sales, and every guy in the office talked about her, including Glen and Larry. I believed that Nicole was hands down the sexiest woman at my dad's company. I had heard plenty of stories about her getting wild and crazy at the annual Christmas party, and while I hadn't had a ton of interaction with her, she even seemed to be a bit flirty with me. After a few weeks, my trips to the Sparkletts bottle became more frequent: "Hey, Larry, you need me to fill the coffee pot?" I'd offer the boys as a "favor," when all I really wanted was an excuse to get out of the smoky office for ten or fifteen minutes for some water cooler chat with Yvonne and sometimes Nicole as well. One way or another, I made sure the four hours a day I was spending at my dad's office went by as quickly as possible.

Meanwhile, at school, the basketball team cruised through the City playoffs all the way to the city championship game in late February. It was such a big deal that it was held at the Sports Arena downtown. We opened up a big lead in the first half, but Coach Warren played it too conservatively, going to a four-corner offense early in the second half in an attempt to protect his lead. In the end he allowed Washington High to creep slowly back into the game, and when we had to go back into our normal offense, we had lost all of our flow and couldn't put the ball in the basket. It was a crushing loss considering how we badly we had outplayed Washington in the first half, and I guessed that the players were understandably pissed at Coach Warren for essentially taking the ball out of their hands.

In spite of everything, Hank remained his usual sunny self after the game. He had played well, with another solid effort off the bench. And because he could run any offense better than most guys, Coach Warren had played him almost the entire second half because he trusted him more in the four-corner than pretty much any of the starters—with the exception of Willie Randolph, of course.

"Tough loss," I said to Hank once the team's bus arrived back at school. A sizable crowd had headed from the game to the Woodrow Wilson parking lot so they could greet the players when they returned. Despite the fact that everyone had been hoping for a celebration instead of consolation—the marching band had even turned out for the occasion—spirits remained high, and the affair turned out to be much more of a party atmosphere than one would've anticipated after such a crushing loss. But, when I thought about it, the team had had an incredible season, and with not one but two highly recruited tenth graders coming to Woodrow Wilson in September, there was a good chance we'd be back in the Sports Arena this time next year.

"Yeah, what can you do?" Hank said. "Some of the guys are mad at Coach Warren for stalling."

"I don't blame them," Moose, who had gone to the game with me and Andrew, added, sounding more than a bit agitated. "Who does Warren think he is? Dean Smith, for fuck's sake?"

"He was playing scared," Andrew agreed. "We should've continued to ram it down their throat, gone for the jugular."

"I know," Hank said. "But he's such a great coach, it's hard to get too mad at him. After all, we did make it to the championship." Hank was loyal to a fault, and his coaches always loved him for it. He would never come down too hard on a teammate, coach, or friend, and was easily the most supportive person I knew.

"So," I said, taking a deep breath before broaching the subject, "did the guys from Oxy show up?" Coach Warren had told Hank a week or so ago that the coach from Occidental had asked for four tickets to the game.

Hank shrugged. "I don't know. Coach left tickets for them at will-call, but he hasn't said whether or not they picked them up. I don't even know if he knows."

Not two minutes later, Coach Warren approached us. "Hey, fellas." Unlike everyone else, Coach's spirits did not seem very high.

"Hi, Coach," we said in unison.

"Sorry about the loss," I added, "but congratulations on a great season."

"Thanks, Efron." Coach was pretty good with names, and after seeing us around the basketball courts for several years, he knew who we were.

"Hank, can I talk to you a second?" Coach put his arm around Hank and walked away to talk to him in private.

"What's that about?" Andrew asked.

"I'm thinking it's about Occidental," I answered.

"Cool," Moose said, "only, what the fuck are you going to do if Hank ends up at Oxy, Douglas? I thought you two were going to room together."

"I guess I'll be finding a new roommate," I answered.

"Well, you're always welcome to room with me," Moose offered for the umpteenth time.

"Thanks, Moose. Let's see what happens. I also might live off-campus with my sister in Pacific Beach." There was no way in hell Julie wanted me living with her, but I needed to keep all my options open without offending Moose.

"Pacific Beach?" Moose questioned. "That'll be a hell of a long drive to school every day."

Hank finished his conversation with Coach and came back over to us, smiling.

"What was that about?" I asked.

"Oh, you know, he was just telling me how proud he was of me and how much he enjoyed coaching me these past three years. The usual stuff."

"Did he say anything about the coaches from Oxy?" Andrew asked.

"Yeah, he said the tickets had been picked up, but he had no idea who exactly showed up. He told me he'd give them a call next week."

"So, what do you characters want to do now?" Andrew said in his inimitable snarky manner.

"I heard everyone's going back to Erica Conway's house," I offered. Erica's mom was a star on the long-running soap opera *General Hospital*, so they had a pretty nice house. When Erica threw a party, you knew the food and booze was going to be top-notch. They were always catered affairs.

"*Allons-y!*" Moose exclaimed, not wanting to pass up a free, high-quality meal.

"I don't know, guys," Hank sighed. "I'm pretty beat. I don't think I can handle a party. Anyone up for a Big Boy run?"

"Are you kidding?" Moose guffawed. "We can eat great food for free at Erica's house!" I knew he had zeroed in on this fact the moment he'd heard Erica was hosting the after-game party.

"Sorry, Moose. You guys go ahead to the party. I think I'll just head home."

"No way, Hank," I said. "I'm not leaving you. We should be celebrating your great season! If that means Bob's Big Boy, then so be it." I wasn't about to let my best friend down.

"Thanks, buddy," Hank said. I could tell he didn't want to go home alone. He had played well, and the season had been a success, but losing a championship game was devastating, any way you slice it.

Andrew must've recognized the same thing. "All right, I'll join you guys."

"Are you serious?" Moose couldn't believe we were passing up a party at Erica Conway's. But if Hank, Andrew, and I didn't go, he had little chance of getting in. "Whatever. Okay. Bob's Big Boy it is."

And with that, the four of us trudged off to Bob's to drown our lost championship sorrows—and to celebrate a terrific season—in burgers, fries, and milkshakes. We even toasted to the possibility of Hank getting a scholarship offer from Occidental, though I believe I accidentally choked on an errant French fry in the process. Or maybe it was just the lump in my throat?

When I got home that night, I was surprised to see David's Capri in front of the house. It was late, and my mom and Art had probably gone to bed hours ago. The only light was the glare of the television in the conversation pit. David was lying on the couch, watching a movie.

"Hey," I said, approaching the steps leading down into the room.

"Hey, Douglas," he muttered, either distracted or disinterested or both.

"What are you doing?"

"Watching *Take the Money and Run.*"

"Seriously?" I loved Woody Allen. David and I had seen his movies over and over again, especially the early, funny ones like *Take the Money and Run* and *Bananas*. "Move your feet," I ordered, wanting to sit down on the couch to join him.

"Sit over there," David said, pointing to the leather chair in the corner. "I'm comfortable."

"Fine," I said, heading over and collapsing into the soft, overstuffed chair. "Your feet smell anyway."

"Where've you been?"

"Woodrow Wilson played in the city championship tonight."

"Did they win?"

"No."

"Figures."

We watched and tried to stifle our laughter as best we could so that we wouldn't wake up Mom and Art, but it was almost impossible to do when Woody tries to rob a bank and nobody can read his handwriting. There were certain lines in movies that David and I would pull out and use whenever the situation called for a laugh. "Birdie num num" from *The Party* was certainly one of them, as was "It's pronounced Frankensteen," from *Young Frankenstein*, and, of course, "Apt natural, I have a gub," or something like that, from the scene we were watching.

"How's work going?" David asked during a lull in the movie.

"Okay, I guess." While David also worked for my dad, we rarely saw each other in the office because he was in sales and was constantly out in the field either meeting with existing customers or trying to get new ones.

"Larry and Glen are pretty crazy guys."

"Yeah," I laughed. "Our rubber band fights are legendary."

"Listen, Douglas," David said, his tone growing serious, "now that you're settling in over there, you should know that you're going to see and hear stuff—much worse than rubber band fights—that would probably get people fired if Dad ever found out. I know I had to make a decision early on that I would never squeal on anybody, and I advise you to do the same."

"You mean, like, tell Dad if someone was doing something that would likely cause him to fire them?"

"Exactly. I don't want that hanging over my head, and

you shouldn't, either. Besides, if Dad is happy with their performance and doesn't know about the bad stuff, then it shouldn't matter anyway. As long as it's not hurting the company, of course."

"But, like, what stuff are you talking about? Stealing?"

"No, no. If something like that is going on, of course you have to tell Dad." David sat up so he could face me. "Look, you're gonna learn real quick that adults are even more fucked up than kids. Just because they have an important job and seem like they have their shit together, I can almost guarantee you they don't. Yeah, yeah, there's some high-quality people working in the company, but most of them are struggling every day that they walk through those doors. They're either in over their heads at work, lack the knowledge or confidence to do their job correctly, are addicted to drugs or alcohol . . . every one of them is battling something, trust me."

"Including coffee and cigarettes," I joked.

"Yeah, right. Is Larry still drinking several pots of coffee every day?"

"And smoking like a fiend."

"Unbelievable. That guy's gonna be dead before he's forty."

We turned back to the TV and watched as Woody was tortured in prison by being forced to spend time in a steam box with an insurance salesman, and once again attempted to stifle our uncontrollable laughter. As our giggles subsided, David continued.

"Anyway, you're gonna learn a lot about people while you're working there. Just figure it's not your place to go squealing to Dad."

It had never occurred to me to tell Dad about the

rubber band fights, and I wasn't really sure what else I'd see or hear that might shock me. But David would never have broached this whole subject unless it was important, and I appreciated the heads up. "Okay," I answered. "Message received. Thanks for letting me know."

"You're welcome," David said as we both watched Woody again. "If you ever need to talk to me about anything, I'm here for you."

I looked over at my brother and smiled. He really did seem to be changing for the better as of late. "What are you doing over here, anyway?" I asked.

"Mom invited me over for dinner, and Art kept pouring me J&B and sodas until finally Mom took away my car keys. So I'm crashing on the couch tonight."

I had to admit, it was nice having my brother home. We hadn't sat and watched a late-night movie together in forever, and it felt like old times again, back when we were kids and the whole family was still together. I remembered a photo I had seen in one of my mom's photo albums not too long ago. I was just a baby, and my dad was lying on his back on our living room floor, a large wooden stereo console with gold speaker grills sitting behind us. In the photo he's gripping me tightly in his hands, arms thrust upward above his chest, and we're both looking toward the camera. I'm not exactly smiling as I hover in the air like Superman, but I'm not crying either. In my fantasy interpretation of the moment, Frank Sinatra is singing on the record player behind us—maybe something from *Songs for Swingin' Lovers*—as my father gazes at my mother with loving eyes and, after lowering me to his chest, blows her a kiss. . . .

February is usually the worst month, weather-wise,

in L.A. It's cold, especially in the Valley at night, where we often woke up to what was actually quite a beautiful sight: white frost spread across the lawn which, if you squinted just right, could pass for a thin layer of fresh snow. As the sun rose, however, and continued its ascent into the morning sky, glints of light would reflect off all the lawns in the neighborhood, the frost soon to melt. February also tended to be the rainiest month, both in terms of the number of days it rained and the amount of rain we got. Some people might argue that January was worse than February, but they forget that it's *always* beautiful in early January, and most of the bad weather comes much later in January, so you might as well chalk it up to February.

Just like the weather, life gets a bit choppier in L.A. during February. There are more accidents on the streets and freeways because of the wet roads, and it gets dark early, so people are always in a rush to get home at the end of the day. It just seems like the most tense and depressing time to live here. I don't know. Maybe it's the same everywhere. Everyone's just sick of winter.

School was beyond boring at that point. The only thing keeping me interested was my work on the *Wire*. Ms. Pearlstein loved my piece on Mrs. Livingstone, though the photo that Jackson Turner, the head photographer for the *Wire* and a really talented, creative guy, took of Mrs. Livingstone was what truly made the piece. As Hank had promised, Mrs. Livingstone was beyond stunning, with movie-star looks. Jackson positioned her on a brick wall just in front of the tennis courts, sitting on top of the wall with her right leg stretched out and resting in front of her, while her left leg dangled down below. Her tennis skirt was pulled up high, though tastefully so, and the lighting was spot on. It was a glamour shot, and I truly believed the image helped raise the level of my profile; there was no denying that this was someone most of the guys at the school—and a good chunk of the girls—would want to read about. In fact, the piece generated the second-most number of letters to the editor for the year—a grand total of three! Hank's piece on the riot at the Junipero Serra basketball game got five responses, which actually tied with the paper's record for most responses to a published piece.

When we returned to school after Christmas break, I handed Ms. Pearlstein a review of Blue Oyster Cult. It was amazing that I remembered as much as I did about the show, considering all the Boone's Farm I had consumed that night. Deep down, I really wanted to write about music—you know, become the next Robert Hilburn or something.

Ms. Pearlstein thought my review was a top-notch piece of Arts and Entertainment journalism, and since it was a truly special show featuring a very popular band in a very tiny club, and on New Year's Eve no less, she decided to run it. On top of that, she laid a brand, spanking new copy of Elvis Costello's *Armed Forces* on me to review. I wasn't a huge Costello fan, though I did admire his gumption on *Saturday Night Live* when he freaked everyone out by switching songs in the middle of his performance, thereby throwing off the timing of what was a very tightly paced live television show. *Armed Forces*, however, turned me into a Costello fan. It was different from the previous two albums, more rock and roll and less punk, though still fast-paced, and I liked it better than his earlier stuff, especially "Accidents Will Happen" and "(What's So Funny

'Bout) Peace, Love and Understanding."

Next, Ms. Pearlstein assigned me a piece on the history of the nearby Valley Music Center, now a Jehovah's Witness Kingdom Hall. While it wasn't exactly what I had in mind when I convinced her to let me attempt some Arts and Entertainment coverage—free albums and tickets to concerts were my true motivations—it ended up being a really fun piece to write.

As I learned and wrote about in the article, it turned out that, back in the '60s, the Valley Music Center hosted concerts; everyone from Ray Charles and the Byrds to Buffalo Springfield and Three Dog Night had played there. A bunch of famous comedians, including Woody Allen and Don Rickles, had worked the stage as well. I was able to find people—friends of my parents, mostly—who had attended shows there, and one of Art's golf buddies even had a photo of Sammy Davis Jr. that he'd taken that night with his Kodak Instamatic. It ended up being the main photo in the piece—along with a historical shot of the theater that the Jehovah's Witness people gave me—and that's how some guy named Donald Finkleman got his first photo credit in a school newspaper, though he probably wasn't still around to enjoy it.

My most recent assignment from Ms. Pearlstein was to review an album coming out later that month from a new singer-songwriter named Rickie Lee Jones. I hadn't listened to the record yet, but judging from the cover—which featured Rickie Lee in a beret and smoking a cigarette—and the press material the record label had sent along with the LP, she was some kind of hipster, maybe a throwback to Ginsberg and Kerouac and the Beat Generation. Miss Duncan had recently given us Ginsberg's

Howl to read and had taught us a bit about the Beats. I had to admit, while I'd had my doubts about Miss Duncan at first—she seemed super uptight at the beginning of the year—the stuff she'd been having us read all year had been pretty amazing. Along with Ms. Pearlstein, they'd been the two most influential teachers I'd ever had.

Just like Belushi so famously said, March came in like a lion. "Douglas, come look at this!" my mom yelled early one morning. "It's raining cats and dogs." The four of us— me, Art, my mom, and L—just stood there in the kitchen, looking out the glass doors toward the backyard, where it seemed like a monsoon had hit.

"Jeez," Art said, taking a sip of his Yuban, "will you look at that."

I glanced down at L, who peered up at me with a pained expression. "Has L been out yet?"

"I don't think so," my mom said, not taking her eyes off the near hurricane for a minute.

"Sorry, L," I said to the poor creature. "The doggie door is open if you want to use it." I pointed to the small rectangular opening in the wall in the corner of the kitchen, behind the table, that led to the backyard. All L had to do was push the rubber flap open with her head, and she could go outside and pee to her heart's delight. "But I don't blame you if you want to hold it a little longer. Hopefully it'll let up in a little bit." L's ears perked up and she cocked her pretty tan-and-white head, which I took as a sign that she understood me and would hang in there for at least another few minutes or so.

As March dragged on, everyone was on pins and needles about college. Well, Moose and I knew we were shoo-ins for SDSU, but Hank was waiting on Oxy and Andrew was still optimistic about UCLA, and tons of other kids were stressed because they didn't know where the hell they were going to end up in September. It was the week before spring break, and college letters were expected to show up in the coming days.

Annie and I continued to see each other fairly regularly. At times I thought she seemed a little distant, but for the most part, things seemed good.

Until they weren't.

It was a Thursday, and I hadn't seen Annie at school since Monday. She had seemed a bit nervous and jittery that day, but when I asked her about it she said she had just drank too much coffee that morning. But when she didn't show up at school on Tuesday, I called her a few times that afternoon from work and a couple more times that evening, but nobody answered. On Wednesday, she was absent again, and this time when I called her from the office her mom picked up the phone and said Annie couldn't talk to me right then, but that she would be sure to have her call me later that night. I stayed up until nearly midnight, but never heard from her. Now it was Thursday, and still no Annie at school. Immediately after class let out, and before I went to work, I raced over to Annie's house. As I walked up the driveway, I could feel my heart pounding. I was sure something awful had happened to her. I rang the doorbell. Once. Twice. Then three times. Finally, Annie answered the door. She looked pale and thin.

"Jesus, Annie. What's going on? Are you okay? Are you sick? I've been so worried about you." The words came out like a torrent.

"Can we go sit in your car?" Annie asked meekly.

"Sure. Of course." I reached out and hugged her, but

she went stiff in my arms. I took her hand and led her to my car, opening the door for her and waiting for her to slowly get in before I softly closed it. My head was spinning as I walked around the front of the car, opened my door, and got into the driver's seat.

Annie took a deep breath. "Douglas, I think I'm pregnant."

"What? Really? But how? I thought you used that diaphragm thing?"

"I do," she said, tears beginning to roll down her face. "I don't know how this could've happened!"

"Jesus." I was stunned.

"But there's more," Annie cried. She was now nearly sobbing.

"What do you mean?"

"I'm not sure if it's yours, Douglas. It could be Kenny's."

Talk about a punch to the gut. I felt like throwing up. "Kenny's?" I asked, tears now forming in my eyes.

Annie stared down at her hands, which were shaking, refusing to look at me. "You remember that night you said you saw my car in front of Kenny's house?" she asked haltingly.

"Yeah," I answered, by now certain I didn't want to hear what was coming next.

"Well, I *was* there that night."

"Oh, fuck," I exclaimed as another punch landed, this one square to my heart.

"I'm sorry, Douglas," she pleaded, her voice rising and her pace fast. "I went there to get my dad's watch back."

"Your dad's watch?" I questioned incredulously.

"I had given Kenny one of my dad's old watches as a present a long time ago, and I wanted it back. He refused to give it to me for the longest time, but he finally agreed, and he insisted I come to his house to pick it up. That was it. I had only planned to stay a minute and then get out of there."

"And?" I asked, though again, I really didn't want to hear the answer.

"I don't know, Douglas," Annie sobbed. "He was so persuasive. And one thing led to another and the next thing I knew we were in his bedroom and he was on top of me." She paused and took a deep breath. "Before I knew it we were having sex."

"Did he rape you?" I could feel the anger welling up inside of me. Black belt or no black belt, I would kick Kenny's ass.

"Well, no, I mean . . . I don't know! It was all so confusing." Annie covered her face in her hands and was crying hard now, and so was I. My head felt like it was going to explode. I wanted to kill Kenny, but was also experiencing a weird mixture of anger, resentment, love, and concern for Annie.

"I have to go," Annie said suddenly, opening the door and flying out of the car.

"Annie!" I called out after her, jumping out of the front seat as she ran toward her front door. "Annie, wait!" But she disappeared into her house without so much as a glance back. I stood there in total silence for I don't know how many minutes. My world had been shattered, as had Annie's, and at that moment I didn't see how we were possibly going to put it back together again. I knew that no matter the outcome to this whole mess, my life would never be quite the same again.

I just couldn't go to work that day. I couldn't even

listen to the radio or music of any kind. I knew that if the right song came on, I'd burst into tears. I'd just call in sick. I drove straight home in silence. My mom was surprised to see me walk in the door in the early afternoon in the middle of the week. She had become accustomed to seeing me come home in the late afternoon every day for a couple of months now.

"Douglas?" she called out before I had even entered the den. "What are you doing home?" She was sitting on the couch, reading *People* magazine. I could see Billy Joel's face on the cover and something about a concert in Cuba.

"I'm not feeling great and didn't feel like going to work."

"What's going on? Is something the matter?" It was nearly impossible to hide anything from Mom, though I'm sure the pained expression on my face was like a flashing red sign.

"Come here," she said, patting the sofa next to her. "Sit down."

I did as she said, and once again the words came out like a torrent. "Annie thinks she's pregnant. But she doesn't know if it's mine or Kenny's. I saw her car at Kenny's one night a couple of months ago and even though she had convinced me it wasn't her car, it turns out it was. But she also says she just went there to get her dad's watch and that Kenny practically raped her, or maybe he did rape her. I don't know." I suddenly burst into tears. "It's all so confusing."

Mom pulled me in tight, and I rested my head on her chest. "Annie the whammy," she muttered. "Annie the whammy." Instead of saying she'd told me so, she said,

"Look, first things first. What exactly did she say? Did she miss her period? One period? Two? Has she taken a pregnancy test?"

"I don't know," I answered.

"Douglas, you have to ask her these things."

"She hasn't been at school all week. Maybe she's been to the doctor?"

"Well, until you know more, you can't assume anything with that girl. She might be pregnant, she might not. It could be yours, it could be Kenny's." I had told her all about Annie and Kenny, so even though she didn't know the guy, she felt like she did. "Listen. Try not to make yourself sick over this, because there are too many unknowns at this point. But I hope you learn something from this: You have to use protection, even if the girl says she's using something. Do you hear me?"

This was the last place I wanted the conversation to go. How did she know I never used a rubber when I was with Annie? "Yeah, Mom. I hear you."

"How 'bout some lunch?" she kissed me on my head and hugged me tightly one more time before getting up. "I'll make us both grilled cheeses and we can watch a movie together."

"Sounds good, Mom, thanks," I said, looking up at her. "I love you."

"I love you, too, my sweet boy. And don't you worry." She turned to leave the room. "Everything is going to be fine."

I desperately wanted to believe her, but the gnawing pain at the pit of my stomach was telling me otherwise. I hadn't felt this kind of hurt since early in junior high, after my parents had divorced and we had moved across the

Valley in the middle of the school year, when it got so bad that my mom took me to the emergency room because she thought I might have an ulcer. I didn't, but the pain back then, like the pain I was experiencing right now, was real.

Annie skipped school once again on Friday, the last day before spring break. The mood around campus was mostly joyous, as kids had started receiving their college acceptance letters and most of them seemed pretty happy with the results. Andrew most of all: He'd made it into UCLA and was going to be a Bruin. He celebrated by wearing an old Bill Walton jersey to school. Later that afternoon, Moose and I, as expected, both got word from SDSU; the letters waiting for us in our mailboxes had informed us that we were officially Aztecs.

Hank, however, still hadn't heard anything. That changed on Saturday morning, when there was a knock at our front door, and I was surprised to see Hank standing there.

"Oh. Hey, Hank. What's going on?"

"Hey Douglas. Is it cool if I come in?"

"Sure. Is everything all right?"

"Yeah, yeah. Fine." Hank stepped into the house and followed me into the den, where we sat down on the couch. "So," he began, taking a deep breath, "I heard from Oxy and felt I owed it to you to tell you in person that they've offered me a partial scholarship to come and play basketball for them."

"Wow. That's terrific, Hank. Congratulations." My happiness for Hank was genuine, though the fact that we wouldn't be rooming together at SDSU stung.

"I know we had plans to live together at San Diego State, Douglas, but I just can't pass up this opportunity."

"Don't worry about it, man, I completely understand."

"You sure? I really would hate for this to hurt our friendship."

"Everything's copacetic. We're cool."

"Thanks, buddy. And look, I'll be able to come down there and visit you and you can come up and visit me. We'll only be a couple of hours away from each other."

"For sure. I can't wait to come up and see you play ball." We sat there for a few moments in what felt like an awkward silence. "So, I guess those Oxy coaches that watched you play really liked what they saw, huh?"

"Yeah, but you want to hear something crazy? It turns out that Ms. Pearlstein went to Occidental, and when she got wind that I was trying to get in, she got in touch with someone she knows in admissions and talked to her about me. She even sent them the column I wrote about the game with Junipero Serra. The admissions person sent it to the faculty advisor for the student paper, who loved it, and it turns out he is close friends with the head coach of the basketball team. They were apparently deciding between me and another player, and my column tilted the decision in my favor. Crazy, huh?"

Once again, fate had come along to slap me in the face. After all, I was the one who convinced Hank to write for the *Woodrow Wilson Wire*. Had I not done that, there was a good chance he would have ended up with me at SDSU just like we had planned all along. "Totally," I agreed.

"So I guess I owe you some thanks for pushing me to write for the paper." It was like he'd read my mind.

"Yeah," I said, unsure of whether I really wanted to take credit for any of this. "I guess so."

"So we're cool?" Hank checked again.

"Yeah, yeah. Totally cool." I debated whether to tell him about Annie, but I knew he was probably really excited inside about the Oxy news in spite of his calm demeanor with me, and I didn't want to bring him down.

"Awesome," he said, rising up from the couch. "I gotta go over and see my grandparents. I'm going to tell them the news."

"All right, man." I led Hank to the door and before we parted, we executed Soul Brother Handshake #3.

"I'll see you soon, okay?" he said.

"Yeah, maybe we can catch a flick early next week. I heard the new Albert Brooks movie is pretty funny."

"Oh yeah? Sounds good. Let's go on Monday night."

"Okay, buddy," I said as I watched Hank, my almost-roommate, walk down the front walkway toward his Camaro. As I shut the door behind me, my mom came down the stairs.

"Was that Hank's voice I heard?"

"Yeah. He came over to tell me he was offered a partial scholarship to Occidental and that he's going to accept it, so we won't be rooming together in San Diego."

"Oh, I'm sorry, honey," my mom said, coming over to give me a hug. "It's been a couple of rough days for you, hasn't it?"

I could feel the tears welling up in my eyes once again, and a lump started to form in my throat. I couldn't even reply. My mom pulled away from me a bit and held me by my shoulders in front of her, our eyes locked. "Everything happens for a purpose, Douglas. And it's all going to work out just fine. Besides, didn't you say you could always room with Moose?"

"Yeah, but I'm not sure I want to go that route."

"Well, it's your decision, and whatever you decide will be for the best. Just trust your gut. You'll figure it out."

"Thanks, Mom. I love you."

"I love you, too, Douglas. How about some breakfast?"

Art appeared at the top of the stairs. L was by his side. "Breakfast? I'm starving."

"Has Lassie been outside yet?" my mom asked.

"Don't know," was Art's reply. "I doubt it. She was asleep in the hallway when I came out of the bedroom."

"Come on, L!" I called, tapping my thigh. L didn't exactly come running—she wasn't really capable of running at her age—but tiptoed gingerly down the stairs. Upon making it all the way down, she stood at my feet, and I reached out to pet her. "Good girl, L. You're a good girl." At least I could always count on L to be there to comfort me, and she knew that I would always be there for her as well.

Spring break was pretty low-key this year. It seemed like everybody had their own thing going on. Some guys, like Andrew and Sven, went skiing. Others, like Hank, who was hitting the weight room every day and then playing basketball with guys from Woodrow Wilson as well as some dudes from Oxy the coach had put him in touch with, were focusing on their sports endeavors. Moose's mom insisted he go to Arizona to visit his grandparents, who had recently moved there from New York. Marco's dad made him work full-time on the stunt cars he kept in a large garage somewhere near the Van Nuys Airport. My dad didn't tell me I had to switch from part- to full-time over the break, but with nothing much else going on, I figured I'd put in the hours and make some bank.

One day during my lunch break at work, I decided to make a run over to Licorice Pizza to see if the new

Supertramp record was in stock yet. *Breakfast in America* was sure to be a huge hit and the first single, "The Logical Song," was already all over the radio. As soon as I walked through the glass door, I heard my name.

"Douglas!"

I turned and saw Genevieve waving; she was holding an album in her hand. We made our way toward each other and hugged warmly. "Hey, Genevieve. How you doing?"

"Good, good," she replied. "Well, except for this Three Mile Island catastrophe."

"Oh, man, I know. Just awful. I've been following it on the news."

"I tried to warn everyone about this in that Op-Ed piece I published in the *Wire* last semester."

"You sure did!" It *was* impressive. Genevieve had written that this exact nuclear power plant meltdown scenario was a possibility, and here we were only a few months down the line and her prediction had come true. I gestured to the album in her hands. "What do you have there?"

"Patti Smith!" she said excitedly, holding the record, titled *Easter*, toward me so that I could see the cover. "Do you know her?"

"Yeah. Well, I know her cover of Springsteen's 'Because the Night.' And I think I saw her on *Saturday Night Live* once. Wait, isn't that character Gilda Radner does based on her?"

"I wouldn't know about that," Genevieve offered. "But I love Patti Smith. In fact, I'm buying this because I've already worn out the first copy I bought!"

"You're kidding!" I laughed.

"Not at all! You know, this is the record that has 'Because the Night' on it."

"Oh, cool!"

"Crap," Genevieve suddenly said, spying someone over my shoulder.

"What's the matter?" I started to turn around.

"Don't. Stop," she insisted. "Gary Wernicke is over there. He's been asking me to go to the prom, and I really don't want to go with him. Shit. Here he comes. Hey, Gary," she said over my shoulder. "Will you tell him you're taking me to the prom?" she frantically whispered to me.

"What?" I said.

"Hey, Genevieve," Gary walked up. "Fancy seeing you here. Hey, Douglas."

"Hey, Gary. How's it going?"

"Good, good. Well, could be better if this little lady here would agree to go to the prom with me." Gary had this way about him that was a throwback to our parents' generation. There was something about him that just screamed 1950s. Before Genevieve could respond, I decided to do her a solid.

"Sorry, dude, but I beat you to the punch."

"What do you mean?"

"I'm going to the prom with Douglas," Genevieve said flatly.

"But, but, aren't you going with Annie?" I wasn't sure, but Gary's eyes seemed to be tearing up.

"We broke up," I announced.

"Gee whiz. Well, okay, then." He looked down at his shoes and paused for a moment. "I'm sorry, I have to go." Gary then rushed off and out the store.

"Oh, man," Genevieve said, biting her lip. "I really didn't mean to hurt him, but he can be such a pain. I kept trying to tell him I wasn't interested, but he wouldn't give up. Thanks for helping me out. Sorry for making you lie like that."

"Well, it's not exactly a lie," I said, locking eyes with Genevieve.

"What do you mean?"

"I'm really not sure what's happening with me and Annie these days. We probably won't be going to the prom together."

"Oh, well, sorry, I mean—"

"It's okay. Things are just a little confusing right now."

Genevieve caressed my arm with her hand. "Well, look, if you don't have a date for the prom, well, maybe we could go together."

Wow. Her words washed over me like a powerful wave. *Go to the prom with Genevieve? Well, why not?*

"You don't have to—"

"No, no," I interrupted. "I'd love to. I mean, assuming things don't work out with Annie, of course."

"Of course, of course," Genevieve insisted. "I don't want to be the one who—"

"Oh, I would never put that on you," I said before she could even get the thought out. There was no way she would be the cause of Annie and I breaking up. It was far more complicated than that.

"Well, look, you let me know, okay? I really should get going."

"Okay, Genevieve, I'll be in touch."

Genevieve leaned in and gave me a long hug. "I'm sorry about you and Annie," she whispered. "But, who knows, maybe it'll all work out in the end."

"Thanks," I said as we stepped apart and locked eyes before she walked away.

It was true about me and Annie. For Christ's sake, she had gone MIA for the entire spring break. She wouldn't return my phone calls or even pick up the phone, and whenever her mom answered she would simply say that Annie wasn't home, but that she'd give her the message. I actually l drove by her house a couple of times over the break, and in both instances her mom came to the door and sent me away. "Annie will call you when she's ready," her mom promised sympathetically when she saw the crestfallen look on my face.

Kenny Killian's house was sort of on my way to and from work, so I'd often take a detour and pass by just to see if Annie's car was there. It never was, but then again, neither was Kenny's. I sometimes imagined they were off in Mammoth skiing together, and the knot in my stomach would grow increasingly tighter. Finally, on the Sunday night before we were going back to school for the last two months before graduation, Annie called.

"Hello?" I answered, not expecting that the call would even be for me. I was standing in the kitchen, helping my mom clear the table after dinner. I still had a couple of plates in my other hand.

"Hi, Douglas." Her voice was quiet, somber.

"Annie?" I asked. I could feel the skin over my entire body come alive, as if the nerve endings had just been fed a bolt of electricity. My palms immediately became sweaty, and I could sense my breathing becoming unsteady.

"Well, who else do you think it is?" she teased. "Are you already seeing other girls?"

"Me? What? No, of course not." I was confused by both her light tone and her question. "Hang on a second. Mom, I'm going to take this upstairs. Will you hang up?"

My mom, who had been watching me with a wary eye the whole time, sighed and said, "Sure, honey."

"Hang on, Annie. I'm going to switch phones."

I handed the phone to my mom, who looked at me with a great deal of concern. She covered the mouthpiece and whispered, "Be careful, Douglas. Don't believe everything she tells you."

"Mom!" I shushed her as I made my way out of the kitchen and ran up the stairs, my heart pounding. I grabbed the Garfield phone from the hallway and ran the long cable from the wall into my bedroom, shutting the door behind me. I couldn't believe the most important conversation of my life was going to take place while I was holding this stupid, orange plastic cat in one hand and nervously gripping the handset in the other.

"Mom? You can hang up now."

"Okay, honey." I waited to hear the click before launching.

"Annie, where have you been? Why haven't you been returning my calls? I've been so worried about you." The words rushed out of me like they'd been bottled up inside of me for days, which they had.

"I'm sorry, Douglas," Annie replied, now more quiet and downbeat than she had been when I first answered the phone. "There's been a lot going on." She paused and went silent.

"Well, are you going to tell me?" I asked. "Are you okay?"

"Douglas, I lost the baby."

"Wh-what do you mean?"

"I lost the baby," she repeated. "I had a spontaneous abortion and had to spend a couple of days in the hospital."

"Oh my God, Annie. I had no idea. Are you okay?"

"Yeah, I'm fine. . . . I think they wanted me in there just to be safe." Annie's voice was starting to break. "Oh Douglas, it was so horrible!"

"I'm sorry, Annie. But I mean . . . you weren't planning on keeping the baby, were you?"

"No, of course not," Annie said. She was crying now. "But I was planning on getting an abortion, not losing it this way."

"How'd it happen?" I asked.

"Oh, Douglas, it was awful! I can't even talk about it."

"I'm sorry, Annie." We both went quiet again, though I could hear her softly crying. "Did you ever figure out whose baby it was?"

"Douglas! How can you ask me that? Of course not! How would I ever figure that out? And does it even matter?" She was now sobbing.

"I'm sorry, Annie. I didn't mean, I mean . . . I'm sorry." I didn't know what to say. I guess it was a stupid question to ask her at that moment, but it was important to me, and I still wanted to know. I felt I deserved to know.

"Is that all you care about?" Annie asked.

"No, of course not," I lied. "But what's going to happen to us?"

"What do you mean?"

"I mean—do you still want to see me?"

"Douglas! Of course I still want to see you. I've been missing you terribly."

"But-" I stammered, not wanting to ask the question but knowing I had to, "but what about Kenny?"

"What *about* Kenny? You're my boyfriend. You're the only one I care about."

I was stunned, confused. It suddenly felt like the room was spinning. I stopped the back-and-forth pacing I'd been doing during the whole conversation and sat down on my bed.

"Don't you believe me?" she asked after I didn't respond.

"Of course," I lied once again. "It's just, I don't know, it's all been so confusing. Why didn't you return my phone calls? Why didn't you come to the door when I came to your house?"

"Douglas! Didn't you hear me?" Her sobs had transitioned to anger. "I had a spontaneous abortion. It all just poured out of me one morning while I was on the toilet. It was the most awful thing I've ever experienced. I had to spend two days in the hospital. I needed to get through this before I could talk to you. Don't you understand?"

"Yeah, yeah, of course I understand." I suddenly felt like I was going to throw up. "I just wish I could've visited you in the hospital. That you would've told me what was happening."

"I thought you were going to be happy to hear from me . . ."

"I am!" I insisted.

"I thought you'd be sympathetic, help me get through this."

"I am! I will!" I insisted once again.

"I have to go, Douglas. This isn't the conversation I thought we were going to have." *Click.*

"Wait! Annie!" It was too late. She was gone. The fucking redial button on the Garfield phone had been broken forever, so I had to furiously dial Annie's number again and again. Each time I called, I'd let it ring four, five, even six times before hanging up, and then dial again. Annie refused to answer.

Giving up, I lay back on my bed, the Garfield phone resting on my chest. I stayed there for a good thirty minutes, hoping against all hope that the phone would ring and it would be Annie on the other end of the line. But did I really want to talk to her? Did I believe her? Had there really been a baby? Did she really still love me, and was I still really her boyfriend? Did I even want to be her boyfriend? My stomach was on fire, and I finally curled up in a ball on my bed. I could feel tears running down my cheeks.

Knock, knock, knock. The soft tapping on my door was followed by my mom's voice. "Douglas? Is everything okay?"

"Not now, Mom," I sobbed. She immediately opened the door and came into my room. Sitting on my bed, she stroked my hair as I remained in my fetal position.

"What happened, sweetheart?"

I looked up at her, wiped the tears from my eyes, and answered, "Annie lost the baby."

"What do you mean she 'lost the baby'?" my mom asked skeptically.

"She had a spontaneous abortion."

"A what?"

"She said everything just poured out of her one day when she was on the toilet and then she had to spend a couple of days in the hospital. Mom—what if that was my baby, too?" I again started to cry. This was just too much for my recently turned seventeen-year-old brain to handle.

"Oh, Jesus," my mom whispered, pulling my head and

shoulders toward her and hugging me tightly. She then wiped the tears from my eyes and looked at me with a serious gaze. "Listen to me, Douglas. You have no idea if this was your baby. You don't even know if she was really pregnant."

"But the spontaneous abortion . . ." I interrupted.

"She could be making that up as well," my mom suggested. "It all sounds very fishy to me, Douglas. Healthy teenage girls do not usually lose their pregnancies this early in the process."

"But why would she make all of this up?"

"I think she's still trying to cover up for seeing that Kenny character you told me about. Maybe this is just her way to manipulate you into continuing to see her."

"I don't know, Mom. Why would she do that?"

"Maybe because she's a selfish seventeen-year-old girl who's a pathological liar."

Her words stung me, and she could see it by the expression on my face.

"I'm sorry, honey, but it's the truth. I've stood by and watched as she's told you lie after lie and manipulated you to suit her needs. Whether it was that business about canceling on you at the last minute before New Year's Eve, or the story about why her car was in front of Kenny's house, or the trip to Mammoth she swore she didn't go on even though your friend saw her there—"

"But Sven could've been mistaken," I offered in defense.

"Maybe, but it's just one thing after another. And now all of this pregnancy business. Douglas, if this were all true, if she had truly broken up with Kenny and you were the love of her life, then why the hell did she keep you in the dark about everything? Why didn't she return your calls? Refuse to come to the door?"

"I don't know," I answered. "Because she was so traumatized about everything that was happening?"

"Douglas, that's *exactly* when you need those who are closest to you. If she truly loved you, if you were truly her one and only love, don't you think she would've immediately reached out to you while this was all going on? If you went through something horrible, wouldn't you want to rely on her to make you feel better, to help you get through it?"

I didn't answer, but I knew Mom was probably right. I just couldn't understand why Annie would feel the need to lie to me, to create these elaborate stories. Was she, as my mom suggested, a pathological liar? Was this all an act to keep me in her life while she was free to also see Kenny or someone else on the side? Was I a dupe? A fool? A gullible teenage boy in way over his head?

"How am I going to get through these next couple of months?" I wondered out loud. "I'm going to have to see Annie at school, and I have all these mixed feelings about her. What am I supposed to do?"

My mom gently stroked my hair. "My advice, Douglas, would be to stay as far away as possible from that girl. Besides, you'll be leaving for San Diego in a few months, and you'll be on to new adventures filled with all kinds of wonderful girls."

Right now, San Diego felt a million miles away. As much as I hated to admit it, I still loved Annie, maybe even more than ever. But that love was mixed with so many other emotions; I just couldn't shake the overall dread that had enveloped every ounce of my being.

"Honey? You home? Where are you?" Art's voice wafted up into my room from downstairs.

"Hang on, honey," my mom called out. "I'll be down in a minute." Mom looked at me with a mixture of concern, love, and pity in her hazel eyes. "You gonna be okay?" she asked.

"I guess so," I responded, unsure of my answer.

"Why don't you just take it easy today. Let me go see what Art wants and I'll come back up with a snack for you." She rose from the bed. "Everything is going to be okay," she promised. "Sometimes these things just take some time to figure out."

"Thanks, Mom," I said as she turned to walk out the door. "I hope you're right," I murmured to myself.

I didn't sleep very well that night, alternately feeling angry and deeply, deeply in love. At 2:00 AM I woke up in a cold sweat, my teeth chattering; at 4:30 I was so hot I had to throw all of the covers off my bed and fell back asleep on top of my mattress clad only in my underwear. By the time I had to get up for school, my stomach hurt so bad I would've thrown up had I had anything in my system to puke.

I was pretty quiet during breakfast, muttering the occasional "yes" or "no" or "okay" as my mom peppered me with questions and told me mundane stories about her cousin Jeannie, anything to try and break through my obviously tense demeanor. I went out the door without so much as a goodbye, though I did hear my mom try to call out after me. I just didn't want to talk about it anymore, just wanted to get to school, see Annie, and get this over with. I don't remember driving that day, couldn't even find my car in the parking lot after school, because I couldn't for the life of me remember where I had parked that morning.

As soon as I stepped inside the entrance to the school, the Senior Quad was spread out before me, looking so green it felt like something out of a movie. In fact, the next few minutes of my life seemed like something out of a movie. Like a vision, I saw Annie almost floating across the Quad directly toward me, and no matter what I was feeling inside, I couldn't help but respond in kind. Two magnets, we were powerfully drawn to each other. We met just inside the front edge of the lawn before we were in full embrace, kissing each other madly, tears running down both of our cheeks.

"I'm sorry I hung up last night," Annie sobbed. "I love you so much."

"I missed you," I whispered lovingly, inhaling the sandalwood in her gorgeous thick, wavy black hair. Our bodies felt so good together. It was so perfect. Why couldn't we be like this all the time?

I would ask myself that question over and over and over again during the days and weeks that followed. Annie and I would fight, then make love, then argue, then break up, then get back together, then make love, then fight . . . it was a vicious cycle, and by the time May rolled around I was like a wet rag, every nerve ending fried. My mom had lost patience with me and refused to even discuss Annie any longer. She wouldn't even allow me to speak her name in her presence, and if the phone rang and God forbid my mom answered it and it was Annie on the other end, Mom would simply hang up on her. Needless to say, I did a lot of racing to pick up the phone before the second ring.

The weekend before prom—which Annie and I were

either going to together or not going to together, depending on what day of the week it was—Moose and I were shooting around in the driveway. "The prom's next Saturday, dude," Moose admonished. "You better make up your mind. Do you have any backups?"

"Yeah, Genevieve Carlson said that if things didn't work out with Annie, she'd be happy to go with me."

"That's cool that Genevieve is being so cool about everything," Moose said, missing a layup and cursing at himself.

"Yeah," I said, grabbing the rebound, dribbling out past the "clear" line that was actually just the thin channel between two large slabs of cement, and turning and calmly draining a seventeen-footer. "It's too bad she doesn't have a date. And I certainly don't want to leave her hanging, but she also knows about all of the drama between me and Annie, so she's being totally mellow about the prom situation." Moose fed me the ball, and I swished another shot.

"I can't wait for Saturday," he said. "It's gonna be a blast. Especially now that Marco got his uncle to let us use his place for the pre-party. And you have your friend's apartment for the after-party. It's gonna be an awesome night."

The prom was being held at the Beverly Hilton, which sat right at the edge of Beverly Hills. Everybody complained that they weren't using a hotel in the Valley— even the Sportsman's Lodge would've been fine—but the committee that put the prom together said the best combination of price and availability was the Hilton. It just so happened that Marco had an uncle who lived nearby, and Marco somehow talked him into letting us have our pre-party at his house. Meanwhile, Larry, who was going to be out of town, generously offered me the use of his apartment in Sherman Oaks for the after-party. I knew he was probably just trying to score points with my dad—though why he thought I'd even tell my dad was another matter—but I happily accepted his offer anyway. If Annie did end up going to the prom with me, Larry said he had no problem with us spending the night in his bed.

"Somebody might as well get some action in there," he'd joked when he handed me a spare key.

"What time are you picking up Marcie?" I asked Moose. His date was a long-time acquaintance who had been in French class with Moose since junior high. They had actually gone out a handful of times over the years, and I knew Moose was hoping against hope that he was going to get laid on Saturday night.

"Around four thirty, I think."

"Why so early?"

"Well, I figure if I get there by four thirty, by the time Marcie's ready—she's always late—and her mom takes a thousand photos, it'll be five o'clock. The party starts at six, and with Saturday night traffic it'll probably take close to an hour to get over the hill and find parking by Marco's uncle's place."

"Yeah, you're probably right." I dribbled up toward Moose, challenging him to defend me, and then went to my patented fadeaway from the corner. *Swish*.

"Fuck you, Douglas," Moose said.

Just then, David pulled up in front of the house. "Hey geeks," he said as he got out of his car, "don't tell me you two are still trying to learn how to play this game," he added snidely.

"I seem to recall a game when we kicked your ass a few

years ago," Moose teased as he had done dozens of times before. In fact, he mentioned it or alluded to the victory nearly every time he ran into David.

"Well, maybe today is the day for me to avenge that loss," David challenged.

"Are you serious?" I asked.

"We beat you as tenth graders. What makes you think you can beat us as seniors?" Moose guffawed.

"I'm bigger and stronger, too," David said, proudly making his biceps pop and even wiggle.

"How much?"

"Name your price, Moose."

"Ten bucks apiece. Your twenty to our twenty combined."

David had just come from the gym, so he was already in shorts and tennis shoes and a workout T-shirt. While Moose and I were wearing jeans and regular T-shirts, we did have our tennis shoes on. "You're on!" David challenged as he tossed his gym bag on the lawn beside the driveway.

This time around, I wasn't going to question the amount of money on the line. I couldn't believe David seriously thought he could beat us, and I wondered if this was just him showing off that he was doing so well in life, making a pretty good living working at my dad's company, that he could easily afford to throw twenty bucks away like it was nothing.

As Moose and I predicted, the game was a blowout—11 buckets to 4—and even though we kicked his ass, David would make us both pay with an assortment of elbows to our ribs and arms, which accompanied forearm shivs to our backs that sent us flying into the garage whenever we had inside position for a rebound. Bruised and even bloodied—one of David's elbows glanced off Moose's lip, slightly cutting him and drawing blood for a few min- utes—we nevertheless emerged victorious and elated, having thoroughly humiliated my older brother on the court. He would not get revenge for our original, and what was still our greatest, victory. Not today. Not ever.

"So, I assume it'll be months before we ever see our money," Moose wisecracked after the game.

David was sitting on the grass next to the driveway, breathing fairly hard, and Moose and I stood a few feet in front of him on the cement. While David *was* in great shape, Moose and I had spread the court and really made him work on defense, crisply passing the ball back and forth, sometimes unnecessarily, just to make David run and tire him out. The strategy had worked like a charm.

David unzipped his gym bag, reached in, and pulled out his wallet. "Nope," he pronounced, "I am debt-free these days, and intend to stay that way." He took two ten-dollar bills and tossed them toward our feet.

"Wow," Moose said, immediately reaching for his bill. "I'm impressed. Is this a new David we're seeing?"

"Well," my brother said, casually tossing his wallet back into his bag and looking up at us, "I don't know about a new David, but I hope I'm not the same prick I was a few years ago!"

With that, we all shared a long, knowing laugh. David got to his feet and headed toward the front door. Raising his gym bag above his head, he said, "I'm gonna go hit the shower," before disappearing into the house.

"Wow," Moose repeated, looking at the ten-dollar bill in his hand. "He really has changed."

"Let's not get carried away." I laughed again, reaching down to pick up my ten bucks. "He's still David."

"Yeah, I guess so," Moose acknowledged.

"But, no, he's definitely mellowed out. I think working full-time and living on his own has been good for him."

"Speaking of which . . ." Moose looked at me expectantly. Ever since Hank announced he was going to Oxy, Moose had been anxiously awaiting my decision about rooming with him.

This was a conversation I had been avoiding. I recently had a long talk with my dad about the whole matter, and he'd convinced me I'd be better off rooming with a stranger. "Look, Moose," I began, suddenly feeling like a girl writing a "Dear John" letter to her boyfriend-soldier in the army, "I think it's best if we don't room together. I just think we'd be better off opening ourselves up to new people, new experiences."

"But you were gonna room with Hank," Moose pointed out.

"I know, I know. But you know what? It might've destroyed our friendship. And the same thing could happen to us. It's not easy living with somebody. And it's not like we're not going to be hanging out all the time. We'll probably spend more time together if we *don't* live together."

"Yeah," Moose said resignedly, "maybe you're right. But what if I get a psycho for a roommate? Or someone I can't stand?"

"Or," I suggested, "maybe your roommate will be a guy who will one day introduce you to a girl, who in turn introduces you to a girl who ends up being your wife and the mother to your three children."

"Yeah, right," Moose laughed.

"I'm serious, man," I said, trying to get Moose to look me in the eye. "We've both been through a lot these past few years—you especially—and if there's one thing I know I've learned, it's to be open to what life brings to you, whether it's good, bad, or indifferent. We can't control the shit life throws at us. We can only react. But in that reaction, we have a choice, and those choices we make are dependent on the fact that we must remain open to all possibilities."

"What, are you fucking Plato all of a sudden?"

"Ha! Touché!" I laughed.

"But I hear you," Moose said. "It's no different than sports. In basketball, what does Hank say that Coach Warren always tells him? Let the game come to you."

"And in golf, according to Art, anyway, it's the same thing: you have to work with what the course gives you."

"Exactly, *mon ami*," Moose said.

From that point on, things were never better between me and Moose. We knew we'd be living in the same ten-story dorm at SDSU, maybe even on the same floor, but we wouldn't be sharing a room. And that was okay, because the psycho we'd each inherit as our roommate could one day introduce us to the love of our life. Or something like that.

Chapter Seven

Prom week was beyond nerve-wracking. I had gone to the expense and hassle of renting a tux—a powder-blue job that matched my eyes—but even up until Thursday morning, things were still a bit up in the air between me and Annie. I had grown tired of the long phone calls late into the night, re-hashing over and over again the details of everything that either had or had not happened between me, Annie, and Kenny over the past few months. To be honest, I wasn't even sure I loved Annie anymore. Or at least I was questioning whether she was worth all of the bullshit we were going through.

But in the end, everything worked out, and on Saturday morning I went over to my dad's house to switch cars with my stepmom, who had graciously offered to let me drive her rad, cherry-red 240Z to the prom so that Annie and I could arrive in style. It was super cool of Cindy, and even though I suspected my dad had pushed her into doing it, I thanked her profusely, which made my dad happy.

The gas crisis had gotten really bad, so Cindy was cool with me picking up the car fairly early in the morning so I could get in line for gas. According to the latest rules, you could only get gas on odd days when the last number on your license plate was odd or even days when the last number on your plate was even. It was an odd calendar day, and Cindy's plate ended in 7, so I hustled over to the Mobil station near my dad's house where I discovered about eight cars lined up for gas. *Not too bad*, I thought. But then I realized the station wasn't even open yet. Checking the clock on my dash, I saw it was 7:50. *Probably opens at 8:00*, I figured, so I got in line behind the others.

At about ten minutes after 8:00, a green Chevy Nova came roaring up into the station and a fat, harried man got out, waving his arms. By now the line had at least tripled in size. That's how bad things were at that point: if you saw a relatively short line at a gas station, you got in it, even if was just to top off your tank.

"No gas! No gas!" the man shouted, sweat pouring down from his forehead and across his chubby, unshaven face. "We are closed for gas! Only open for service!"

"Why didn't you post a sign, asshole!" I heard someone yell from a car somewhere up in front of me. Several other shouts and threats from drivers throughout the line followed.

"I am sorry! Please, come back tomorrow. Tomorrow I'll have gas!"

Everyone began to drive off at the same time, which was madness, of course. I got out of there safely and hopped on the freeway, enjoying the speed and low ride of the Z. Such a cool car! Getting off at Canoga, I headed north until I found a station with a long, but not insane, line up near Sherman Way. I got in back, reclined the seat, turned up the radio, and a little under an hour later I was on my way, with a full tank of gas and what promised to be an insanely fun night ahead of me.

The plan was to pick up Annie at 4:45 to take some photos at her house, and then drive over to Marco's uncle's place, which was off Olympic, not far from the Beverly Hilton where the prom was being held. When the prom was over, Hank, Moose, Andrew, Marco, Sven, and I and our dates would head back to Larry's place, near Victory and Balboa, for the after-party. What a night it was going to be!

With my hair feathered to its Travolta best and my powder-blue tux looking sharp, I grabbed Annie's corsage from the fridge and headed out the door. My mom was waiting for me with her camera.

"You look so handsome!" she enthused, snapping a photo.

I had to hand it to her; in spite of her feelings about Annie, she'd put it all aside once Annie and I had committed to attending the prom together.

"Turn around, let me see how you look," Art said as he walked down the stairs wearing his navy one-piece jumpsuit. It had a gold buckle with an anchor on it and had been one of Art's favorite pieces of clothing for years. From the tattered edges around the bottom of the pants, you could tell it had seen better days, and my mom had forbade him from ever wearing it outside of the house again. But since they were staying home this Saturday night, Art had obviously decided to get comfortable and slip on the jumpsuit.

I turned to face Art. "So handsome!" he smiled, looking over at my mom proudly. Mom continued to snap away until I practically had to force my way past her to the door.

"Have a good time, sweetie!" she called out as I headed down the walkway toward the Z parked in front of the house. "I love you! Drive carefully!"

"I will!" I called out over my shoulder.

Cindy's stereo wasn't actually as good as mine, since I had upgraded it with some of the money I had made working for my dad. Her standard Datsun setup was no match for my new Pioneer deck with the Harman Kardon power booster and JBL speakers. Pacific Stereo had been offering an incredible deal on the package, and I went for it and couldn't be happier. Anyway, who needed a killer stereo when I could relish the speed and handling of the 240Z? I took my time driving to Annie's, enjoying the curves of Wells Drive for as long as possible before finally turning on Winnetka and heading past Woodrow Wilson and Ventura Boulevard and up to Oxnard and Annie's neighborhood.

Annie, of course, looked beyond stunning in a soft, pink chiffon gown with white lace. Her mom, hyper and frenzied as always, must have snapped a thousand photos of the two of us, standing in front of the house, next to their dog in the driveway, by the maple tree in their front yard, and finally beside my car as I hustled Annie in and said goodbye to her crazy mother. My dad's words came into my head: "Remember, you're marrying the mom. Always look at the mother. That's who you are marrying."

"Now, you come home at a reasonable hour, Annie," her mom warned. "I don't want a repeat of what happened last year." She was referring to last year's senior prom, which Annie had attended as a junior—with Kenny, of course. Annie had once told me that she'd gotten so drunk that night, Kenny had to carry her from the car into the house when he dropped her off at three in the morning.

"Douglas," her mom called through the passenger-side window as we were about to pull away, "I don't want to see you carrying my daughter passed out in your arms at the end of the night, you hear? She better be able to walk through that door on her own two feet," she said, gesturing heatedly toward their weathered front door.

"Don't worry," I promised. "I'll take good care of her." And with that, I peeled away from the curb, burning a bit of rubber in the process.

"Jesus, Douglas, I know you wanted to get away from my mom, but that was a little over the top!" Annie laughed and smiled that big, wide smile of hers. "Who do you think you are? Mario Andretti or something?"

"Sorry," I said. "This car is a lot more powerful than my Honda."

"This is so cool!" Annie said, looking around the interior of the 240Z. "That was so nice of your stepmom to let you drive it tonight."

"Yeah, they wanted us to stop by, but I told them we probably wouldn't have time. Besides, I think your mom took enough pictures of us that there will be plenty to go around."

"She's a nut!" Annie cracked up again.

Traffic out to the city was predictably slow, but Annie and I were having a great time, laughing and gossiping about different kids at school. "Did you hear about Diana Durgin?" Annie asked at one point while checking her makeup in the small visor mirror.

"No, what happened?"

Annie dabbed her pinkie on the lipstick at the corner of her mouth and said, "She ran away to become a Moonie."

"Are you serious? Why would she want to join a cult?"

"I don't know. There were always rumors that her dad was abusing her."

"Wow. That sucks."

"Yeah, I hear she's on her way to New York right now."

"New York City?"

"No, I think it's somewhere out in the boonies. Ha!" Annie laughed her beautiful laugh. "You get it? The Moonies are in the boonies!"

I laughed with her, and she rubbed my thigh.

"Yeah, it's probably way up in the other corner of New York, in the woods or something," I surmised as our laughter subsided. When I'd heard that the next Winter Olympics were going to be held in Lake Placid, New York, I'd looked it up in our atlas and was surprised by how forested the state was. I guess in Southern California, our perception of New York is formed by New York City, just like people who live in New York City think we all live in Hollywood.

You'd think that, after all the freaky cults of the '70s—from the Manson family to the Jonestown Massacre at the end of last year—people would know better by now. The Moonies had been in the news as of late, with rumors that teenagers and young adults were being kidnapped off the streets, brainwashed, and forced into becoming members of the cult. Nobody really knew what was true and what wasn't, but I couldn't imagine why in the world someone like Diana Durgin would run off to join them. Even if she had a troubled home life, wasn't there anyone else she could turn to?

"I think it's really sad," I finally said after a few moments of silence.

"I know!" Annie agreed. "She was always so nice, too!"

The conversation thankfully turned to happier topics. Annie told me a funny story about her younger sister getting busted by her mom for smoking pot, but that ended with Annie, her sister, and her mom all getting high together. "And you know me," Annie giggled, "I hardly ever get high! And I'm such a lightweight. All I did was laugh all night. And eat popcorn! We were all so silly!"

Even with the traffic we hit, time seemed to fly by with Annie next to me keeping the conversation moving. We soon pulled up in front of a really cool 1940s complex of what seemed like townhouses. Each unit had two floors and was like its own separate house, even though it was connected on each side to another similar apartment. They were almost like what you'd expect to find in a duplex or triplex, only there were at least a dozen or even fifteen units arranged in a U-shape around a central garden area that was planted with dozens of birds of paradise plants and mounds of red bougainvillea, all of which were spectacularly in bloom. There were two sets of stairs leading up from the street into the garden and the walkway that encircled the courtyard; we went left.

"This is so cool!" Annie marveled. "Whose place is this again?"

"Marco's uncle," I answered, looking up at what I could only describe as a small tower, or turret, on the side of one of the end units. It had a small, narrow window and a weathervane at the top.

As we approached the front door, we could hear that the party was in full swing. Even though we were right on time, people had evidently arrived early, and I felt a surge of disappointment and annoyance that Annie's mom had kept us for so long. I rang the bell several times. When no one answered, Annie tried the door and we walked right in. The first thing I saw was a group of people huddled around the coffee table in the den—Marco, Hank, Moose, Sven, Malinowski, a couple of other kids from school, and an adult who I presumed was Marco's uncle.

"Hey, Douglas!" Marco called out excitedly. "Hey, Annie! Come on in!" As we approached the table, I saw what could only be a small pile of cocaine spread out before them. Sven was leaning over with a rolled-up dollar bill and sniffing up a line of the white powder. He leaned his head back, and then shook his head wildly from side to side. "What a rush!"

Malinowski suddenly turned his head away from the table and sneezed.

"Holy shit!" Sven laughed maniacally. "You almost pulled a Woody Allen!"

"I turned my head!" Malinowski defended himself.

"Here, want to try something cool?" I heard Marco's uncle say. "Do this." He then proceeded to dab his pinkie along the edge of the pile of coke and then rub it along his teeth and gums. "It makes your teeth all numb and shit. You don't need much," he cautioned as Moose was about to stick *two* fingers directly into the pile.

Everyone followed suit. "Cool!" Moose said.

Andrew, who was standing behind the group with all of their dates but not participating, looked over at me and made the "crazy" signal by twirling his outstretched index finger next to his head. As far as I knew, this was the first time anyone from our group had tried coke. Sure, we all knew about it, but it was insanely expensive, and the opportunity just hadn't presented itself.

"Douglas, Annie, this is my uncle, Jerry," Marco said. "He's my mom's brother."

"The non-Italian side!" Jerry laughed, and then waved at us. "Nice to meet you."

"Thanks for having us," Annie smiled.

"Yeah, thanks so much," I added. "It's really cool of

you to do this." I glanced around at our group; everyone was looking sharp in their tuxes, though a bit wild-eyed from the coke. Their dates, who were chatting away with Andrew and each other, looked beautiful in their long gowns in various shades of pink, pale green, and yellow. Hank, much to everyone's surprise, had brought snobby Jessica Farmer. Marco had been seeing Elizabeth Blake for the past few months, so they were together tonight. Andrew, who could never get a date, had brought his cousin Andrea. Sven was with his longtime girlfriend Cecilia, while Malinowski was dateless. Moose, of course, was with Marcie, as planned.

"You guys want some?" Jerry asked, holding out the rolled-up dollar bill. Just then, a drop-dead gorgeous blonde emerged from the bathroom, a little unsteadily. I recognized her, but wasn't sure why, and then I remembered: Jerry worked in the movie business like his brother-in-law—Marco's dad—only he was a director, or at least an assistant director, anyway. I had heard he was always dating beautiful actresses, and this was obviously one of them, though I couldn't quite place her. She plopped down on the couch next to Jerry and placed her hand on his chest, running her fingers through his thick, golden chest hair. His shirt was unbuttoned down to his navel, and I spotted a gold chain with a gold spoon gleaming around his neck.

I hesitated and looked at my friends. Pot and alcohol, sure. And even though I'd never done either, I was cool with acid and mushrooms as well. To me, though, cocaine had always been more on the level of heroin and speed—until these last few years, when it had suddenly become the chichi drug of choice for seemingly all of Hollywood and rock and roll.

"Go for it, Douglas," Sven urged. "We've all tried it. It's no big deal."

When I looked at Hank, he just shrugged. "Your call ..."

"Sure," I said, "why not? It's prom night, right? Annie, do you want any?"

"No, thanks," she replied. "You go ahead."

Hank slid over and made room for me on the couch. Jerry chopped up the powder with the edge of a razor blade, made a small thin line, and handed me the rolled-up dollar bill, which I noticed was actually a fifty-dollar bill. "We'll start you off small," he said. "Do half of that line up one nostril, and then the other half up the other nostril. Like this." He proceeded to demonstrate on the line he had just created for me. "Sorry, I bogarted your line!" he laughed, a little too loudly, before making me another one.

Within seconds after I had snorted the powder up my nose, I knew exactly what Sven had been talking about: what a rush! It was exhilarating, totally different from pot. I could immediately sense why this shit had become so popular—hell, half the guys in the NBA were rumored to be doing it—and clearly understood why it could also turn into a very big problem for some people. Fortunately, my friends and I didn't have enough money to get addicted to coke, so I doubted we'd be doing it again any time soon. On this night, however, we each did several lines, and by the time we were ready to leave for the prom, we were all high as a kite from the combination of coke, pot, and the Dom Perignon champagne Uncle Jerry had generously donated for the occasion and that flowed freely throughout the pre-party.

"Do you want me to drive?" Annie asked as we stumbled back down the walkway leading from the party to our car.

"Are you kidding? How many glasses of champagne did you have?"

"I don't know," Annie giggled, leaning into me hard. "I lost count after the fourth one."

"Fortunately, it's only a few minutes away. We'll make it. I took a couple of hits off of that joint they were passing around right before we left. I'm good."

"Great," Annie rolled her eyes as I opened the door to the Z to let her in. After closing her door, I practically danced around the front of the car on my way to the driver's side, laughing with Annie as she watched from the window and saw me knock my knee into the front bumper, where it stuck out a bit unexpectedly from the stylish front end of the car.

"Ouch!" I cried.

Annie covered her mouth with her delicate hands. "Are you okay?" she exclaimed with genuine concern, followed once again by her special smile and laugh. I felt my heart melting; in that moment I could've sworn I was Paul Newman to her Katharine Ross in the bicycle scene from *Butch Cassidy and the Sundance Kid.*

I slid into the driver's seat, leaned over, and gave Annie the biggest, wettest kiss of my life. "Whoa, now, cowboy!" she turned away after several long, luscious moments. "You're gonna mess up my makeup." She pulled down the visor and checked herself in the mirror, once again using her pinkie to try and patch up whatever I had just done to her lips. She sighed and reached into her small Gucci clutch to search for her lipstick while glancing at me sideways, pretending to be annoyed when she was actually amused, amused and in love with me at the same time. She shook the bag, momentarily frustrated, before fishing the lipstick out from the bottom.

"What the heck do you have in there?" I asked, pointing at her purse and then glancing into the side mirror before pulling out into traffic. "Your entire bathroom?" Her dad had given her that clutch for her sixteenth birthday, and while I didn't dig the green-and-red stripes, I knew it was special to her.

"My momma always taught me that a girl's gotta be prepared, silly!" Annie responded with a faux Southern accent.

"All right, Scarlett," I joked.

Within what seemed like seconds we pulled up to the front of the Hilton and handed over my stepmom's precious Z to a valet guy, who—based on the smile on his face—looked like he was definitely going to take it for a joyride at some point during the evening. We walked through the lobby and followed the signs announcing Woodrow Wilson Prom until we arrived at one of the hotel's many ballrooms. The strains of KC and the Sunshine Band's "That's the Way (I Like It)" blasted through the walls, and when we opened the doors and entered the room, it was a kaleidoscope of colored laser beams and disco balls, all with a bunch of stoned, drunk, or otherwise high seventeen- and eighteen-year-olds gettin' down and boogeying. Hey, disco was done, and I was never into it anyway, but if you wanted to just have fun and dance, it was tough to beat.

"Look," I said, pointing across the room to where Hank and Moose were standing with Jessica and Marcie. "That must be our table over there."

"Go ahead," Annie said as she kissed my cheek. "I'm going to run to the bathroom."

"Okay. Meet you at the table?"

"You betcha." Annie winked and sashayed off, while my heart swelled with pride. Damn she looked fine tonight.

As I made my way over to my friends, I spotted Genevieve. True to her independent nature, after I told her that Annie and I had worked things out, she decided to go to the prom without a date and was now standing with a group of teachers—including Ms. Pearlstein—engaged in an animated discussion. I decided now would be as good a time as any to say hello.

"Hey Genevieve!" I called out as I approached her.

"Hi Douglas!" Genevieve's eyes lit up and she immediately gave me a hug. "Are you having fun? Where's Annie?" Her eyes searched over my shoulders.

"She ran to the bathroom. We just got here," I explained. "Are you having a good time?"

"Absolutely! We were just discussing Margaret Thatcher becoming Prime Minister and how that might affect next year's Presidential election." She turned and gestured to the group of teachers surrounding her, who returned my gaze with expectant eyes.

"Well," I stammered, trying my hardest to be witty and smart. "I guess it's not a matter of if, but when will we elect a woman as President?"

"That's exactly what I just said!" Genevieve marveled.

"You two are like two peas in a pod," Ms. Pearlstein teased. Turning to the other teachers in the group, she said, "I've gotten to know these kids pretty darn well over the last few years." The other teachers nodded knowingly.

"I hope that was a good thing!" I laughed, and everyone laughed with me. Turning to leave, I said, "Thanks for everything, Ms. Pearlstein. Enjoy the rest of the evening," I smiled at the teachers.

"Oh, can't you join us for a little longer?" Genevieve asked.

Looking directly into her warm eyes, I quietly replied, "I'm really glad you came. It was great seeing you. But I better get back to Annie."

"Of course. I understand. See you soon, okay?" She grabbed my hand lightly between the palms of her hands. Her fingers were soft and long and I noticed a small scar on the back of her wrist.

"Absolutely," I replied, and then headed over to my table.

The rest of the night was a blur of overcooked chicken, spilled drinks—it seemed like everyone and their mother had snuck in small bottles or flasks of every type of liquor under the sun—and sweaty dancing to the likes of "Le Freak," "Super Freak," "Stayin' Alive," "Funkytown," "Boogie Oogie Oogie," and "Dancing Queen." By the time the actually-pretty-good cover band launched into "We Are Family" to end the evening, it seemed like the whole senior class was on the dance floor, throwing their hands up and around while shouting the chorus joyously in unison. It didn't seem like we'd been all that tight these past few years, but now, looking back on everything that we'd been through and accomplished—some of us had been together since junior high and others since grammar school—we reveled in our ties, celebrated how lucky we were to have survived to this point when many we knew had not, and for this special evening, anyway, we were one. As my hero Muhammed Ali so famously said: "Me / We." What a high.

Sven took a photo that night and made a bunch of copies and gave them to all of us a few days later. In the shot, Hank is seated at the table, where half-drunk glasses of smuggled liquor and Coke or 7 Up are scattered around. Someone—we think it was Marco, but Sven always claimed it was his idea—has poured a bunch of either salt or sugar (again, the point has been hotly debated ever since) on a long, flat knife and is holding it up to Hank, who's glancing at the camera, wide-eyed and with a huge smile on his face, as if he's about to snort the longest, thickest line of cocaine ever put in front of anyone, anywhere. For some reason, that shot always seemed to sum up the night. I did feel sorry for Hank, though: Who knew where that photo could show up one day? And even though it's obviously a joke to us, it might not seem that way to someone else, especially if they were your coach or your boss or your future wife or something.

As for Annie and I, we had a blast. We danced our butts off, laughed at the bad food, and each spent time gossiping with our friends, sometimes on opposite sides of the room, but always keeping an eye on one another. She would wink at me sexily as our eyes met from wherever it was we happened to be standing, and I would smile back and blow her a kiss.

But perhaps the highlight of the night came after a string of disco hits and before the last build-up to the "We Are Family" climax. We were sitting back down at the table, picking at our desserts—something that seemed to be somewhere between Jell-O and flan on the disappointing custard dessert scale. The band had calmed things down, pretty much clearing the dance floor with the exception of a few diehards for a particularly vapid cover of the Little River Band's "Lady." When the strains of America's "I Need You" started, I shared a knowing glance with Hank, who had his arm wrapped sloppily around Jessica. It seemed painfully obvious to the both of us that the lead singer had cut a deal with the band for a "mini-set" just before the final few dance tunes of the evening. He probably argued that the partygoers would need a rest before they launched into the final series of frenzied hits. Or threatened to quit the band if he didn't get his moment in the spotlight.

Hank and I then shared a laugh as Marcie pulled Moose onto the dance floor for a slow dance to what was undoubtedly America's most banal song. I glanced down at Annie and pulled her close, happy she wasn't the type of girl who'd pull me out on the floor for such a lame tune. But when the girl back-up singer stepped into the spotlight with a fairly soulful version of Maria Muldaur's "Midnight at the Oasis," Annie grabbed my hand and led me onto the dance floor. I actually didn't mind at all because this was a pretty sexy song, which meant that Annie and I'd be doing some deep body-locking action.

Within moments we were in each other's arms, holding each other as tightly as can be, my sheikh to her belly dancer. A few other couples had also joined the original die-hards, but there was still plenty of space on the wooden floor, enough that we could get lost in our own world and in each other's eyes. I was intoxicated by the smell of Annie's sandalwood perfume, the back-up singer doing a damn good impression of Maria, my hand caressing Annie's spectacular butt, her hand caressing my cheek. . . .

My head was swirling; the combination of everything I'd ingested over the course of the evening colliding with love and lust on the dance floor brought about a peak experience, right then, right there, in that very moment. *Why couldn't we always be like this?* I thought to myself. Pure magic.

Which made what happened only a half-hour or so later all the more devastating.

It began in the car, on the way to Larry's apartment from the hotel. We had all left the prom together and were traveling up the San Diego Freeway in a long line; there must have been eight or ten cars in total, and everyone was following me. While we were driving, Annie decided to change into some casual clothes that I had assumed she'd brought for the following morning after we'd spent the night at Larry's.

"What are you doing?" I asked as she pulled the top of her dress down to her waist, revealing her bra.

"This dress is so damn uncomfortable. I couldn't wait to get out of it."

"But everyone's still going to be all dressed up," I argued. "You'll be the only one who's changed."

"So?" Annie said, continuing to strip.

"I think they can see you," I said, looking in my rearview mirror at Hank and Jessica, who were driving behind us in Hank's Camaro.

Annie turned around and looked out the Z's sloped back window, which was covered with black louvers. "No, they can't, silly," Annie said. Within a few moments, she was in jeans and a green top. I had to hand it to her: she pulled off that outfit change like a magician in a box. Our ears were both ringing, and we drove in silence for a minute or two.

"I told you it wasn't that big of a deal," Annie suddenly said.

"What's that?" I asked.

"The prom," she said, pulling a small hairbrush out of her clutch and brushing her long, dark hair. "It's just another party."

It felt like an arrow to my heart. Here I had experienced one of the greatest nights of my life, something I would treasure forever, and Annie had tossed it into the dumpster as "just another party." I couldn't even respond.

"I mean, it was fun," Annie said, still focused on brushing her hair and not noticing the carnage she had wrought, which I'm sure was plainly visible on my face. "But, you know, nothing that special, right?"

"Yeah," I managed to mumble. "I guess."

"What's the matter?" Annie asked, finally sensing my hurt.

"I don't know. I had a really good time. I thought it *was* actually kind of special."

"Well, of course it was, Mr. Magoo!" She leaned over and kissed me on the neck. "I loved being there with you." She ran her fingers through my hair. "It's just, you know, there was so much drama leading up to tonight. I'm just saying it wasn't really worth it."

"Yeah, I guess," I said, still not understanding what she was actually trying to tell me.

The rest of the night didn't go much better. By the time everybody parked and made it up to Larry's apartment and got settled, it was almost 2:00 AM and everyone's energy level had plummeted. I put on some music—Al Green seemed to be a good choice, mellow but groovy—and we lit a few joints, but the conversation gradually grew quiet once we had all shared our best gossip from the evening: who was seen cheating on whom, who was seen fighting, who was seen throwing up in the bathroom . . . that sort of thing. Annie had been particularly silent for nearly the whole after-party, when she suddenly broke a fairly long lull in the conversation with, "I wish Kenny were here."

The other girls in the room gasped and looked directly at me with both concern and pity in their eyes. Hank and the guys just looked at the floor and shook their heads. I was dumbfounded, speechless.

"I mean, you know . . ." Annie looked up, a bit panicked now that she realized she'd said something out loud that she'd probably been meaning to keep silent in her head. "He's always the life of the party, that's all. We could use his energy!" She smiled, trying to keep it light, but the damage had been done.

"Whatever," Jessica said, looking at Hank and giving him the "Let's get out of here" head nod toward the door.

Andrew looked at his watch; it was now after 3:00 AM. "I think it's time to go," was all he said. The others gradually followed suit, and within fifteen minutes, the party had cleared out. That was it. The night was over. Well, almost.

"That was fun," Annie said after Hank and Jessica, the last couple to leave, walked out the door.

"Was it?" I asked sharply.

"Oh, come on, don't be like that." Annie came over and hugged me, kissing me on the lips and running her hand over my crotch.

"I can't believe you said that about Kenny, Annie!"

"I'm sorry. I didn't mean anything by it. Sometimes these things just come out of my mouth. I don't know why, but I can't help myself." She had begun to tear up.

"Well, maybe you should learn some restraint," I said unsympathetically.

She removed her hand from my crotch, grabbed my hand, and led me down the short hallway to the one bedroom in Larry's small apartment. "Come on, Douglas," she teased, "be nice to me, and I'll be nice to you."

We sat down on the edge of the bed, but I just couldn't do it. Sensing my distance after a few minutes of rather passionless making out, Annie said, "Do you want to take me home?"

"Maybe it'd be for the best," I admitted. "It's pretty late, anyway."

We got our stuff together and left the apartment; the walk to the car was just as quiet as the drive home. I turned on the radio to try and provide some sort of a distraction, but I couldn't focus on any of the songs that played. Annie just softly cried the whole sorry ride home, her head leaning against the passenger-side window—cool and cold I'm sure, from the damp, late night/early morning air.

Needless to say, that was pretty much the end of the line for me and Annie. The first week after prom, we had long conversations over the phone: What had gone wrong on prom night? What could we do better going forward? How much Annie loved me. How she had started to see a therapist. How much she was going to miss me when I moved to San Diego.

"You know," Annie said at one point, "my dad said that instead of going to Pierce, I could move to San Diego and enroll at Grossmont."

By this point, I had not only grown tired of the conversations about "our relationship," I had also grown tired of Annie. Did I really want her to come and live in San Diego? If I were honest with myself, the answer was an unqualified "no." I was ready for a new start, a fresh beginning. I wanted to play the field, meet some new girls, have the full-on college experience. Having Annie down in San Diego would only compromise all of that, and only bring me more pain and confusion. Sure, I still loved her, but she had chipped away at that passion, and by now I didn't think I had any left, no matter how much it hurt to think about not being with her anymore.

I found myself avoiding Annie at school, refusing to take her phone calls and not bothering to call her back when she left a message. I threw myself into work, often staying past 5:00 to earn a little extra money and complete extra assignments I had asked to be given. My dad was super proud of me.

"Son," he said to me one night when I joined him and Cindy for dinner, "I've been hearing good reports from Tim Johnston. He said Larry and Glen have both told him what a great job you've been doing and how hard you've been working lately."

"Thanks, Dad. I'm really enjoying the experience."

"That's wonderful, Son. Tim's a great mentor for you."

Tim Johnston was Larry and Glen's boss. A week or so ago, he had called me into his office. The door was shut, and I heard voices behind it. When I knocked softly, they bade me to come in.

"Hey, Douglas, you hungry?" Tim asked. He had a gigantic head of hair, feathered like mine, only sandy blond and with about twice the volume of my mane. "We're going to drive down to Pink's for an extended lunch."

Even though I had already eaten a sandwich on my

way over from school, I felt like I couldn't say no to my boss. "I can always eat!" I said enthusiastically. We took off and drove deep into L.A. for a classic Angeleno treat: Pink's hot dogs. The line was long, as usual, and by the time we ate our dogs and drove back to the office, it was nearly 4:00 in the afternoon. Nobody had seemed to notice we were missing and, heeding my brother's advice, I never said anything to my dad: What he didn't know wouldn't hurt him. If he was happy with the job Tim was doing, who was I to pop his balloon?

I had heard rumors that Tim had a nasty cocaine habit—part of the reason the normally laid-back dude could occasionally be an absolute terror as a boss. I remember one time when Larry hadn't finished a report Tim needed and Tim absolutely tore Larry a new asshole. He was screaming so loudly, my dad came running down the hall to see what was up and then called Tim into his office and gave him a lecture about the proper way to handle his staff. Nevertheless, sales had increased nearly 25 percent since Tim had taken on his role as VP of sales and marketing, so my dad was willing to put up with his at-times erratic behavior. My dad just chalked it up to Tim's focus, intensity, and passion for the job; everyone else knew his volatile behavior was simply the coke demon gaining control.

One day I went to hit the Sparkletts bottle in Yvonne's office. When I arrived, Yvonne and Nicole were chatting at Yvonne's desk. "And then you pop the capsule right as you're about to cum and it's like the biggest explosion you've ever felt in your life," Yvonne laughed, then stopped herself as she finally noticed me at the water cooler. "Oh, hi, Douglas," she giggled.

"Hey Douglas, you ever tried a popper?" Nicole asked.

"A what?"

"Oh, leave him alone, Nicole. He's much too young for you."

"I don't know about that," Nicole teased. "I'd have you." She arched her eyebrows in a way that simply defined sexy. I looked at her, speechless. On a scale of one to ten, Nicole, with her absolutely perfect body, gorgeously tan skin, and long blonde hair, was a sixteen.

"You better be careful, girl," Yvonne warned. "That's the boss's little boy you're talking to over there."

"He's not so little." Nicole gave me the full, obvious once-over, stopping her pale green eyes for a few moments while looking directly at my cock, which was now getting hard and visible in my tight jeans.

"Honey," Yvonne laughed, "talk about jailbait. Hey, Douglas, you even eighteen yet?"

"No, I-I just turned seventeen," I stammered, feeling my face turning beet red.

"I'm telling you, girl, you better stay away from this young man!" Yvonne shook her head, turned her chair toward her desk, and went back to work.

Nicole picked up the ends of her hair and turned her gaze toward them as if she were looking for split ends. There were none visible that I could see. Glancing back up at me, she cooed, "Always a pleasure to see you, Douglas." With that, she winked at me, turned, and walked out of the room.

By now the water from the Sparkletts bottle was overflowing my cup. "Oh shit," I exclaimed as I felt the water spilling over my hands. I turned off the spigot and headed back toward my office; I could hear Yvonne quietly laughing as I left the room.

"What happened to you?" Glen asked, gesturing to my pants. It wasn't until then that I noticed the water had also spilled onto my right thigh.

"I got distracted," I mumbled.

"Look at him," Larry said, "he's all hot and flushed."

"I walked in on Yvonne and Nicole talking about sex and drugs and then Nicole flirted with me!" I blurted out.

"Ha!" Glen laughed. "I wouldn't get your hopes up. She's flirted with every guy who's ever set foot through the front door of this place. She's all talk and no action."

"Well, I don't know about that," Larry offered, leaning back in his chair and looking like the cat who swallowed the canary.

"Oh, give me a fucking break, Larry. Only in your dreams would Nicole fuck you."

"I never kiss and tell," Larry smiled. He took a long, slow drag on his cigarette, blew a cloud of smoke into the air, and returned to his work while chuckling to himself in that rough smoker's laugh of his.

God damn, adults are fucked up, was all I that I could think to myself.

Sometimes, while driving home from work, I'd find myself behind Glen and his 1974 Hornet. It had a bright-red paint job and pair of white racing stripes that ran from behind the back passenger windows all the way down and through the doors, flowing directly over the door handles on their way to the very edge of the front quarter-panel, where the stripes narrowed into sharp points. It was an impossible car to miss. Glen lived in Canoga Park but, like me, preferred to take the backstreets home instead of sitting on the Ventura Freeway.

It was a Friday night in early May, and I knew Glen was

in a good mood; he had a hot date scheduled for tomorrow night and had been talking about it all week long. Suddenly, without any signal or warning at all, Glen yanked the Hornet over to the curb. I pulled up beside him, and as he rolled down his window, I reached across the passenger seat and did likewise.

"I LOVE THIS SONG!" he screamed. Cranking his car stereo to what must have been eleven, he jumped out of his car and started rocking out to "Sultans of Swing." Of course, Hank and I had already been turned on to Dire Straits since the record was released last October, but "Sultans" had finally settled into the top of the charts in just the last couple of months. Glen was obviously a bit late to the party, but I admired his taste, nevertheless. It *was* a great song.

"What station?" I yelled.

"KLOS!"

I turned my dial from KROQ to KLOS, cranked up the tune, and Glen and I rocked out right there on Rosita, Glen jamming away in the street while I played air guitar in my seat. Cars had to drive around us, the various drivers giving us the stink eye as they slowed their speed and drifted by. When the song ended, I waved goodbye and shouted, "That was fun!" As I rolled the passenger window back up, I yelled, "Good luck tomorrow night!"

Glen flashed me the peace sign before reaching into his car to turn down the radio, which was now blasting the Doobie Brothers' "What a Fool Believes" at full volume. It was funny: Music had really undergone a significant change this past year, and I found myself listening to KROQ instead of KLOS or KMET, where the bands were starting to seem a little stale, a little old. KROQ offered a host of new bands and new sounds, and they were playing some incredible stuff: the Clash, Talking Heads, the Cars, Elvis Costello, the Police, Devo . . . my friends and I were really digging the new music. "New wave," people were calling it. My brother and sister's generation belonged to bands like the Beatles and the Stones; sure, David had tried punk rock on for size for about a minute, but by now he had dismissed the whole scene as "a bunch of poseurs" and was back to listening to the rock and roll of his youth. But these new wave bands were *our* bands, and there was something pretty cool about that. It was like it was finally time for my generation to get its own identity, its own music, out of the shadow of the sixties.

The final weeks of school slowly wound down to the end. Annie and I had officially called it quits, both agreeing it was for the best. I was hurting, but there was so much going on in my life at that point, what with work, and graduation, and college and all, that I fortunately didn't have a lot of time to dwell on Annie and feel sorry for myself, though I certainly had my share of down moments.

A few days before the end of the year, Ms. Pearlstein saw me during lunch and essentially ordered me to come see her in her classroom after school.

"Jeez," Hank said as Ms. Pearlstein walked away, "I wonder what that's about."

"I don't know," I said. "Probably some last-minute assignment she wants to give me."

I thought I had turned in my last piece for the newspaper a week ago—a hard news article about the gas crisis and how it was affecting local drivers—and she had praised me for it. "This is some excellent reporting, Douglas. You've really captured the frustration of the drivers."

"Yeah," I had joked, "though it almost cost me my life."
I was referring to the one angry dude in a pick-up truck
who told me to fuck off and mind my own business when
I approached him as he waited in a long line of cars at a
gas station on Ventura, hoping to ask him a few questions.
Fortunately, most of the other drivers were more than
happy to vent their frustrations *to* me, not *at* me, and I had
gotten some great quotes for the story.

"Hi, Ms. Pearlstein," I greeted her as I entered her
classroom after school that day, "you wanted to see me?"

"Hi, Douglas!" she said warmly, smiling. "Come in. I
have some very good news for you, young man."

"Oh yeah? What's that?"

"Well," Ms. Pearlstein said, resting on the corner
of her desk and adjusting the frames of her rather large
glasses, "I spoke with the faculty advisor for the *Daily Aztec*
and told him all about you."

"You did?"

"I did, indeed," Ms. Pearlstein responded happily. "I
sent him some of your clips, in particular that recent story you wrote on the gas shortage, and he not only thought
they were excellent reporting, he asked if I thought you
might be interested in working for the paper starting this
summer."

"You're kidding!" I blurted out.

"I'm not kidding at all," Ms. Pearlstein laughed.
"You're a very talented journalist, Douglas."

"Wow. Why this summer?"

"He—Mr. Adams is his name—said they always bring
in cubs over the summer so that they are ready to go once
school starts."

"Wait," I said, wanting to make sure I was hearing her

correctly, "you mean he's also going to offer me a position on the paper when school starts?"

"Well, I guess that all depends on how things go this summer but, yes, I believe that is his intention. He'd like you to start the week after the Fourth of July, on July ninth, I think he said."

"Wow," I repeated. I was shell-shocked. This was a lot to absorb. I'd have to quit my job at my dad's. And where would I live?

"I know this is relatively short notice, but you think about it, Douglas. I told him you would call him by the end of the week." She handed me a slip of paper with Mr. Adams' phone number on it. "It's an *excellent* opportunity."

I glanced at the number with its 714 area code and then looked up at her. "Oh, I know," I said, my excitement growing by the second. "Thank you so much, Ms. Pearlstein. I really appreciate what you've done for me."

"It's my pleasure, Douglas. You're the one who did all of the hard work. Congratulations," she smiled. "I'll see you at graduation on Friday."

I walked out of her classroom as if I were floating on a cloud. Working for the *Daily Aztec* over the summer sounded like a great way to start my college education, and the more I thought about it, the more stoked I became. I just hoped my dad, who wasn't entirely supportive of my nascent journalism career, would allow me to go. *Maybe I could live with Julie*, I thought to myself. Dad would like that; he was always trying to bring his sons and daughter closer together, and firmly believed the three of us needed to remain tight so that we'd always be there for one another.

When I brought it up to him the next day at dinner

at his house, Dad was not thrilled I'd be giving up two months working for his company for what was essentially a non-paying job at a college newspaper. "I know, they give you a stipend," he railed, "but that's peanuts compared to what you've been earning working for me."

"But Dad, it'll be great experience, and I'll still come back and work for you every summer." I had landed a body punch—he was wavering—and now I came in for the knockout: "Besides, just think how great it'll be for me and Julie to live together for part of the summer. It'll be an opportunity for us to really get to know each other, to grow closer." I was laying it on thick.

"Have you talked to her yet?"

"No, I wanted to talk to you first. But I'm sure she'll be excited to have me there."

"I don't know," my dad rubbed his chin. "She's got that boyfriend and everything."

"Yeah, but he has his own place," I argued.

"Okay, look, Son, if Julie says it's okay, then I'll support the plan. I like the idea of you spending more time with your sister." Bingo. Mission accomplished. With Dad's stamp of approval, there wasn't a chance Julie would say no, boyfriend or no boyfriend.

I got home early enough from Dad's house that I immediately called Julie.

"Hello?" she answered.

"Hey Julie," I said.

"Who's this? Douglas?"

"Yeah, it's me."

"Hi. Is everything okay?"

"Yeah, of course. How are you?"

"Fine. How are you?"

"Great! Listen, my journalism teacher got in touch with the faculty advisor for the newspaper at SDSU, and they've offered me a job starting in July. Dad thinks it's a great idea and asked me to ask you if I could stay with you for a month or so until I can move into the dorm."

"He did? Dad said that?"

"Yeah. Why, is it not cool?"

"No, no, it's cool. I'd love to have you. It's just a bit un-expected, that's all. And there's Michael and everything."

"Yeah, I wondered about him. How's that going?"

"Great, it's going great. You'll get to know him. You'll like him."

"Cool. He's got his own place, too, right?"

"Yeah, yeah, he does."

"Cool. So, okay, I guess I'll be in touch when it gets closer to July."

"Great. Hey—have fun at graduation. Sorry I won't be able to make it up."

"Thanks. No worries. It'll probably be chaos out there anyway, knowing our class."

"Oh—I forgot to ask," Julie said, sounding a bit con-cerned. "Mom said that Lassie hasn't been doing too well."

"Yeah, she's definitely getting old. She's slowed down a lot and is on a bunch of medications. You might want to get up here sooner rather than later if you want to see her one more time."

"Seriously?"

"You never know," I said. This was partially true—L had been aging fairly rapidly as of late—but I also knew my mom wanted Julie to come up and visit pretty badly.

"Okay, I'll come up soon."

"Cool," I said.

After we hung up, I made plans with myself to call the faculty advisor for the *Daily Aztec* and accept the position. I went to bed that night knowing that my life would soon take a drastic turn. A new chapter was going to open, and while I was nervous about what it would bring, the palpable sense of excitement I felt at the unknown kept me awake until 3:00 AM. Sure, I occasionally started to obsess about Annie, but honestly, I felt like I was in a good place, with an open road ahead of me. I'd be throwing caution to the wind and allowing the fates to deliver whatever it was they had in store for me.

The day of graduation, I was a bit nervous. Even though Annie and I were officially broken up, my love for her still gnawed away at my stomach from time to time; I was still "getting over her," as my mom would tell me during those moments when I felt weak, sad, and confused. What would happen tonight? Would I see her? What would we say to each other? In the end, Annie didn't even bother to show up, which was so much like her since she didn't give a shit about school and had been planning on attending Pierce Junior College since the time she was in junior high.

As expected, Woodrow Wilson's graduation, which had grown increasingly rowdy over the past few years to the point where parents had really started to voice their disapproval, reached a new low that night. Gone were suits and ties beneath the gowns in exchange for shorts, bikinis, swim trunks, T-shirts, and flip-flops. People wore funky hats, pieces of art, and sculptures on their heads. The cloud of smoke emanating from the football field up into the air was plainly, plainly visible to every mom, dad, sister, brother, aunt, uncle, and cousin sitting in the stands. There were well over a thousand of us packed onto the grass, and it basically looked like a Grateful Dead concert, or maybe a "Day on the Green."

There were balloons and streamers and confetti; Frisbees flew across the field throughout the ceremony; some kids had smuggled their ghetto blasters under there gowns, and strains of rock and roll echoed from various parts of the field, making it difficult to hear the speeches, not that anyone was listening anyway. There were even a couple of people on stilts, dressed in their caps and gowns! And, of course, everyone, and I mean everyone, carried a red plastic cup in their hand filled with whatever liquor happened to be passing across the row when their cup was empty. There must've been a couple thousand bottles on the absolutely destroyed football field by the end of the evening.

"What a disgrace," both my mom and dad said afterward.

"I agree," Art added. "The principal should be strung up by his balls."

I shrugged. *Hey, this is where you guys chose to send me to school,* I wanted to say. Instead I just said, "I guess it's just a sign of the times," in a bid to calm them down, though even I didn't really know what I meant.

"It was an abomination," my mom insisted in a tsk-tsk manner. "And you were all guilty. Even you, Douglas." She shook her head with dismay, but then laughed and hugged me. "But I still love you and congratulations, my beautiful son."

Everybody joined in—David, my dad, Cindy, Art, and my mom—with hugs and handshakes all around. Since all of us going out to dinner was never going to happen—it was amazing that my mom and Cindy remained civil for the five or ten minutes we were all together after the graduation—we had agreed to do two separate celebratory dinners on Saturday and Sunday nights, leaving me free to join my friends at one of the many after-parties that were going on that evening. A couple of the guys—Andrew and Sven—would be late because they couldn't get out of family dinner celebrations that night, but Hank, Marco, Moose, and I had all managed to free ourselves for the whole evening, so I quickly expedited the goodbyes to my family so that I could meet up with the gang in the parking lot.

"Well, thanks for coming," I said, once the initial euphoria of the occasion began to fade and the old tension between my mom, my dad, and Cindy began to rise up into the air. "I'm looking forward to seeing you tomorrow night," I said to my dad and Cindy.

"Okay, Son." My dad gave me a hug. "I'm proud of you."

"Thanks, Dad. Bye, Cindy." I leaned in for a kiss on the cheek.

"Bye, Douglas. Congratulations."

"See you, squirt," David said in his best Eddie Haskell impression. Then, switching to Ward, he shook my hand firmly and smiled warmly. "Welcome to your college years."

"Hopefully they'll be a bit more productive than his were," my dad cracked, pointing at David.

"Was that really necessary?" my mom shot back at my dad.

"Okay, okay, let's not end this way." I knew this situation had to be diffused pronto, so I stepped into the middle of our little pack. "Goodnight, everyone! Mom, Art—I'll see you in the morning." I walked toward them and essentially herded them away. When I looked over my shoulder, I saw Cindy leading my dad in the opposite direction. David was heading away from everyone, to the students' parking lot on the other side of Winnetka, I guessed. His shoulders were sagging a little and his head was down.

"Hey, Mom, Art—I'm going to go check on David."

"Okay. Sorry, Douglas. I love you." My mom sincerely seemed ashamed that the evening had ended on a bit of a sour note.

"Don't worry about it, Mom," I said as I turned and jogged over to David.

"Hey David! Hey! Wait up."

David turned and stopped.

"You okay?"

"What the fuck?" David said, visibly upset. "Why does he always have to make cracks like that? Nothing I ever do is good enough for him."

"You know what I've finally realized, David?"

"What's that?

"Remember when you told me about how fucked up all the adults at work were gonna be? Well, our parents are human beings just like those guys, and like all human beings, they aren't perfect. In fact, they have a ton of faults and are pretty fucked up, just like you and me and all of our friends. I think we expect our parents to be these perfect people, but they're not."

"Well, that's pretty fucking obvious!" David laughed, and I laughed with him.

"And, by the way, you were right about everyone at work. Talk about a bunch of fucked-up people!"

"The whole world is fucked up," David said resignedly.

"Then maybe you should just try cutting Mom and Dad some slack. They're going to make mistakes, say stupid shit. They're not perfect."

"Yeah, maybe. But since they're the ones who've been telling us what to do our whole lives, don't they have a responsibility to not be fuck-ups?"

"Well, I guess so. But who says they're not trying their best, you know? And that's really all we can ask of them."

I don't know if I convinced David of anything that night, or if he changed in any way, but I was glad we had the conversation, and things did seem to immediately improve between my mom and dad and David after that evening. David became a little less judgmental, a little slower to get angry at some perceived slight, even a bit more understanding. Gone were the days when dinners with David, me, and either my mom or my dad ended with David rushing out the door after one silly argument or another, and in its place were what seemed like dinners straight out of *Father Knows Best*. Life in the extended Efron households was peaceful for the first time since the divorce. Even my mom and dad were getting along, and there was talk of all of us getting together for Thanksgiving this year, though who would host was still up in the air.

"I'm not giving up Thanksgiving," my mom declared, drawing a line in the sand from the get-go. "She can have Christmas," she'd barb, a more-than-obvious dig at the fact that my dad had married a "shiksa," as my mom would often snidely remark.

The graduation after-party was not far from where Moose and I lived. Carrie Weinstein had a nice home right above the Stromness golf course. From pretty much the moment we got there, Hank, Marco, Moose, and I commandeered the fire pit overlooking one of the fairways you could just barely make out down in the darkness below. And when Andrew, and then Sven, eventually arrived with Malinowski in tow, they joined us. A few people meandered over during the night, but mostly it was just the seven of us around the gas pit.

"Rumor has it that Ali is finally going to retire for good," Hank said.

"Thank God," I replied.

"He's been getting pummeled ever since the Norton fight," Marco pointed out.

"It's been sad to watch," Hank sighed.

Ali was my hero. Hank's hero. Hell, *everyone's* hero. You could already tell that boxing had taken its toll on him. His movements in the ring had slowed, from his footwork to his jabs. Even his speech seemed to slow. Any more damage to his brain or his body and it would surely become tragic.

"Hey. Do you want to go see *Rocky II* when it comes out next week?" Moose asked no one in particular.

"I'm so sick of all these fucking 'Part 2' movies," Andrew fumed. "They should've called it a day after *Godfather*. Total aberration. There will never be another number two that's better than the original. Not a movie, a book, an album, a play . . . nothing. Never again."

"Tell us how you really feel, Andrew," I joked.

"What's wrong with sequels?" Moose asked.

"Name me five sequels other than *The Godfather* that have been worth the price of buying a ticket," Andrew challenged.

"*Jaws II*," Hank shouted.

"*French Connection II*," Moose followed suit.

"Oh, come on!" Andrew interjected.

"*Exorcist II*," Malinowski stood up to announce, his belly hanging over his low-waisted jeans.

"*Diamonds Are Forever*," Marco continued the game.

"That doesn't count," Andrew insisted. "How obvious that you'd pick a stunt movie."

"What do you mean it doesn't count?" Marco rose up, beer in hand, in an almost threatening manner if he hadn't been so wobbly on his feet.

"Sit down, big boy," Andrew said coolly. "Bond is a franchise. It's a different animal."

"Can you believe this guy?" Marco slurred as he plopped back down on the low brick wall encircling the pit area. "He's always got rules, always got little ins and outs."

"And this is why Andrew is going to be an attorney," Moose said in the tone of a mother speaking to a five-year-old.

"I got one!" I said. "*Dawn of the Dead*."

"How the fuck is that a sequel?" Andrew laughed as if I were an idiot.

"The first one was *Night of the Living Dead*," I said smugly. "Gotta love the Z Channel!"

"Give me a break. *Night of the Living Dead* came out, like, ten years before *Dawn of the Dead*. That doesn't count as a sequel." Andrew once again argued as only a future lawyer could.

"See what I mean?" Marco took another big swig from his Foster's and gestured up into the air with both arms held high above his head, almost as if he were being asked to put his hands up by the cops. God, he was shit-faced.

"Everyone knows it's all about the money, but they're

just giving the people what they want," Marco spouted with all of the drunken bravado of someone whose dad was "in the industry."

Sven, who had by now fixed his stoned and drunken gaze on the gas flames of the pit—he rarely smoked pot— very thoughtfully offered, "For my money, you can't beat the *Pink Panther* sequels." Looking up from the fire and around the pit at each of us, in a deadly serious tone he said, "And I'll tell you what . . . I'll watch any of the *Planet of the Apes* sequels anytime, anywhere."

There was a unanimous murmur of consent from everybody seated around the pit. "When the man is right," Hank said, looking at Andrew, the only one who didn't react to Sven's pronouncement, "the man is right."

"Okay, okay," said Andrew, in a surprisingly magnanimous—for him, anyway—gesture, "I'm going to revise my statement." Now he was starting to slur his words, and I'd never seen Andrew drunk. "Any movie besides *The Godfather* and *Jaws* that has a '2' after it, automatically sucks. If you can't come up with a decent title for your sequel, then you probably shouldn't be making it anyway."

"Well, I'm still going to go see *Rocky II* next week, so if anyone wants to join me, let me know," Moose offered calmly, staring up into the sky.

As we all followed his gaze, we could see the smoke from the fire pit heading toward the stars above. It was a clear night, and being on the edge of the golf course, there wasn't a lot of light around us. With no moon as of yet, the stars were out in full force. The chatter about sequels died down, and the only sound we heard was the occasional crackling of the lava rocks inside the fire pit.

"I could use another beer," Hank said, breaking the

silence. "Anyone want one?"

"I'll go with you. I could use a stretch and a top off." I ambled to my feet, and Hank and I made our way over to the kegs.

"What do you think?" Hank asked. "Buttwiper or Coors Pisswater?"

"I can't believe they cheaped out on beer on grad night," I whispered to Hank, perhaps a little too loudly.

"Hi, Douglas!"

I turned around to see Genevieve Carlson standing behind me, smiling. "Hey, Genevieve!" I said a bit too enthusiastically, following it up with a big hug. I was definitely feeling no pain by this point in the evening.

"How are you? How did you like graduation?"

"Oh, I had a fine time," I proclaimed. "But my parents . . . well, let's just say they didn't appreciate Woodrow Wilson's rather casual approach to the event."

Genevieve laughed. "Ditto!" She raised her cup and we clinked beers. "So, you looking forward to going to State?"

"Totally. In fact, I'm moving down there at the end of the month."

"You're kidding! Me, too!"

"Really? Why?"

"My aunt is an attorney, and she's letting me work in her office over the summer. It's going to be fantastic. She works on behalf of a bunch of non-profit organizations tied to a variety of amazing causes." Genevieve placed her hand on my arm. "What about you? Why are you going down there so early?"

"I got a job working on the SDSU *Daily Aztec*."

"The school newspaper? No way! How cool! Congratulations!"

"Thanks. Yeah, Ms. Pearlstein did me a huge solid and called the faculty advisor and sent him some of my stuff and, well, they offered me a job as a cub reporter."

"That is so awesome, Douglas! Where are you going to be living?"

"I'm going to stay with my sister in Pacific Beach."

"Well, that's not far at all from Del Mar where my aunt lives! Maybe we can get together!"

"I'd like that," I smiled, looking into her warm eyes.

I had always known that Genevieve liked me, and I had liked her as well, only never with any romantic feelings on my part. But maybe what I thought were romantic feelings—the ones I'd had for Annie, for instance, or even Natalia so many moons ago—were something else altogether. Maybe what I felt for Genevieve—comfortable, compatible, and copacetic—was actually love. Maybe that's what solid relationships, like my mom's and Art's, for instance, were really made of.

"Okay, then," Genevieve smiled happily. "You still have my number, right? Call me before you leave and give me your sister's number, and I'll give you my aunt's."

"Sounds like a plan, Genevieve." And then I leaned in and gave her a friendly kiss on the cheek, holding the other side of her face gently in the palm of my hand. She smiled and turned a little bit red, took my hand, squeezed it, and then slowly released it as she backed away, our fingers touching lightly just before she turned and walked back into the house.

"Wow, that looked friendly," Hank joked, coming up to me from the other side of the patio, where he had retreated in order to give me and Genevieve some space.

"Genevieve's going to San Diego early as well. She

wants to get together."

"Cool," Hank smiled. "You guys have known each other for so long. Who knows? Maybe there's something there."

"Maybe," I shrugged, not wanting to say anything that could possibly tempt the fates to turn against me. I didn't know what I was feeling toward Genevieve, and I didn't want to get overly excited, but it was definitely a road worth exploring. The possibility of a new relationship would certainly take the sting out of the pain I was still feeling from my break-up with Annie. San Diego was giving me a fresh start just when I needed it most and knowing that Genevieve would be down there made it that much more enticing. Even if nothing ended up happening between us, it would be great to have someone to hang out with during those first couple of months before school started.

"Hey. Douglas? Douglas?" Hank slapped me on the arm.

"Huh?" I said, my reverie about Genevieve broken. "What?"

"You want to go back over to the guys?" he asked, pointing to our gang around the firepit.

"Yeah, sure," I answered. As we were walking back to the group, we saw that Dennis Martin, a kid who played in the Turkey Bowl with us every year, was talking to the guys. He walked away before we reached the pit, but from the looks on everyone's faces, we could immediately tell that whatever Dennis had told them was pretty bad news.

"What's up?" I asked as we reached them. "What was Dennis talking about?"

"Mark Schiller," Andrew said.

"What about him?" Hank asked, concerned.

"The Big C," Sven replied.

"Jesus," I said. "How bad is it?"

Moose shook his head and wiped a tear from his eye. "He's on chemo, but they don't think he's going to make it through the summer." Even though he was still pissed at Schiller for telling Andrew to clobber him in the last Turkey Bowl, Moose and Schiller had been friendly rivals on the football field for years, dating back to junior high.

"Fuck," Hank said. "I wonder if we should go see him."

"You probably know him the best, Moose," I said.

"Yeah, but we weren't exactly friends. Might be kind of awkward."

"Maybe we can send him a card," Marco suggested.

"Who are we, Miss Manners?" Andrew cracked.

"You're such an asshole, Andrew," Marco spat.

"Jeez," Andrew said, "what's gotten into you? You've been a bummer all night long."

"Sorry." Marco was suddenly beyond downbeat, head down, staring at the ground.

"What's going on, Marco?" I asked.

He took another big swig of beer—not that he needed any more—and without looking up, responded, "You know, high school is over, and you guys are all sitting here with big plans—you and Moose are going to San Diego State, Hank to Oxy, Andrew to UCLA, Sven and Malinowski to Northridge . . . I'm happy for you all, but my life is shit right now."

"What the fuck are you talking about?" Moose looked at Marco like he was out of his mind. "You're going to be working with your dad, eating endless amounts of that incredible craft services food, mingling with the stars, probably attending red carpet movie premieres. What the fuck are you complaining about?"

"No," Marco said quietly, "none of that is happening."

"What do you mean?" Hank asked, concerned.

"My dad's not giving me a job," Marco admitted. "At least not right now. He said I have to go to Pierce, get a degree first."

"Okay, well," Andrew said, trying his best to lift Marco's spirits, "that's not the end of the world. You'll go to Pierce, transfer to somewhere like Northridge, and then go work for your dad."

"And I bet he'll start letting you work part-time once you get a couple of semesters under your belt," Sven suggested, taking a swig of his beer and obviously pleased with himself for the wisdom he proffered.

"I hate fucking school, and I suck at it," Marco said angrily. "Besides, he also said I have to help pay my way through school, so starting Monday I'll be apprenticing as a tow truck driver for a friend of his."

"Seriously?" Andrew laughed. I knew he didn't mean anything by it and he couldn't help himself, but Marco suddenly became enraged.

"What's so fucking funny, you little prick?" Marco shot up unsteadily to his feet and stood over the terrified Andrew, beer bottle raised in a very threatening manner. Hank and Moose jumped up and tried to calm Marco down while Andrew simply cowered in fear. It really did seem like for a moment there that Marco was going to slam the bottle into Andrew's skull, but he didn't. Instead, he turned and threw the beer bottle out onto the darkened golf course below us, stumbling as it left his hand; we heard the bottle crash on what I could only presume was a rock or maybe even the cement cart path, the sound of breaking glass echoing up into the air.

"Fuck you guys," Marco said as he blew by us, bumping into people as he drunkenly left the party. We were so stunned we just stood there, staring at each other open-mouthed.

"Somebody should go calm him down," Malinowski suggested.

"Not me," Moose said. "He's way too pissed off."

"I'm certainly not doing it," Andrew said, wide-eyed and still obviously traumatized by what had just transpired.

Hank and I sighed and took off after Marco, but by the time we made it to the front door and out into the street, he was gone.

"Damn," I said, "I feel bad for Marco."

"I know, dude. Driving a tow truck and going to Pierce. Ouch."

"Must be hard, too, being around all of us and our college plans."

"Yeah," Hank agreed, "I'll give him a call tomorrow."

"Yeah, me, too," I said as we walked back to the house to rejoin the party. However, between the news about Mark Schiller and Marco's revelation, the shine to the celebratory evening had been tarnished.

"I think I'm going to call it a night," I heard Moose say just as Hank and I returned to the pit.

"Yeah, it's getting pretty late," Andrew agreed. Hank and I just shrugged, and the six of us straggled back toward the front door.

"Hey guys, wait up, I forgot my sweater," Sven called out.

Sven and his sweaters. When the weather got too

warm for him to wear his ski jacket, he had a favorite sweater he'd put on, and it was genuinely the ugliest thing any of us had ever seen. "We'll wait for you outside," I answered. Malinowski joined him, and they went back inside the house.

As we walked out to the driveway once again, where Hank and I had stood just minutes before, we saw Kenny Killian's Mustang pull up across the street. Sure enough, Kenny and Annie emerged from the car.

"Oh, fuck," Hank murmured.

"Be cool," Moose warned, placing his hand on my shoulder.

Annie glanced at me as she was crossing the street, but then cast her eyes downward. Kenny looked at all of us with a smirk, and as he passed he made eye contact with me, but said nothing. *Did he even know who I was?*

Sven and Malinowski passed Annie and Kenny at the front door, and when Sven caught up to us he asked, "What did you guys say to Kenny?"

"Huh?" I said. "What do you mean? We didn't say anything."

"Well, I just heard him say to Annie, 'I don't know what it is about that guy, but one day I'm gonna beat the shit out of him.'"

"Holy fuck!" Andrew laughed in that obnoxious laugh of his.

"Was he talking about you, Douglas?" Moose asked.

I looked at him like he was an idiot. "Who else?" I answered glumly.

"Let's get out of here," Hank suggested.

I was frozen; the emotions soaring through me were a disturbing mixture of love and hate, of anger and despair.

I thought I was going to throw up.

"Douglas?" Hank said. "You okay?" I hadn't noticed when he had put his hand on my shoulder, but I suddenly saw it resting there.

"Let's just go," I managed to say, holding it together long enough to make it to my car and say a relatively calm, if somewhat disconnected goodbye to my friends.

As I drove home, I rolled down the windows, let the pleasant June evening air rush over me, and breathed in deeply, over and over and over again. Eventually, my brain settled down, my heart rate returned to normal, and instead of focusing on Annie, I thought about Genevieve, about the *Aztec*, about San Diego and the endless possibilities lying ahead. I didn't sleep well that night, but I slept.

Chapter Eight

My dad insisted that I work full-time between graduation and the weekend I would leave for San Diego. Working the nine-to-five gig wasn't quite the drag I thought it would be, although I'm sure it helped to know that it was only for a few weeks. The fact that it was the beginning of summer lent an easygoing, almost festive atmosphere to the office. My dad's printing business had never been busier or more profitable, and he predicted that a new Republican administration would be coming into power in a little over a year. "There's no way Carter is going to get re-elected with these gas shortages and inflation issues on his hands," he insisted, going on to declare that he'd be making even more money in the '80s. "Lower taxes and more relaxed regulations are good for business," my dad, the ultimate capitalist, lectured me. "And good for my wallet, as well," he laughed.

I hadn't yet broken the news to Dad that I was planning on signing up for a Marxist Economics class my first semester at State. I knew he was going to throw a fit. I could just hear him now: "Is that what I'm paying for? Some Commie to shit all over capitalism and poison your mind?"

"It's just about getting a well-rounded education, Dad," I'd try to reason with him. "It's about learning about different points of view and then making your own informed decision."

"Sounds like bullshit to me," he'd dig in. "Just remember what puts food on your table."

For now, I kept quiet about the classes I had been perusing in the course catalog. He probably wouldn't be thrilled about the creative writing class I was planning to take, either. "You can write on your own time," he'd surely advise. "Take something more practical." I figured I could put off the discussion until at least August, or maybe even September, under the guise that I really had no idea what classes I'd be enrolled in come fall, since so much was dependent on what was open and available to me. SDSU was notorious for being so crowded that popular classes at convenient times were hard to get into, especially for an incoming freshman.

The next couple of weeks in the office went by pretty quickly. We continued having rubber band fights at the drop of a hat, and I had even gotten high with the guys during a couple of our "Fine Cuisine Lunch Club" treks, where we'd explore the best food the city had to offer: Tommy's at Beverly and Rampart, Phillipe's and Langer's downtown . . . We often returned to the office well after 2:00, and one time we barely made it back by 3:00, though of course that included a stop at Famous Amos on Sunset for some munchies after we had smoked a post-lunch doobie.

Meanwhile, Nicole continued to flirt with me at work, and when she joined the lunch gang at Pink's one afternoon, she sat next to me at one of the long tables we took over. Though she never got overtly flirty, she definitely leaned into me while laughing several times over the course of the lunch, even running her hand along my thigh a couple of times. Nothing ever happened between us, but

I had to admit the attention from this older, insanely hot woman was pretty sweet.

Annie had phoned me a few times, but I refused to return her calls. My mom finally told her flat out that I didn't want to talk to her anymore. Even though I was still feeling pain about the whole affair, I knew I needed to cut her out of my life completely, and there was no way I wanted her to follow me to San Diego. I thought that if I just gave her the silent treatment, there was no way she'd come down to attend Grossmont instead of staying up here to go to Pierce, as she had suggested she might do. But who knew if she was ever really considering doing that, or if it was just another one of her lies? I didn't really care by this point.

One day, returning home from the office, I walked in the door and heard my mom immediately call out, "Douglas, is that you?"

"Yeah, Mom. It's me."

"Come in here, honey."

I followed my mom's voice into the den, where I found her sitting with Art. "Douglas, I'm afraid I have some bad news. Your friend Marco has been in an accident."

"What do you mean? What kind of accident? Is he okay?"

"Evidently he was changing a tire on the Ventura Freeway when a car struck him from behind."

"Oh, my God! Is he okay?"

"Yes, he's okay. I spoke with Hank, and he said Marco had jumped out of the way at the last second, which saved his life. But . . ." my mom stopped and looked at Art.

"But what?" I asked. "Tell me!"

"He lost his arm, Douglas," Art said. "They had to amputate his right arm from just above his elbow. It got caught in the collision, and it was crushed."

"Jesus," I said, stunned. I sat down on the love seat next to them.

"He's at Tarzana hospital. Hank said he was allowed to have visitors tomorrow and that he and some of your other friends were going to go over there around eleven o'clock. I'm so sorry, Douglas." My mom reached out and grasped my hand.

"Well, at least he's alive," I said, thinking immediately about Weddy. Then a thought suddenly occurred to me. "Will he be able to drive again?" I asked. "I mean, his whole life, all he wanted to be was a stunt driver like his dad."

"I'm sure he'll be able to drive," Art said. "As for professional stunt driving . . ." he raised his eyebrows. The answer was obvious: Marco would never be able to follow his dream.

The next morning, at a little before 11:00 AM, the five of us—Hank, Moose, Andrew, Sven, and I—gathered at Bea's Bakery across from the hospital, and then pooled our money to buy a box of cookies for Marco before heading in to see our injured friend. Our collective mood, instead of being sad and morose, was actually quite light. Yes, we were there under serious circumstances, but we also understood that Marco's life had been spared. Plus, I think we all realized that this might be the last time all of us would be together for some time to come. I was headed to San Diego, Andrew had already moved out to Westwood and was working at his uncle's law firm for the summer, Sven had gotten an early start at CSUN and was already taking a couple of classes in summer school, and Hank was busy playing ball. Moose would be around for a couple of months working at the local Baskin-Robbins, and then he'd be in San Diego as well. Each of us had plenty of reasons to be optimistic and firing on all cylinders.

Entering Marco's room, we were hit with a large dose of reality: his stump of a right arm was very visible, and seeing it up close and personal smacked us all in the face as soon as we walked through the door.

"Hey, Marco," we said in a somewhat broken unison.

"How's it going, man?" Hank offered, trying his best to remain upbeat.

"Oh, you know," Marco managed to laugh. He then attempted to raise his heavily bandaged right stump. "It is what it is."

"Dude, we're so sorry," Moose said.

"We're glad you're okay, though," I said. "It sounds like you could've been killed."

"Yeah, it wasn't entirely her fault, though."

"What?" Andrew asked. "What do you mean?" His lawyerly instincts were obviously aroused.

"The guy whose car I was fixing should've pulled off the freeway instead of pulling over to the side where he did. I mean, there was a shoulder and plenty of room, but we were only fifty yards or so from the exit. It would've been much safer."

"So why didn't you make him do it?" Andrew interrogated.

Marco sighed. "The dude was driving a 911. He didn't want to fuck up his rims. I understood and told him it was all right."

"Fuck," Sven said, saying out loud what each of us had been thinking. He might as well have followed it up with, "Bad decision."

"What can I say, guys?" Marco continued. "I'm a fuck-up. I make stupid decisions. My parents always told me I was trouble, and I believed them."

"Oh, come on, Marco," Hank said, somewhat angrily. "That's bullshit."

"Thanks, buddy," Marco smiled. "But it is what it is. Just like my arm. You know what this means, right?"

We all shuffled our feet and cast our eyes downward. We knew what was coming.

"I'll never drive again. I mean, they said I'll get a prosthetic and can drive like normal people, but a career as a stunt driver? Forget it." He chuckled weakly.

"You never know," Sven said. "Maybe with some practice, some new technology, you'll be a lot better than you think."

"Yeah, come on, Marco," Hank urged, "it's way too early to be giving up on that dream."

"Thanks, guys. Really, I mean it." Marco looked about as sincere as I'd ever seen him. But then he sighed again and glanced around at the various IVs and monitors that were hooked up to him. "But it is what it is."

Moose tried to steer the conversation to other topics, and the rest of us followed suit. After a good fifteen or twenty minutes of gossip about various kids from high school, which Marco seemed to have little interest in, the topic switched to sports when Moose asked, "So, do the Lakers take Magic tomorrow?"

"Well, that's sort of a no brainer!" Andrew laughed, spraying Moose as he pronounced "brainer" with a large capital "B."

"Say it, don't spray it, moron," Moose said, angrily wiping his arm.

"The bigger question is: Who's going second?" I pointed out.

"If it were me, I'd take Sidney Moncrief," Hank said. "That guy can play." When it came to basketball, Hank was certainly the most knowledgeable out of all of us.

"I heard the Bulls are picking Greenwood second," Andrew said knowingly. "As a longtime Bruin fan, I'm happy for David, but I think they'd be better off with that center from San Francisco. What's his name?"

"Cartwright," Hank answered. "Yeah, I think you're probably right. I don't think Greenwood has an NBA body, but Cartwright certainly does."

"They're both good," I said. "But Magic is head and shoulders above any of them. Even Moncrief."

"I heard West actually wanted Moncrief more than Magic," Moose added, "but Buss told him to forget it, that Magic was his guy."

The next thing we knew, Marco was snoring. "With all the medications he's on," Sven whispered, "he probably naps off and on the whole day."

Sure enough, the nurse walked in and said, "Hey, guys, he's been up all morning waiting for you to come. He might need to rest for a bit. Can you wait outside until he wakes up? It shouldn't be long. He just needs a little catnap."

We all shuffled out the door and huddled in the hallway outside, trying our best to stay out of the way of the nurses and doctors who frequently hustled by. It took a bit longer than the nurse had suggested—more like forty or forty-five minutes—but when we went back in, Marco seemed to be in a better mood. Perhaps it was because of whatever it was the nurse gave him before we entered—morphine, I was guessing—but he was actually making jokes about his new disability.

"Hey guys. Being an amputee is both a blessing *and* a curse."

"How so?" we played along.

"On the one hand," he said, raising his left hand, "I have fingers. On the other hand—" he laughed, somewhat moving his stub "—I don't."

"Oh, that's awful," said Moose, who was probably laughing the hardest.

"Here's another one the therapist told me," Marco went on. "What do you call karate for amputees?"

"Um, one-armed karate?" Sven guessed.

"Partial arts," Marco smiled.

"That's good," I said, admiring the wordplay.

"Okay, last one," Marco promised. "Why didn't the police arrest the amputee?"

"Oh, I've heard that one before," Moose said. "Because he was unarmed."

"Very good," Marco chuckled. "Thanks, guys. It was really great seeing you. It means a lot to me that you all came together to see me. Who knows when this will happen again?" He was talking a bit dreamily, softer than normal, obviously due in part to the drugs. But who knew, maybe a different Marco would emerge from the tragedy, a better Marco, even.

We were all at a crossroads that day, every one of us in that room. Our lives would never be the same from that point on. New beginnings lay ahead, new challenges— some obviously greater than others, as was the case with our amputee friend. After saying our goodbyes and promising to keep in touch and support Marco, the five of us walked out to the parking lot next to the hospital. All the guys wished me luck in San Diego that summer. I promised to visit often, and they promised to do the same. The only way to describe how the other guys and I, and even Marco in a strange way, were feeling was, well, *free*.

Of course, Hank and I would still see each other before I left for San Diego the following weekend. In fact, we already had plans to go see a bunch of new punk rock bands in Los Angeles at a club in Chinatown that had just recently opened called the Hong Kong Café. "You know that guy at Licorice Pizza," Hank said when he called me to tell me about it, "the one who's always wearing, like, suspenders and plaid shirts and leather boots and shit?"

"Yeah," I said, "I know the guy you're talking about. He's impossible to miss."

"Well, as strange as he might seem, the dude knows his music, and he told me all about this show with Black Flag and X—two of the hottest punk bands in L.A. right now. We should definitely go check it out."

"Sounds like a plan, Stan," I had readily agreed.

We met at Hank's townhouse just a few days before I was going to leave for San Diego. Hank had already pulled out his Thomas Guide and figured out where this place was; he had even written down directions and handed the paper to me after we had hopped into his Camaro. He also handed me a flyer for the show with the address for the Hong Kong Café. "Oh, this is easy," I remarked. "It's right smack in the middle of Chinatown, just below Dodger Stadium. I don't even need this." I tossed the paper with the directions into the back seat.

"Hey!" Hank complained. "I spent a lot of time on that!"

"Well, you should've known better when you've got

me in the car," I laughed.

"That's true!" Hank laughed with me. "You're the master of driving in L.A. Lead the way, my friend."

I had learned how to get around L.A. from the true master—my dad, whose encyclopedic knowledge of the streets of not only Los Angeles, but the Valley and a good chunk of Southern California, including Orange and San Diego counties, was legendary. It came from all the years he spent as a traveling salesman, before he got into the printing business. He had passed a lot of that knowledge on to the entire family, just by constantly telling us what route he was taking whenever we drove anywhere as a family in the pre-divorce days. But even after the divorce, the lessons continued.

Whenever we drove to the Forum or Dodger Stadium, for instance, he would take new and different shortcuts and describe them to us as he was doing them, turn by turn. It was impossible *not* to learn and remember routes, especially those we took again and again, sneaking into Dodger Stadium through the Chinatown entrance, for example, or coming down Florence instead of Manchester to get around the Forum traffic. Even the Coliseum, notoriously difficult to get to whenever the Rams or the Trojans were playing a big game, was not immune to my dad's knowledge of shortcuts; we'd exit the Santa Monica Freeway early at Arlington and then cruise down Santa Barbara Avenue, parking in a front yard just west of the stadium that belonged to Leroy, a guy whose yard my dad had been parking in for over twenty years.

While Hank and I drove downtown, we smoked joints and I checked out the flyer he had handed me. It was pretty crazy stuff, and featured a nude woman with pretty large tits, wearing only a black top hat and black leather boots that went almost to her knees. Her one hand was balled up in a fist, and the other was holding a knife. A guy in front of her was also holding a knife in one hand and had his other arm and hand outstretched, as if he was telling the woman to stop. Behind the woman, a dress of some sort was evidently pinned to a wall with an array of knives similar to the one the man had in his hand. There was also some odd text about a new movie called *The Disco Strangler*.

"This is some pretty crazy shit," I remarked.

"I know, dude. Have you ever seen a poster for a concert like that?"

"Look," I pointed out to Hank, "at the bottom it says, 'Blame this on R. "Burgie Boy" Pettibone.'"

Hank just shrugged and turned up KROQ, where the DJ announced he was going to play Iggy Pop's "Five Foot One."

"Oh," Hank said excitedly, "the dude at Licorice Pizza says this guy is the original punk rocker. He said we have to check out his old band called the Stooges." He smiled and we both started jamming along to Iggy, our heads bobbing up and down to the mega-fast beat and killer guitar riff.

Even though neither Hank nor I knew exactly what to wear to a punk concert, we figured jeans, a plain T-shirt, and tennis shoes would be safe. As we walked up to the club, literally right in the center of the original Chinatown, I was stunned to see that the concert was happening at what appeared to be a very traditional, very ornate Chinese restaurant.

"Wow, what a trip," I marveled.

"The guy at Licorice Pizza said they're having these shows in old restaurants," Hank said. "That way, they can serve food, and it becomes an all-ages concert. Besides, the restaurants were about to go out of business anyway. Same thing over there." Hank pointed across the way at another Chinese restaurant, Madame Wong's, with a line of punks waiting to get in. "The dude said the restaurants are now making money hand over fist."

By the looks of the kids in the line we joined—which seemed to be 95 percent male—everyone was about our age, give or take a year or two. Thankfully, there were plenty of kids dressed like we were, but there was an obvious preponderance of black boots with silver chains wrapped around them. Some kids wore black or red suspenders, or lots of buttons with names of bands on their jackets, and there was a fair amount of leather even though it was a warm, late-June evening.

The white-and-gold exterior of the restaurant featured a large sign that read, Hong Kong, and beneath it in smaller letters were the words, Genuine Chinese Dishes. A classic golden pagoda roof loomed above the whole structure. There were two stories, and the line of kids was headed straight up the stairs to the second floor, which was actually the restaurant's banquet hall. Evidently, while families ate "genuine Chinese dishes" below, punk rock shook the building from above.

As we made our way up the narrow stairs, the air grew hot and thick with a mixture of sweat and the nervous energy of the crowd, which seemed unusually amped up. Most of the kids were too young to drink, and there was no way the restaurant was going to risk its business by serving underage kids. The crowd definitely wasn't wealthy enough to be able to afford coke, but still ... something was driving the manic energy in the room. The music playing over the PA was deafening, an assortment of songs by local punk bands I had heard occasionally on KROQ. Unexpectedly, there were a couple of warm-up bands, and we had apparently already missed the group who'd opened the show.

"How can they possibly have five bands in one night?" I asked Hank. As the next band took the stage, playing an angry but very brief set of short songs, we got our answer. Number one, every song was about two minutes long—three, tops. Number two, the guys in these bands were all so young, and the bands were so new, they only knew a handful of tunes! So you could have a show with five bands, and the whole night would be over in a few hours, just like a normal rock and roll concert. The short songs and short sets only seemed to feed the energy in the room, which was unlike anything I'd ever experienced before. It seemed to build as each band came and went, with small groups starting to push and shove each other by the time the third group of the night finished their set.

When the lights went down after yet another brief break and Black Flag took the stage, there was a surge forward, and Hank and I were caught in the wave. Suddenly the band exploded; their lead singer—Keith Morris, according to some punk we talked to later in the evening, who said Morris had grown up in nearby Hermosa Beach—was unlike anyone I'd ever seen, careening around the floor and throwing himself into the crowd with no regard for his body or his safety. He screamed out threatening—and mostly indecipherable—lyrics, though you'd occasionally be able to grasp some words about a nervous breakdown or revenge or depression.

The band, meanwhile, seemed to know only a handful of chords at best, but they pounded away with a speed and ferocity those old fogies the Rolling Stones could only dream about. The crowd of teenage and just-past-teenage punks slammed into each other like atoms bouncing off one another. There was no intent to injure, nevertheless elbows flew, feet kicked, and hands even slapped or punched on occasion. It was just a part of the whole experience, and Hank and I dove right in, ricocheting off kids and laughing and screaming along with any recognizable chorus we could make out at the top of our lungs.

Sometimes kids would even join the band onstage, jumping around before diving back into the crowd, and the band didn't seem to mind at all! By the time Black Flag had finished their set, which probably consisted of fifteen songs but only lasted about thirty or forty minutes, we were drenched in sweat, exhausted, but having a hell of a time.

"Well," I said to Hank once the music stopped and the crowd started drifting toward the sides and back of the room to either head for the bathroom or grab some water or a Coke to drink, "this certainly ain't Fleetwood Mac!"

Hank shook his head in amazement. "That was awesome, dude! There were even a couple of chicks dishing it out!"

"I know! I couldn't believe it! I started to apologize to one of them because I thought I had pushed her too hard, but she just turned around and threw an elbow into my chest!" I rubbed the center of my chest, where I thought I might actually have a bruise.

X took the stage next, and they were unlike anything

I'd ever seen. The dude at Licorice Pizza had told Hank that X featured a guy who went by the name of John Doe and a lead singer who called herself Exene, and they were evidently either married or lovers or former lovers or something. Doe played bass and shared singing duties with Exene, I mean, if that's what you called Exene's wailing.

While the members of the band seemed a bit older than the guys in Black Flag, and their hair was definitely longer, they rocked just as hard and just as fast. The way Exene and John Doe's voices intertwined was haunting, and as they sang songs about being desperate, vomiting, and one intense tune about a phone being off the hook—seriously!—we once again careened around and around the pit of fans crashing into each other with wild abandon.

Perhaps the funniest thing of all was the guitarist, a character straight out of one of those '50s rockabilly bands with a pouf of blond hair that was almost a full-on pompadour, and a leather jacket, of course. He just stood in the middle of all the chaos, as cool as a cucumber, posing in various guitar hero stances while he belted out stinging guitar solo after stinging guitar solo. The drummer was beyond unbelievable, keeping up a ferocious beat that drove the music louder and faster than I had ever heard. Meanwhile, Doe would pump away at his bass as he and Exene screamed and howled through a brief set of their two- or three-minute songs. They even threw in an amazing cover of the Doors' "Soul Kitchen." By the time the band ended their set with "Los Angeles"—the song I had heard on KROQ a couple of times in the last week or so that seemed destined to become a SoCal punk anthem—we were simultaneously begging for more while at the same time desperate to get out of the steaming hall and breathe in some cool, fresh, late-night air.

"Oh, man," I said, practically collapsing on Hank as we stumbled outside, beyond exhausted. I had never felt this way after a show. Elated, yes. Dog-tired? No. What the hell was this new music?

"How fucking great was that?!" Hank had one of the biggest smiles on his face I'd ever seen.

"Dude, we gotta go thank that guy at Licorice Pizza for turning us on to this."

"For sure," Hank agreed.

On the way home we decided to take some back roads instead of immediately hopping onto the freeway; we needed to smoke a doobie and chill for a bit after the intensity of the last couple of hours. I told Hank to take Stadium Way out of Chinatown, and we followed it all the way around Dodger Stadium.

"Fuck, I don't think the Dodgers have it in them to win the division this year," Hank said, breaking the silence as we drove beneath eucalyptus trees and the smells of the surrounding hills flooded into the Camaro through the open windows.

"They still haven't gotten over last year," I said somberly. The truth was, nobody had gotten over last season. After young Bobby Welch struck out Reggie Jackson with men in scoring position, we were up 2–0 against the Yankees in the World Series and seemingly had them on the ropes. But then Mr. October took over and the next thing we knew, we had been swept off the field.

As we made our way past Dodger Stadium to Riverside and into Griffith Park—I had decided to take us through the park and over to Forest Lawn Drive, where we'd eventually hook up with the Ventura Freeway—the cool air that had settled into the surrounding hills and canyons washed over, around, and through us and we both breathed in deeply and exhaled, realizing our twin behavior and then laughing hysterically.

The pot was kicking in, and we were both definitely starting to relax and let go of all the energy, spent and otherwise, in our bodies; it was similar to how we'd feel after a particularly long, hard day on the basketball court. That completely satiated feeling where you know you've given everything you had to give, left it all on the court—or inside the concert hall, as it were. Our ears were still ringing so loud that we hadn't even bothered turning on the radio, and we didn't even talk that much, at least not until after the euphoria that had carried over from the show to the car began to wear off.

I think we both realized we had just turned a corner musically. By June of 1979, disco was dead. The rock stars of the '60s were starting to become has-beens and burnouts. After tonight, both Hank and I were certain that punk rock and new wave were going to be the music of our generation. As Genevieve was always preaching, the '70s were over, and the '80s was going to be our decade; we would find our own battles to fight. Just like the generation before us had Vietnam and Civil Rights and '60s rock and roll, we'd have punk rock and new wave to power our own struggles, whether it was stopping nuclear energy or nuclear war, or the world's crazy dependence on Mideast oil, or who knows what.

"It's our time now," I'd heard Genevieve say time and again, and I was now starting to see the light: punk rock seemed to be a clear demarcation between what was, and

what was to come. Genevieve had me convinced that politicians like Jerry Brown represented the future of the
country and that the days of Richard Nixon and his ilk
were over.

"We can get on here or drive all the way around to Bar-
ham, whatever you want to do," I said to Hank as we approached an entrance to the Ventura Freeway just before
Forest Lawn and Mount Sinai, two major cemeteries on
the edge of Griffith Park overlooking the eastern part of
the San Fernando Valley.

"Let's take the long way," Hank suggested. "I got a lot
of family members buried up there at Mount Sinai. I can
wave as we go by."

"Ha!" I chuckled. "I'll do the same." I also had a bunch
of relatives buried up there. Pretty much every Jew I
knew in the Valley did.

It was pretty late by the time we got back to Hank's
townhouse. After Hank pulled the car in the garage, he
walked me out to the front of the complex where I had
parked on Lindley—right across from the apartment
building next door, in fact, where I had once had my infamous battles with Mr. Asshole over whether or not L could
pee on his building's parkway. Standing there in the exact
spot where I had once dropped my Dodgers mini-baseball
bat on the sidewalk while trying to threaten Mr. A and his
German Shepherd, Prince, Hank and I both knew this was
the last time we would part as high school buddies living
in our parents' homes.

"This is sort of weird, isn't it?" Hank said as we stood
on the sidewalk near my car, keys jingling in both of our
left hands.

"Yeah, but it's exciting," I smiled. "We should make

plans for you to come down to San Diego. It'll be a blast."

"You kidding?" Hank smiled as well. "I can't wait. I'll look at my basketball schedule for the rest of the summer, and when I have a couple of free days, I'll drive down."

"Maybe we can go to TJ, dude! My sister always tells me how they'll serve anybody in the bars down there. They don't even check IDs."

"Sounds like a plan, Stan." Hank extended his right hand, and I did likewise, and we executed a perfect Soul Brother #1 Handshake. And then #2. And #3. And #4, #5, #6, and #7. It was the first time in years that we had run through our entire repertoire of Soul Brother handshakes at once. And then we hugged each other tight, even pounding each other's backs with the inside of our fists. That was something else we had really never done before. Well, off the basketball court, anyway.

No more words were spoken. We each backed away— Hank toward the brick steps leading to the front gate of the Encino Royale, and me across the grass parkway toward my brown Civic—and then we both raised our left hands, which also held our keys, gave a brief wave, turned, and disappeared, he behind the black wrought-iron gate and me into my car. It felt like we had both just closed the door on a past life.

Coda

The plan was for me to finish out the week at work, then have dinner with my dad and Cindy on Friday night, have dinner with my mom and Art and David on Saturday night, and then drive down to San Diego on Sunday, ready to start at the *Daily Aztec* bright and early Monday morning.

The last day at work was your usual lunchtime celebration, only this time we went to La Fiesta and all of my workmates drank margaritas. There were a couple of speeches that veered into roast territory, with Glen making a crack about my fledgling skills with an adding machine and Larry presenting me with a hockey mask and a box of rubber bands.

After telling all those assembled what a lousy shot I was, and how he and Glen would pummel me during our rubber band wars, he joked, "Remember what they told the struggling musician: 'Do you know how to get to Carnegie Hall? Practice, practice, practice.' Douglas, I expect that when you next grace us with your presence within the hallowed walls of our offices—next summer, perhaps—that you will have at least advanced into being a worthy opponent." With that, he pulled a copy of Sun Tzu's *The Art of War* out of a bag and handed it to me, strongly advising me to read it; little did he know, I had already absorbed the book during Power Reading in junior high.

At one point, I got up to go to the bathroom, and when I

came out, Nicole was standing there waiting for me. "Hey, Douglas," she said, smiling slyly. I could hear the laughter coming from our group at our table around the corner, but nobody we knew could see us. She placed her hand in mine and gave me a peck on the cheek. I could smell the tequila on her breath. "I hope you'll give me a call once you turn eighteen," she said. "Maybe I can come visit you in San Diego." As she took her hand away, I realized she had placed a piece of paper into my palm. I glanced down and saw that it was her phone number. Looking around to make sure once again that nobody could see us, I put my arm around her waist, pulled her closer, and gave her the wettest, messiest French kiss I could muster.

"I'll take that as a 'yes,'" Nicole laughed as she suddenly pulled away, her green eyes on fire. She then slapped me on the butt and pushed open the door to the ladies' room, disappearing inside while sashaying that fine ass of hers, just bursting to get out of her tight jeans. I returned to the table, walking on several cushions of air.

That night, I pulled up to my dad's house right at 6:00 PM as planned. Dinner was a casual affair, and by the end of the evening I realized the true reason my dad had wanted to see me before I left for San Diego. In addition to saying goodbye, it was his one last shot at lecturing me about, well, you name it: studying hard, staying out of trouble, staying away from drugs and alcohol, using protection if I was going to have sex, choosing my friends wisely—all good advice, to be sure, but seriously? It was sort of like the time he decided to teach me about the birds and the bees—when I was already in seventh grade! Hell, my older friend Nick Einhorn had told me everything I needed to know back in the third grade. Point being, it was a little late in the game for these kinds of lectures.

"Yes, Dad. I will, Dad. Yes, I understand, Dad."

I dutifully repeated the words he wanted to hear, and when he had mercifully run out of topics to lecture me about, he put his hand lovingly on my shoulder and said, "I just want you to be safe, Son."

"I know, Dad."

"I love you, Douglas," he said with genuine warmth in his soft, hazel eyes.

"I love you, too, Dad," I said. He gave me a light squeeze on the shoulder and returned to his dinner. I looked up to see Cindy smiling, a tear forming in her right eye.

"So," my dad said, changing the subject to our favorite topic of discussion: sports, "what's wrong with the Dodgers?"

"I think they're still in shock from losing to the Yankees. We won't win the division this year, that's for sure."

"How about this Magic kid the Lakers drafted? He any good?"

I looked at my dad like he was crazy.

"I'm just kidding," he laughed.

We spent the rest of dinner talking about how great it was going to be seeing Kareem, Magic, Nixon, and Jamaal play together. Cindy had to leave to go pick up Rebecca from Cindy's mom's house, where she had spent the day with her grandparents.

"Take care, Douglas," Cindy said on her way out the door. "Have fun in San Diego. See you soon."

"Thanks, Cindy. And thanks for dinner—it was delicious."

"You're welcome, Douglas," she called out over her shoulder.

My dad had recently subscribed to ON-TV and they were broadcasting a handful of Dodger home games. It was super cool, as we'd never been able to watch the Dodgers on TV when they were playing at home unless it was a nationally televised playoff or World Series game. Tonight they were playing the Braves, but the Dodgers were in the midst of a losing streak and would fail to turn it around as they fell 5–2 to Atlanta—the result of an inability to hit and a rough, wild performance by Dodger pitcher Rick Sutcliffe, who walked seven batters while only striking out two.

"Tough to win when your pitcher can't find the plate," my dad said as he walked me to the door. Cindy had returned with Rebecca earlier and taken her upstairs to bed, where she herself had evidently fallen asleep; she never came back down to join my dad and me as we watched the game.

"Yeah, Sutcliffe sucked tonight," I agreed.

"All right, Son. You take care of yourself in San Diego. Call me once you get settled. Maybe Cindy, Rebecca, and I will come down and pay you and Julie a visit next month."

"That'd be great, Dad." We gave each other a big hug, and I got into my Honda and drove home. Things were pretty good these days between me and my dad. Even though he was still prone to being a bit heavy-handed when it came to lecturing me about stuff, I knew it all came from a good place in his heart. And I think my commitment to work these past months, and the good job I did at the office—in spite of Glen's cracks at my farewell lunch—had raised my dad's level of respect for me, and perhaps, just perhaps, made him a little bit more confident in my ability to make good decisions, take care of myself, and stay out of trouble. He basically just wanted me to put my nose to the grindstone once I went off to college, and I believe my stint working at his company had been reassuring for him. Time would tell whether I was truly worthy of the newfound trust and respect I had earned from him.

It was pretty late by the time I got home. Baseball games were now regularly lasting well over two hours, and even two and half hours on many occasions; the days of the sub-two-hour game seemed to be over. But my mom was up and waiting for me when I walked in the door. She looked as if she'd been crying.

"Hey, Mom," I said, "what's wrong? Are you okay?"

"It's Lassie," my mom sniffled. "I don't think she's do-ing very well."

"What's the matter?" I asked, immediately growing concerned.

"She won't come inside. No matter how much Art and I plead with her, she won't move from that spot at the edge of the yard." She gestured vaguely toward the backyard and then started sobbing. "I think she might be dying, Douglas."

"Jesus," I said softly. I walked by mom, placing my hand on her shoulder briefly and kissing her on top of her head, and went straight to the kitchen, where I opened the sliding glass door. It was a moonless night so far, and the stars were blazing away in the sky. I could just make out L sitting quietly at the edge of the yard overlooking the canyon. She seemed calm and relaxed as she turned at the sound of the door opening and saw me, pausing for a moment as if inviting me to join her before turning her head back to the canyon. I grabbed a couple of thick blankets that were lying across a kitchen chair—my mom had probably used them to sit with L before I got home, I guessed—and went out to the back and sat beside her.

I had pretty much experienced my whole life with L. We got her when I was only four or five years old, and she had been through everything with me—the divorce, the move from Northridge to Encino, my trials and tribulations with Natalia, the death of Weddy, our move to Tarzana, my high school years, Annie . . . and while my dad had moved out, and then Julie, and then David, I had always been there for her. My mom eventually had Art, so, in the end, out of the original members of the family L had been brought home to, I was the last one standing, the last one she depended on for food, for companionship, for fun.

For many years now, I was the one who fed L, walked her, and played ball with her, and she repaid my kindness, care, and attention by always being there for me. At my lowest moments, I could always depend on her to comfort me. She'd sleep at the foot of my bed when everything was going well, but when I was having problems with Annie or school, or having a tough time after Weddy died, she'd sense that I needed a little extra comfort and would cuddle up with me, her soft little head even resting on my pillow at times.

To be honest, everything had been so crazy lately with graduation and Annie and work, I hadn't really thought too much about how much I was going to miss L when I moved to San Diego. And while I knew she had aged tremendously in the past couple of years, and that the vet had said her age and health issues would eventually get the best of her, I figured we at least had another year or two where I'd be able to come up to visit from San Diego and she'd be there waiting for me.

Did L somehow know I was leaving on Sunday?

I spread out one of the blankets on the grass and lay down beside L. She got up and joined me on the old quilt, seeming at first to struggle to get comfortable. Her fur was soft and still gorgeous, that classic Sheltie light brown-and-white coat, always immaculately brushed by my mom, not a knot to be found. L eventually settled down and cuddled up next to me, her head and snout nuzzling into the curve of my arm. I don't know how long I was lying there, just looking up at all the stars with L resting comfortably next to me, her breathing even and slow, when all of a sudden a shooting star, as big and as bright as I had ever seen—whether it be in the mountains or the desert or over the ocean on a moonless night—appearing like a streak of fire across the sky out toward the west, appeared high above the dark hills surrounding the canyon below. It lasted longer and burned brighter than any shooting star I had ever seen, and when it was over I wondered if I had just watched a comet; I'd never witnessed a meteor that bright and that long in my entire life.

Weddy's goofy, smiling face came into my mind, and I immediately thought of the sign with the neon shooting stars above the liquor store at the intersection where he had died. The sign had acted so strangely that night as Hank and I were finally leaving the scene of the accident, after the cops had asked their questions and the ambulance had taken Weddy away. Was the comet Weddy's way of communicating with me once again, just as he had with Hank and me on that tragic night? Was this his way of telling me that everything was going to be all right? That he would be there to welcome L when she passed? That he would take good care of her, play with her, feed her, throw a ball for her, and maybe even brush her hair to keep the knots out?

These thoughts and others swirled around in my brain as I continued to stare at the sky, dark and mysterious yet full of life. I continued to pet L as she slept soundly, my fingers tracing their way calmly through her fur. I pulled the second blanket on top of us to get warm, as it was pretty chilly outside.

At some point, I joined L in a long, peaceful sleep. When I woke up, the sun had yet to rise but dawn was breaking, and it was plenty light outside. My arm was still wrapped around L, who was cuddled beside me just as she had been when I'd seen the comet or the shooting star or Weddy or whatever it was that I had witnessed. As I struggled to awaken and the memories of the light show in the sky filled my brain, it all seemed like a dream that had happened a long time ago. Suddenly, I realized that L was very still. Too still. She wasn't breathing any longer. I turned her head toward me. Her eyes were open, but vacant. L had died during the night.

The rest of that day was undeniably sad. We had to load L into the car and take her down to the vet, where we all cried as we said goodbye to her small, lifeless body. My mom took a scissors and cut a chunk of her fur as a keepsake. But as the day went on, our mood shifted as we told each other our favorite L stories. Mom mentioned the time L broke her leg when she leapt off a bench to chase a bird and landed awkwardly. She was only a puppy, but the cast she had to wear was practically bigger than her whole body! But L was a gamer and dragged that thing all over the place; nothing could stop that little dog.

David always blamed Julie for L's broken leg,

claiming that she either should've held L more tightly so she couldn't have jumped at all or just let her go; instead, David maintains to this day, Julie grabbed at L awkwardly as the little dog went after the bird, causing L to land the way she did and break her leg. It was still a sensitive subject and something I wouldn't touch with a ten-foot pole, but whenever David is really pissed at Julie about something, or if he just wants to get her goat, he'll bring it up.

I talked about how much I always loved L's roll-overs. Sure, any dog can be taught to roll over, but L would do it again and again and again and again. If you got her on a large lawn, she'd roll over fifty times if you told her to do it. She absolutely loved to roll over and never got dizzy or anything. Being a relatively small dog, I guess it was just something easy for her to do. And fun, of course.

That night, as I packed a suitcase and loaded my car in preparation for my drive to San Diego in the morning, Moose came out of his house to say goodbye. It wasn't really necessary since he was going to be coming down the following night after he got off work to help me get settled. We were also planning on spending Sunday checking out the campus and the dorms we'd be living in come fall.

"All packed up?" Moose asked as he was crossing the street.

"Yeah, pretty much," I answered, leaving my car and walking toward him.

"Hey, isn't this about the spot we were standing when we first called our truce?" Moose pointed out, looking down at his feet.

"No, I think it was more over here," I said, gesturing to where I stood.

With that we both laughed, each acknowledging just

how far our friendship had come since that day.

"So you think you'll get down there around eight tomorrow night?" I asked.

"Yeah, give or take thirty minutes. It all depends on when they let me leave the store. Now that it's summer, we've been incredibly busy. It seems like the whole world wants ice cream."

"Okay, I'll be waiting for you. You still have that paper I gave you with my sister's address on it, right?

"Yep. It's sitting in my car, ready to go."

"Okay. I'll see you tomorrow, buddy."

"See ya, Douglas."

Moose moseyed back over to his house, and I went back to my Honda, shut my trunk, and headed into the house. Just as I reached the top of the stairs, the phone rang. I took a few more steps and then picked up the Garfield receiver.

"Hello." Silence. "Hello," I repeated.

"Hi, Douglas." It was Annie. "Please don't hang up!" she begged. "Douglas?"

"Yeah," I said. "I'm here."

"I heard you were leaving for San Diego soon."

"Who told you that?" I asked.

"Is it true?"

"Yeah. I'm leaving tomorrow morning."

"Can I please see you before you go?"

"I don't think that would be a good idea." I was trying to be strong. Steel. A stone wall.

"Please, Douglas. You know, we moved."

"You did?" Not that I cared.

"Yeah, my mom had to sell the house and we moved into an apartment in Encino, sort of near where you used to live. Near Hank's place."

I didn't respond. What was I supposed to say?

"Douglas, the building has a sauna," she said in that flirty voice of her. "Nobody ever uses it. Maybe we could go in there together."

"I don't think that would be a good idea," I repeated. Did she really think I wanted to go over there and have sex with her in some sauna? And how did she even know it was never used? Had she already had sex in there with Kenny? Or someone else?

"Come on, Douglas, don't be like this. You know I love you."

"Seriously?"

"Douglas, I've decided I'm going to come down to San Diego and go to Grossmont," Annie suddenly announced. "So we'll be able to still see each other all the time."

"You know what, Annie? You can do whatever the fuck you want to do, go wherever the fuck you want to go. I just don't give a shit anymore. Stay the fuck out of my life!" I slammed down the phone.

My mom was standing in the hallway; she had apparently been there for the bulk of the conversation, and I hadn't even noticed her. I was angry, breathing hard, but I wasn't crying, at least not until my mom approached me and wrapped her arms around me. We both stood there, in the middle of the hallway for who knows how many minutes, both of us crying our eyes out. Over L. Over Annie. Over my leaving tomorrow. Mom and I had a long history of comforting each other, especially after the divorce, and this moment was no different. I was going to miss Mom, and she was going to miss me, and there were no two ways about it.

"I love you, Douglas," she whispered.

"I love you, too, Mom," I said.

We squeezed each other tightly for a moment longer, and then I went back to my packing. The phone rang several times over the next hour or so, but nobody picked it up; we just assumed it was Annie and decided to let it go.

I wanted to beat any Sunday traffic that might be on the road, so the whole household was up bright and early the next morning. My mom cooked a nice breakfast. "It's a long drive; you need to be well-fed," she said, though I knew it wasn't that long of a drive and making breakfast was just something she could do to distract her from the fact that the time had finally arrived for her baby bird to leave the nest and fly away. She held it together pretty well, actually. It wasn't until I was in the driveway, hugging her and Art and even David, who had joined us for the ceremonial departure, that she finally broke down and starting crying, her whole body heaving up and down in what were deep, almost violent, sobs. Art encouraged me to leave; no amount of hugging and promises to visit often would comfort her at this moment in time. I just needed to go.

Driving away from the house, I watched in my rearview mirror as Art pulled my mom close to him and started dancing with her, slowly and softly, right there in the driveway, David standing a few feet away with his hands in his pockets, watching me drive off. I imagined Art was singing one of their favorite songs to her, probably Billy Joel's "I Love You Just the Way You Are." I could swear I saw my mom smile as I caught one last glimpse of the three of them before I disappeared down the hill.

Instead of hopping right onto the Ventura Freeway, I

decided to take Ventura Boulevard to the San Diego Freeway just for old time's sake. I turned the radio to KROQ
and drove along for a bit, eventually passing Reseda Boulevard and then Lindley, where the Encino Royale sat just
a block or two down the street. "Blockhead," a song from
Devo's forthcoming album, was playing and Jed the Fish
was hosting, as I went through the intersection where
Weddy had died. I passed through the light at Ventura and
Zelzah where Weddy had made that fateful decision on
Halloween night to turn left instead of crossing Ventura
like the rest of us had done—proving once again my theory that fate and choice can combine to suddenly and unexpectedly change your life in an instant. I turned up the
radio and settled in for the drive to Pacific Beach.

"Next I'm going to preview a new release from the
folks at Dangerhouse Records," Jed said. "This is a six-
song EP coming out in August, and it features the most
cutting-edge bands currently setting the Los Angeles
punk rock music scene on fire. I'm talking the Bags, the
Eyes, the Alley Cats, Black Randy and the Metrosquad,
the Germs featuring local hero Darby Crash, and . . ." Jed
paused for effect, "perhaps the best band on the scene today, X, with their incredible song 'Los Angeles.'"

"Holy shit!" Once again, life had thrown another
"psych" at me. Sometimes they were small, just little
pokes to let you know the fates were there, watching,
waiting. Sometimes they were major and represented
tremendous shifts in your life. They could be good, bad,
or indifferent. Today was good. And small, yet significant
somehow. As John Doe belted out the opening lyrics and
Exene joined in, singing/screaming the name of my beloved city in her own inimitable way, I thought to myself:

Yep. The time is right. The fates have conspired, I've made my choices, and just like John and Exene's heroine in the song, I also had to leave Los Angeles.

I was ready for a new adventure, ready to open myself up to new possibilities, whatever those might be. Traffic was light, fortunately, and the open road south lay ahead as I made my way onto the San Diego Freeway and climbed the hill that led the way out of the Valley.